Spring Unbroken

Martian Spring Series
Book 2

Patricia Cooper Baker

ISBN: 978-1-7359250-6-6
Spring Unbroken
Published by Cooper's Peak, Publisher, 2024

Cover art licensed from Shutterstock.com.

Dedication

To my family: Thanks for saying you love me, even when I've spent too much time in Wonderland and not enough with you. Thank you for sharing your creative pursuits: music, art, sports, design, and careers, and showing me how your problem-solving relates to mine.

To my friends: Thank you for believing in me against all odds and shoring me up when my faith is low. You are my heroes.

To my writer communities: Whether we keep in contact through meetings, from across the net, or in one-on-one sessions, you inspire me and offer unique ideas that stretch me to new limits. You make me laugh, cry, and ponder over the things you write and the institutions you support. My writer buddy, Bob, deserves a special callout. He goes the extra mile with spot-on feedback, then edits (OMG!), and offers inspiring examples of perfect prose.

To my readers: Thank you for your kind comments, reviews, and the time you spend reading my work.

You give me hope that I may yet write that magnificent book that brightens lives as pages are turned with characters who live on after the covers close. Keep asking me the most treasured of questions: What will you write next?

Contents

Part I: Visitors from Home and Afar

1 New Home, New View

Will that cooker never ding?

Finally!

I grabbed the cup from the multiwave cooker, and the first precious sip revved my body, heart, and spirit with a jazzy tingle, fit for the start of my new life. We had been in love for months, but this was the first day Collin and I lived under the same roof.

The delicious anticipation of life together reminded me of the day I took my first steps on Mars. Months ago, the exhilaration of moving into WayPoint Station had been tamped down by a lack of confidence and a healthy dash of fear. Today was pure joy.

Collin's galley window showed different rugged ridges from the view in my old quarters, but the same two Martian moons raced through their courses past the sun. Collin and I were another tag team racing through the stars. I couldn't predict where the cosmic wheels would take us, but we shared the journey, and that was enough. His love steadied me, and no matter what twisted path lay before us, I believed our happiness would endure.

On the Martian terrain, the rocks, ridges, and dust devils touched the sky, and now, so did I. True, I couldn't walk on the surface without my terrain gear and wouldn't survive inhaling the raw Martian atmosphere. Yet I was unbound … floating, breathing easily for the first time since as far back as I could remember.

On Earth, I had been abandoned and rejected. But now, Mars lifted the weight of self-doubt, leaving me free to embrace a happy life.

A rustle of bedclothes tore me from a wonder-filled universe and back to making breakfast. So, I plundered through Collin's galley staples. Elly had kept a different selection in the Icehouse, but a biodegradable wrapper promised me breakfast bread—multigrain, protein-fortified, enriched with vitamins. And it was pre-crisped. Wasn't Martian convenience fantastic? After the bread was warmed in the cooker and freshened in a stingy hint of misting, the toast was ready.

It was an old-fashioned notion, but deep down, I wanted Collin to think I was a good cook, but this breakfast wouldn't convince him. Toast and coffee were as far as a multiwave cooker and Collin's larder could take me. Oh well. It was my best. So, I dropped a silk rose on the plate, balanced a tray in one hand, and pushed through the galley door.

"Ready or not, here I come."

***

Collin yawned, but when he spotted my tray, he scooted to the middle of the bed, saying, "OK, fine, if you insist." He sounded grouchy but grinned as he finger-combed his thick blonde waves and made a spot for the breakfast platter on his knees.

"Coffee. Bring it!" He reached for the tray, and once he held it steady, I jumped in next to him.

"Oh, nice and warm," I said, scooching close to his shoulder.

"Warm coffee? I was hoping for red hot and highly caffeinated," he said, rolling his eyes as he took a satisfying sip. "Ah, yes. Perfect."

I reached for my cup, saying, "I meant the bed. You kept it warm."

"But that's my job, isn't it?" he asked. With a mischievous grin, he added, "You had no bed, so you shoved me over, and here we are."

"It wasn't as easy as that," I replied. My lips brushed Collin's cheek as I reached for toast. But he held my wrist, pulling me closer for a proper kiss.

"Warmer than an icehouse, isn't it?" he asked, kissing my red curls before turning to the tray.

"Much warmer," I agreed.

After a bite of toast, he said, "I'm glad you like our new arrangement. It was hard work tugging the strings to make it happen."

Laughing, I replied, "You had nothing to do with it. The Icehouse booted me when it gave Wolfgang Fulbright his old room back."

He sat the tray on the far side of the bed and put his arms around me. "Who said I had nothing to do with that? It was all my idea. Where else would you go, anyway?" he asked, being careful of coffee spills as he snuggled.

I finished a sip, admiring the sparkle in his sea-blue eyes. Then I sat my cup aside to enjoy the taste of his lips and the scratch of his stubbly beard against my fingers. "I wouldn't want to be anywhere but here."

"And that's as it should be," he replied, returning his cup to the tray. "So, what trouble can we get into this weekend? What's going on around town?" He smiled, moving into the embrace, but paused as a new idea struck. "We can travel and stay home, too. If it's virtual, we can go anywhere we want. How about Hawaii? Or a quick trip around the world? I've always wanted to dig for gems in Iceland; it would be more fun with you there." He took my coffee, set it on the tray beside his, and propped on one elbow, waiting for my answer.

Sadly, a message interrupted our first weekend breakfast together.

"It's Luis Kaneko," I whispered, pulling back a little.

Collin moaned as he reached for the tray and shouted at the voice in my wristband. "What is Mr. Prime Minister micromanaging now?"

Giggling, I replied, "he says for you to hush." Then, when I ended the message, I added. "He just wanted to be sure everything was in place for the meeting."

"Ah, right—the meeting. I hope working on Saturday isn't part of my new routine. How will this go?" he asked.

"It's part of the tour. We're to show Luis and some of the newcomers the memorial I set up in the Temple room. I guess I'll have to answer questions; Westergaard will be there."

"Oh, right. So much for Hawaii; I'd better get shaved," he said, leaning in for another kiss. Then, as Collin rounded the bed past me, he lifted my chin. "You aren't worried, are you?" he asked.

"Of course not," I said, forcing a smile.

He shook his head, smiling. "Liar."

"OK, I'm worried," I said. "Westergaard is here to investigate the deaths of Dexter and Bernadette. We were witnesses, and we have secrets to keep."

"Those secrets aren't about Craig and Duval, and I wouldn't dare blab about the other thing." He turned as he reached the door of our hygiene room, adding, "And if you need backup, Luis will be there. He won't let anyone blindside you."

"That's why I'm bringing *you*," I winked.

"*Two* backups then," he replied, grinning. "And don't forget our secret weapon."

I whispered across the room. "Do you mean *Ray*?"

"No," he laughed. "I meant Mrs. Kaneko. Not even Luis gets past Michelle."

I rifled through my side of his closet until Collin returned.

"Wear that purple thing," he said. "Nobody can resist you in that."

"Are you sure?" I asked. "It stands out, and it might not be a good idea to remind folks of flashy Bernadette."

"Bernadette is gone. They will only see Spring, and you have no reason to hide."

I shrugged. A little more confidence couldn't hurt. So, I put my WayPoint tan and black outfit back on the pegs and pulled out the purple wrap dress.

***

We stepped through the door and onto one of the spoke streets leading to WayPoint's Central Park. Being so close to the social center of Mars was a change for me, and the lighting was different, too. A meters-thick Martian concrete canopy covered the town center, but only a thin layer of translucent ice protected me from the sun in the

Icehouse and yard.

To the left, the canopy hovered over gathering places and eating establishments. But if we went right, we'd intersect the inner and then the outer ring streets, shielded by a thick coating of dragon skin. The ring streets ran around the town center and intersected other spokes, which led to other work divisions.

"I can see the roof of the Council Hall from here," I said, pointing left. "It's not a long walk."

Collin shrugged. "We could escape if you'd rather. Do you need more time to calm your nerves?" He gave me less than five seconds to decide before he said, "I think you do." Then he spun me to the right, and we took a longer route. "We'll start our weekend with a brisk morning stroll, and we can walk as long and far as you like." But we paused when we reached the inner Ring Street.

"Which way now, Captain?" I asked.

Collin chuckled. "Ring Street is a circle, so it doesn't matter. Whether we go left or right, all spokes lead back to the center. We can run around all day if you like, or we can grab our terrain gear, go straight ahead, and jaunt out through the fields."

We headed left, and at the next spoke, he paused. "Better now?"

One arc segment was all the rebellion I could take. I chuckled, saying, "I hate being late. I'm ready."

"You certainly are," he said, linking elbows with me. "Let's show the newcomers what it's like to be real Martians. After all, you're the new Secretary of Human Services."

"Secretary-in-Training," I corrected.

"Well-trained, I'd say," Collin replied. "Be proud of what you've done. We're on home turf. The newcomers are not. Not yet."

Then he stopped me and squared my shoulders to his. "You agree that we have the home-turf advantage, right?"

"Sure. But what do we say when Westergaard finds out we were at Sanctuary Cave the night Bernadette and Dexter died?"

Collin squeezed my shoulders tighter. "Neils isn't much of an investigator if he hasn't read the depositions. On the evening in question, our prime leader was held captive in his quarters, and you were locked in the clinic. Proof surfaced that Luis had been illegally ousted as WayPoint's Prime. We moved you to a safer place, and Duval found us at the cave. Things went downhill for her from there. It's up to Luis to explain the coup. Bernadette, Dexter, and Garrison Mathis were responsible for that—not us."

"But ..."

"But nothing. We aren't ready to tell our other reason for being there, are we?"

I sighed. "You're right. The world isn't ready to hear about the other stranger on Mars."

He nodded. "No one needs to know that we have a resident alien, and we surely don't want anyone to know where he was that night. Not yet. We'll stick to our story. You needed to escape, and Sanctuary Cave was the perfect place to take cover till Brian and Linda delivered the proof Kaneko needed." With a shrug, he added, "It worked; he's back in power."

"Thank goodness for that, but our *friend* is still in jeopardy. What should we do?" I asked.

"The question isn't what, but when, and we will know when the time comes. But aliens among us—it's no exaggeration to call that Earth-shattering news."

I sighed. "We must step carefully."

My worry lines deepened, and Collin pulled me closer, wrapping me in his arms. "Between Ray and us, we will figure it out."

I was as safe as a baby in his swaddling embrace. After one more long sigh against his chest, I looked into his eyes, smiling broadly.

"We've got this," he said. "You, me, and Ray."

I nodded. "We've got this."

Then he linked arms with me, and we walked proudly together to the door marked *Destiny*.

2 In Memoriam

The Rim of Forever, the center chamber of Destiny Temple, was a moving theater of virtual cosmic art, reflecting the magnificence of space and how our tiny WayPoint Station was part of it.

The seating would accommodate hundreds of WayPointers, but often, citizens gathered in smaller groups for private contemplation or services tailored to any of Earth's faith communities. I had frequently sat alone there, lost in the whirl of space, seeking solace in troubled times.

But today, we walked past the *Rim's* portal to the Memorial Chapel, a room I had designed. My heart quickened, and I sucked in a deep breath as Collin pushed at the door marked *Memorial in Progress*.

He chuckled as he tightened his hold on my waist, whispering, "Relax. It's not deep-sea diving, only a demonstration."

It may not have been a tiny sea cabin, but the Memorial Room was the smallest in the temple, and to me, the six people there made a crowd.

The WayPoint colony, tucked inside Echo Crater, was too young and diverse to have well-established rituals. But Luis decided we needed it, and he wanted the Memorial Room to be part of his tour to indoctrinate newcomers to WayPoint Station. It was no coincidence that the first tributes were for the people Neils Westergaard came to investigate. By honoring Bernadette and Dexter, we highlighted their contributions to WayPoint while giving their deaths needed perspective.

The investigation surrounding Mathis' trial would likely prove all three were involved in the coup to snatch power from our Prime Minister. Still, until a coup attempt was proven, Luis believed we should focus on their efforts on behalf of WayPoint Station.

Like the Rim of Forever, our Memorial Chapel was partially virtual. Today, I'd demonstrate it to newcomers Lilith Marchand and Neils Westergaard. Perhaps our recent returnee, Wolfgang Fulbright, didn't need the tour. After all, the multipurpose Destiny Temple had been his idea, and The Memorial Chapel was merely a recent addition.

WayPoint's first lady, Michelle Kaneko, rushed to greet us with a peck on each cheek. "Ah, you both smile even though Luis makes you work on your day off. You must forgive *mon mari*," she begged beneath sad, puppy eyes.

Collin flashed his contagious grin. "Nothing to forgive," he replied. "It's why we're here."

"Ah, Dr. Graviston, you greeted our newcomers the day they landed," Luis said as he beckoned the others to stand near us. "Lilith Marchand and Neils Westergaard, please meet Collin Grant, a member of our geology team." After they shook hands, Luis continued, "Dr. Graviston designed this memorial, and I'll let her explain how it works."

Collin drew his arm from around my waist and gave me a tiny push at the small of my back. "Yes, Spring, show us what you've done here."

I smiled as I stepped to the exhibit wall and turned toward those gathered. "If I've done my job well, this should be self-explanatory, but if I missed my mark, you may always ask Marvin about anything in WayPoint." I twirled a finger toward the ceiling, and the group tittered, acknowledging our ubiquitous AI servant, always in the cloud and ready to answer any question.

"Indeed, Marvin is always nearby, isn't he?" A smile wrinkled the corners of Lilith's pale, sparkling eyes. "Sometimes I feel Marvin is peeking over my shoulder, even though he always sounds disinterested."

The dapper Dr. Westergaard, dressed in a tweed suit of grey and beige instead of WayPoint standard garb, showed no hint of a smile as he turned to me. "I've met the versatile Marvin, and I find him a useful will-o-the-wisp, but give us your version of this chapel, please, Dr. Graviston. There's nothing like hearing it from the designer."

Michelle twirled toward them. "Our Spring does much more than this to bring humanity to WayPoint. Besides her work in psychiatric sciences, she piloted our newcomer's Supper Club. She is very thorough. You shall see. Luis is grooming her to be WayPoint's new Secretary of Human Services."

I ignored my friend's praises as I stepped toward barely visible outlines of three human-sized parabolic arches. The top of each curve was marked with the symbol for Mars adjusted for WayPoint Station. Instead of a circle sprouting an arrow, this arrow ended in a star shape, indicating Mars as a steppingstone to the stars.

"Luckily, WayPoint has lost no more than a handful of citizens, but this room can display eight full-sized memorials at a time," I said. "However, the number and size of the doors can be customized. As you see, three niches were requested today, so we have room to make them life-sized."

"Three was by my choice," Neils added. "In a way, I'm here to represent Dexter Craig and Bernadette Duval as I investigate their deaths. As for Ross Hashimi, we met on Earth for a seminar on Martian geology, and I want to learn more about his work here."

"Then let's start with Mr. Hashimi," I said, pointing to an electronic panel on the wall. "An individual memorial is activated by selecting from this electronic roster or speaking the name. Try it, please, Neils."

"May we see Ross Hashimi?" he asked.

Hashimi's name appeared across the center parabola and over an *Om* icon, representing his South Asian tradition. But within fifteen seconds, the name disappeared, and a virtual version of the man stood within an arch-shaped niche.

Clad in his iconic striped caftan, Ross Hashimi displayed a hint of a smile. The image nodded as Luis Kaneko's recorded voice recited Ross' assignments with the geology department, including projects he contributed to and honors he acquired, ending with his mysterious death near the edge of the Echo Crater floor. Once Kaneko's epitaph ended, Ross held his hands near his chest, palms meeting, in the traditional pose of Namaste. Then, with a little smile, he bowed his head, and the niche automatically closed. The name and religious identifier gradually faded after another fifteen seconds.

"Was he alone when he died?" Westergaard asked. And since he was an investigator, I imagined him jotting notes on a tiny spiral pad.

Michelle gave a tiny shrug as she replied, "Much of what happened is a mystery, but we have no reason to believe anyone was with him. When alerts went out that his health was threatened, Dr. Fulbright responded as quickly as possible."

Luis added, "Hallucinations plagued some members of our colony for a time. Luckily, Dr. Graviston helped repair that, but Hashimi walked into the wilderness alone before we knew the problem existed. We assume he was one of the early victims of Mars' first unique malady."

"Dr. Fulbright is back on the job, and we believe he will solve our final cases," I added.

Westergaard pursed his lips, asking, "May we see the others?"

"Speak the name of the one you wish to view," Luis replied.

"Dexter Craig," Neils said, and Dexter's name appeared over a Christian cross.

Collin squeezed my hand, and I braced as Dexter's virtual image appeared. There was no trace of the recrimination he had once given me, no sign of his hunger for power or the blind allegiance he had for Bernadette Duval. Dexter's image was of the man I met during my first days on Mars, perfectly dressed and meticulously groomed. He smiled warmly, and his eyes had the old twinkle of interest that sprang from the first blush of attraction. Tears welled as I recalled the friendship we shared before his undignified death.

When his eulogy was complete, Dexter's image winked and waved before he faded behind the virtual door. Westergaard asked, "Was Mr. Craig also a victim of hallucinations?"

Luis shook his head. "No, we don't think so. Dexter Craig died trying to save Ms. Duval."

"Then he must have been a courageous man," Lilith said.

Collin cleared his throat to muffle a scoff, and Luis quickly spoke up. "Those living on Mars display bravery daily. Our job here is to prove long-term survival is possible, but it isn't a given. Death is possible, too. Those here work hard to make survival the expectation, but they know the risks."

Neils nodded and then spoke the last name, "Bernadette Duval."

"What faith does that spiral represent?" Lilith asked, pointing to the position of faith icons for the others.

"Ms. Duval did not specify a faith preference, so this spiral represents our galaxy, the Milky Way—our greater home," Luis explained.

Then, when the door vanished, Lilith sucked in her breath at the image of Bernadette Duval in a flowing red satin gown, revealing bare shoulders and a plunging neckline.

"Why … who chose that gown?" Lilith asked, pushing thin silver-streaked tresses behind an ear.

"Bernadette chose it," I replied. "Ms. Duval left no faith designation, but she left a specific video of the image she wished to use for her memorial. We didn't have the dress, but we could recreate it virtually."

Holographic Bernadette smiled and tossed her hair back. As her image faded, she turned her back to the camera, displaying brunette tendrils that swept down a bare back as she grinned over her shoulder.

"That's very specific," Lilith said. "Who created that visual?"

"It was in the video," Luis replied.

"And was she a victim of the hallucinations, too?" Westergaard asked.

Luis nodded. "We believe so. Her last words revealed a delusion that she was the queen of Mars."

"Such a vibrant woman," Lilith said, her voice trembling. She wiped a tear and added, "It is unfortunate that Mr. Craig could not keep her from running into the terrain."

With a grim face, Neils patted Lilith's shoulder. "There are still questions to answer; that's one reason I'm here."

Luis Kaneko pointed to the open door. "I urge you to visit the other rooms, especially the Rim of Forever. Then, we can move to the clubs, spa, and game rooms. We hope those spots will make your stay on WayPoint more enjoyable."

"And the restaurants," Lilith added. "Those are far more interesting than I ever imagined."

I smiled, ready to say yes, but a latecomer interrupted our conversation.

"Beth Martin!" Collin said, reaching a hand to her shoulder. "It has been too long."

"Did you want to see the memorial, Beth?" I asked. "I can stay behind and give you a quick peek."

It was Luis' turn to interrupt. "Ms. Martin is our driver today, so we rely on her services for the final parts of the tour, a brief trip around the WayPoint complex."

"We're happy you joined us, cherie," Michelle said. "Have you questions about the memorial before we go?"

Beth tucked her chin to her chest, but finally, she said, "I came to see if Ginger Welsh's name is on the roster of the lost. I haven't heard from her in ages."

"The list is posted here, Beth. Her name isn't on it," I said. "As far as I know, she still makes air drops and surface collections between Phobos and Mars."

"OK, then," Beth muttered. "Mr. Torres thinks so, too. I just wondered."

Luis spoke up. "If you have doubts, I'll look into it for you, Beth, but I've heard nothing of her being off the team for any reason."

"It isn't necessary, Sir. She's always been an independent woman." She tucked her service hat under her arm. "I'll wait for you in the transport bay."

Then, with a slight bow, she was out the door.

Collin tugged me in that direction, too. "Hawaii is waiting," he whispered.

***

Hawaii was fantastic, especially the romantic moments waiting for dawn at the House of the Sun in Maui. Virtual travel wasn't the same as a real trip, but there were advantages. We lost no time in transit, and there were no reservations or political conflicts. We scaled mountains if we wanted exercise and relaxed together, spellbound by Maui sunrises.

"It's perfect," I whispered as the sun bathed us in rainbows of peach and gold.

"As it should be on our first honeymoon," Collin said, holding me close.

"Is that what this is?" I asked. "Doesn't that usually come *after* a wedding?"

He grinned, rocking me to him. Then, between moist kisses to my ear, he whispered. "Around the world, first, Sugar Spring. All else comes in good time."

We relished the sunrise as long as we dared. And just like the deity Maui, Collin could slow the virtual sun, giving us a few more minutes in its glow before we ended the show and fell asleep, cuddling in our bed.

3 Old Haunts

Since the tragic night at Sanctuary Cave, the changes at WayPoint Station brought fresh challenges and new worries. For example, my first position on Mars included working as Dexter Craig's assistant, which taught me the scope of his old job, soon to be my new one. The workload and personnel were familiar, but political maneuvering was a skill I'd yet to master. As Collin left for work, he gave me good advice. "*Forget the stressful stuff for a day. Take a break from training*".

It was the perfect time to collect my belongings from the Icehouse, but there was no hurry. I had all day. The spoke street took me to the inner Ring Street, where I followed the curve toward my old Martian home, lingering at every portal to watch the outdoor routine of WayPoint at work.

Nearly every division had field components along the outer rim. Whether they worked inside greenhouse-like chambers, produced rocket fuel, or monitored growth experiments in Martian fields, they kept WayPoint alive.

Finally, I came to WayPoint Clinic and the adjacent Icehouse, my old quarters. I passed through the clinic entrance and waved at Jinae Kim, whose bouncy brunette bob and brilliant smile had become the new face at Bernadette's Welcome Desk. The furniture had not changed, but Kim's single silk rose in a biodegradable vase was nothing like Bernadette's ostentatious desk décor. Why did Duval need a designer paperweight or an antique inkwell on Mars when we barely used paper and ink was obsolete? No one knew, but she insisted on them. Perhaps they were family heirlooms or made a statement that resonated with her.

Westergaard was using my desk in the physician's office pod, so I didn't go there. My knickknacks and books were more at home in Collin's quarters. It troubled me to think of Neils Westergaard mingling with my Icehouse family, but that was none of my business now. Or was it? After all, I was training to be the link between WayPoint's Council and the Division of Human Services.

My destination was my old quarters, so I passed by the Conservatory and continued up the spiral stairs to collect my few Earthly possessions and get them out of Fulbright's way.

I didn't miss my pie-wedge sleeping cabin. It had been a place for relaxation and privacy, but I gladly swapped my cocoon of solitude to share life with Collin in the roomier Science Team quarters. The virtual entertainments I had enjoyed in the Icehouse, such as the gondola rides, weren't anchored to a specific place. They were anywhere in WayPoint; one only had to ask Marvin.

As it turned out, I had no reason to knock or pry into Fulbright's quarters. The adjacent study held a box with my name atop a similar container engraved in French script, probably left by a former resident. But when I paused to open my box and examine my treasures, I found one of Elly's flowery ceramic mugs inside.

"I'm free for coffee anytime," the note said. Elly had better mean that. I'd miss her more than anyone else from the Icehouse.

With my box in hand, I planned to leave by the Ring Street portal near the stairs. But when I reached the landing, my wristband beeped with a message from Dr. Fulbright.

"Nurse Kim told me you were on the premises. If time permits, wait for me in the Conservatory. I'd like to have a word."

So, instead of turning left to the portal, I turned right and entered the Icehouse's garden-like meeting space.

The Conservatory was still set with the standard arrangement I used for group sessions, but it also held memories of the life-changing events that happened there. I could barely look at the terrain exit I had used on the night Collin and Milo helped me escape Bernadette's captivity, but I couldn't forget the expectant faces of the entire house waiting to hear what happened when I returned.

They knew nothing about Rayfarer, and I couldn't tell them about finding him in Sanctuary Cave. I had been tired when I returned that night, and the Icehouse residents were interested in the coup and my well-being, nothing more. So, they were satisfied with a bare-bones explanation that said nothing about finding Ray.

Collin and I weren't ready to reveal our friend to the public, but Wolfgang Fulbright had met Ray before I did and had a few clues about him that others didn't. We found Ray with information and a gift Wolfgang had shared with me. He was the returning third member of our Rayfarer's club, and we hoped to bring him up to speed with what happened to Ray after Fulbright left. So, his meeting invitation was a welcome start to passing information and getting answers from him, too.

The wait wasn't long, but I paced along the walls until Fulbright entered the Conservatory. It was good that he still had his shocking Einstein hair because nothing else reminded me of the man I had met briefly in the clinic. Now, he wore a clinician's jacket over his body suit instead of patient togs, and I could see him clearly without the barrier of blinds and flashing emergency lighting.

Fulbright had been secretive and enigmatic at our first meeting—a man accused of hallucinations and incompetence. But now he was the picture of a calm, if eccentric, doctor. Wolfgang had accomplished his self-imposed mission on Earth and didn't need to convince anyone of his mental state. He seemed pleased to return to his old surroundings and beamed as he offered me his hand.

"You've done well here," he said. "I knew you would. You were the perfect replacement to help my patients while I investigated this mystery at home."

"I regret we didn't have more time before you left for Earth. For some reason, Mr. Craig was set against my meeting you."

"Did he say why?"

"His excuse was worry that I'd be infected with the hallucination malady. I never understood it completely."

"I apologize for our terse meeting. There was an undercurrent of misdeeds even then. It was hard to know who to trust, but it was necessary to trust someone who could care for my patients."

"You must be relieved now. You seem much more at ease and, if I may say so, a lot less frightening."

He chuckled. "You've changed too. Of course, I knew you mostly from your paper trail, but the records showed you had endured hard times on Earth. I depended on the fact that you had survived hardship and that those battles might help you in your struggles here."

"They probably did help," I said, "but so did the people in this Icehouse. They became family to me, better than any I had on Earth. They had my back and stiffened my resolve."

"That may be so, but nothing can push strength to the forefront when there's none to push. Perhaps it was hiding or had never had a reason to rise before, but courage was always inside you, waiting to raise its head when needed."

I nodded. "You might be right, and it might be so with our patients. But their past experiences confused them so much that their courage wasn't quite up to the battle. Finally, with treatment, old fears and torments dissolved in the light, and they made progress."

"Now we're getting to the heart of matters," he said as he moved to the nearest settee and leaned toward me. "I have questions," he whispered. "Bring me up to speed if you can."

I looked around the room again and peered high into the green tendrils dangling from the observation deck. People had listened from up there before. "Is anyone here?" I asked.

"Not in the home quarters. Everyone is at work in the clinic. We are alone in the Icehouse."

I was still apprehensive, but I hesitated to insist on a search.

Fulbright must have understood, so he spoke again, "Marvin, complete privacy mode, please."

"Privacy mode active," Marvin droned. "No recordings. Listening inactive. Is there anything else?" *Lilith was right. Why had I never considered him disinterested before?*

The AI activity light on my armband dimmed until I asked, "Marvin, who is in the clinic?"

My wristband light flickered red as he replied. "One orthopedic patient, one patient in for respiratory therapy. Nurses Jinae Kim and Lilith Marchand are at their stations."

"Will you alert us if that status changes?" I asked.

"Complying." I imagined a sigh behind Marvin's bored tone. His listening light dimmed again.

"Satisfied?" Fulbright asked. And when I nodded, he added, "First, how did you treat our patients? And what became of Brian and Linda?" he asked.

"Brian and Linda helped Luis Kaneko escape his captors and regain his status as our Prime Minister. They earned a favor for that, and they wanted to return to Earth where they can start a family; children aren't allowed here yet."

"Good for them. I thought they were bonding. But how about the cure? Please explain what you know about the hallucinations and the treatment method. Giles and Thaman still need attention."

Even with Marvin's promise of security, I was afraid to tell all out loud, so I chose my words carefully, using jargon-like code. "The hallucinations were not a symptom of normal psychosis. In this case, they were induced by ...." I sought the right words.

"Induced by ...?" Wolfgang prompted. "The past experiences?"

"Yes, their experiences on Earth and aspects of their working environments here."

"The environment? How? They had worked at their jobs for months, years. Did the environment change?" he asked.

I cleared my throat while searching for the right words. "Those who fell to the visions were particularly sensitive to Martian factors and could not explain their experiences. So, we needed to convince them that what they saw might not actually be there. The exact method of relief differed from case to case."

"Hm." Fulbright pondered for a few seconds, then asked, "Were these factors from Martian physical aspects, such as vapors or chemicals in the soil? Or was the problem with things missing on Mars—too little light, water, or food? In other words, was it too much Mars or too little Earth?"

"If I had to choose between your options, I'd say it was too much Mars. But neither choice is exactly right."

He leaned even closer. "So, is it something not of Mars or Earth?" he whispered.

I nodded.

He leaned back, staring into the dangling vines. "Did they encounter the man I spoke of—the one I warned you about before I left Mars?" When I nodded, he leaned in to whisper. "Did they see him? Do they know what he is? Do *you* know what he is?"

"They did not *see* him exactly—not like you mean. And they have no idea he helped cure them."

"Can I follow his plan to cure Thaman and Giles? Will he help with the cure?"

"I'm sure he will if he can. He's currently blocking everyone. He was under attack, and Collin and I helped him hide."

"I haven't felt him since I returned. Will he be able to contact me?" he asked.

"We shall see," I replied. "Let me speak to Collin. The three of us should meet soon."

"Very well. I've reviewed your notes on Giles and Thaman. Giles was bullied in his younger days. And sometimes the bully accused Giles of his own misdeeds."

I nodded, "And Thaman came here with an excellent sense of orientation, but due to Martian factors, his sense of direction, something he always counted on, failed."

Fulbright continued, "He was once the best at finding his way along our routes, and now he is completely disoriented because that skill evades him. Is that it?"

"I see it this way. He had problems long before he came here. Everyone in his family trusted the older son, yet Thaman knew his brother was a compulsive liar. His family members were often at odds with knowing what to believe and when. So even before he came here, Thaman had to fight to trust himself despite what his family chose to believe."

Fulbright nodded, "So, his family experiences weakened his confidence in himself, and after he lost his sense of direction, his confidence to make decisions waivered. He might be tricky to fix."

I nodded. "Both Giles and Thaman may present challenges," I said. "But our visitor is a fit helper. Together, we can repair Thaman."

"Now I have a question for you," I said.

Wolfgang leaned back, "I'll do my best."

"Do you have a new chip now?"

"My chip?" he asked. "Of course I do. They won't allow me back on WayPoint without a chip."

"But how did you get off WayPoint without one?"

"Ah," he said, nodding. "When a WayPointer leaves the planet, the chip remains. If someone dies or leaves permanently, the chip is ceremoniously given to their commanding officer, who destroys it. But in my case, there was hope of my return, so the protocol was muddied. I was not required to return the chip, but I did not want it inside me on Earth. So, I left it here. Did it help you unlock my secret?"

I nodded. "It did. Collin and I used it to send Bernadette hunting for you, which gave me a chance to escape her prison."

"Very well, then," he replied. "What became of it?"

I shrugged. "I hid it." Then I whispered its exact location in the Icehouse yard.

"It could only cause more confusion now," he said. "I'll dispose of it."

He may have had other questions about Bernadette chasing his chip, but a light flashed on Wolfgang's band, interrupting us.

Marvin droned, "Lilith Marchand approaches."

"Allow it," Fulbright said, and we turned toward the panel that hissed open as she arrived.

Marchand didn't have the flippant sarcasm of Jinae Kim, but they shared a nurse's efficiency. And while Jinae's grin was cocky and promised a dose of mischief, Lilith's pale hair and sunny smile warmed the room. Wrinkles around her eyes pegged her closer to Fulbright's age than mine, but her perkiness carried a youthful vibe.

The portal had opened, but she knocked at the wall anyway. "I hope I'm not intruding. Nurse Kim told me you were here."

"Welcome, Lilith," Fulbright said. "No need to knock; you and I have become closer friends than that. Come in, please."

She beamed as she joined him on the settee. "This will only take a moment," she said, then turned to me. "I'm trying to arrange a reunion of my recent traveling companions. Did you two know each other on Earth?"

Fulbright chuckled. "No, Spring and I met briefly before I left Mars," he said. "Dr. Graviston was to replace me, so now, we have patient history to share. What kind of reunion did you have in mind, Lilith?"

"Oh, just a dinner meeting to discuss our trip and compare notes on adjusting to Mars. Will you join us, Spring? Bring your partner, Collin, if you like. I hear he was once Dr. Fulbright's patient, too."

"Do you have a place and time in mind?" I asked.

"I've reserved a group table at Taco Marciano on Thursday night," she said. "But if that doesn't work, we can make other arrangements."

"My date book is open," Fulbright replied.

"And I will have to check if Collin is free," I added. "But Thursday sounds fine for me."

"Very well then," she said, beaming, as she pretended to dust her hands over her lap. "My work here is done. Neils Westergaard has already agreed to that date, and if Jinae joins us, we'll have six." She turned before she reached the door. "I look forward to seeing you all on Thursday—but no business talk," she said, wagging a finger.

We listened as she rounded the doctors' office pod, and when the clinic door opened, I leaned toward Fulbright. "I've told you all I can say here," I whispered. "We'll meet at my new home soon and try to reconnect you to an old friend. Will next Tuesday work for you?"

"Tuesday is perfect. I look forward to it," he said.

I swung by the gym. Even if Fulbright was right and strength hibernated within me, toning couldn't hurt.

4 The Reunion

"You didn't meet any … er … *foreigners* at the gym, did you?" Collin asked.

"No, no one from another planet or anywhere else."

He meant Ray, of course. Rayfarer had used the gym to help separate Collin from the crippling hallucinations that the alien had accidentally planted. That experience gave Collin and me a permanent link to our alien friend, but after we shielded Ray to help him hide from his predators, we had more difficulty contacting him.

Most of the time, we kept Collin's quarters in privacy mode. We trusted Marvin to keep *Listening Lennies* from knowing our private lives, and part of his protocol was to guard our secrets. We worried more about anyone hearing us speak of an alien before Ray was safe and we were set to introduce him to Mars. Who knew when that would happen? Even Marvin might be alarmed at those whispers, and an unexpected protocol could surface.

"Well, I have news," Collin said as he set our takeout pizza on the counter. "Guess who got a new assignment today."

"You?" I asked, giving him a big congratulatory kiss. "Did they make you geology lead? It was only a matter of time since they bumped Roderick Alexander to Secretary of Sciences."

He smiled and teased my kiss with three more. Then he squeezed me, saying, "No, that's not it. But nice that you think of me as leadership material."

"What then?" I asked, setting out plates.

"I've pulled an assignment at the cave."

"*The* cave?" I asked. Then whispered, "*Ray's* cave?"

He nodded. "Since the tragedy with Bernadette and Dexter, the council has been worried that Sanctuary Cave is dangerous. Before anyone visits, Alexander wants me to check for signs of malfunction or flaws in the seal between the safe cave interior and the raw Martian terrain. I know it better than anyone else on the team."

"That works for us, too, doesn't it?" I asked. "Is there a deadline for completing that job?"

"No, and I intend to drag my feet as long as necessary. I can stay in the loop of what's happening in the cave and keep Ray safe."

"You'll have to be careful, won't you?"

"Yes, if anyone is looking for free clues about where to search, they won't get them from me. In fact, I'll keep out of the lava tubes and stick to inspecting the barrier between raw Mars and the safe zones. There is no reason to lead anyone elsewhere."

"But they don't know what they are looking for, right?"

"We have no reason to think that, but we don't know who was behind the energy that scanned Ray. The best we can do is keep them from learning what *we* know till the time is right. We have no idea who watches that cave or what behavior will set them in motion. It pays to keep things on the down-low."

"Isn't Ray well-blocked and hidden?" I asked.

"I should review what's already been done toward security. I want to test what can reach him. Then, I can complete a safety check. Maybe I can set up a few monitors."

When I told him about Lilith's dinner event, Collin begged off. "I'll start my new assignment tomorrow, and I'll need privacy to review my findings and separate what's for our eyes only and what's for more public consumption."

I grimaced at meeting potential enemies without my backup, but

Collin wasn't worried.

"Before you came along, I was restricted to the surface, and none of us got a look at cave samples before Rod Alexander had approved them as safe. But then, you found a way to fix me, and now I might become the Geology lead. You cured over half those affected by hallucinations, and you faced the mystery on Mars before I knew anything about it." He grabbed my shoulders, saying. "You are so much stronger than you know. There's no stopping you, but just whistle, and I'll be there. I've got your back."

"I know you do," I said, "And besides, with Maria Torres there, Taco Marciano is friendly turf. I should be fine."

He pushed back and lifted my chin as he studied my uncertainty. "Tell you what," he said. "Invite Elly to take my place. She'll bring Andy. That's all the backup you'll need, don't you agree?"

He was right about that. My adopted Martian parents had shepherded me through more than one crisis. So, I nodded. "You're right; I've got this."

***

Maria met me at the door of Taco Marciano, and after a kiss on the cheek, she grabbed my hand. "This way," she said. "The party is bigger than I expected." She whisked us past the virtual Mariachi band in the main dining room, whispering, "How are things going so far? Are the new folks friendly?"

"So far, so good," I whispered back. "Do you know otherwise?"

"Westergaard has been to see Milo, but my husband wasn't bothered by it. We'll see."

The invitations I extended to Andy and Elly made perfect sense. The three newcomers had duties at the Waypoint Clinic now, so the Petersens were their working companions.

The gentlemen stood to shake hands, and we ladies exchanged greetings as Andy helped me into my seat. The others enjoyed nachos and fruity tea, and Maria illuminated the tabletop menu as we grabbed a plate.

"You're in luck, Spring," Maria said, pulling a useless pencil from her ponytail. "Would you like to join the others in trying our fajitas? We have a new shipment of freeze-dried chicken."

"What, no crickets?" Elly asked.

"No," Maria replied. "It's freshly grown from chicken cells in Earth's laboratory vats."

I chuckled, "That and a salad sounds perfect to me."

Lilith agreed. "I can't quite adjust to eating meat-shaped cricket powder," she said. "Chicken sounds delightful."

Neils' lips tipped upward in a tiny smile. "Oh, it's not so bad once you get used to it," he replied.

"You ate crickets on Earth?" she asked. "How did that happen?"

"Oh," he blushed. "Some of my associates made me try it. It's a good protein source, and if textured properly and prepared right, it passes for about anything."

"I agree," Andy said, grinning. "After years on Mars, I enjoy it, and our restaurants give it unique twists."

"Andy is just happy that he doesn't have to eat my cooking," Elly said, patting her husband's hand.

Then Andy turned to Lilith. "Our paths don't cross as often as I thought they might, Lilith. Is everything going well so far?"

"Yes, the staff are patient, and Jinae is nearby if I have a question."

"She's doing great," Jinae added. "Lils enjoys her work so much that I think she'd do it in her spare time if we didn't have rules against that."

Fulbright nodded. "Nurse Marchand has a calming influence on two of my patients. I've found her playing cards with Thaman and Giles, and when she's around, there's less bickering."

"They are sweet young men who help fill my evening hours. They want to be released for duty soon," Lilith said. "I hope that works out for them."

"Progress is on the doorstep," Wolfgang replied.

Jinae turned to Westergaard. "How's your desk in the Clinic offices working for you, Neils? Isn't it a bit out of your way?"

"Yes, it's a little walk from the communications pod to work, but the residents of the Icehouse are among those I am due to question. It's easier to catch them between appointments when I'm close to where they live and work. And the Bashirs and Petersens are kind enough to share evening entertainment with me occasionally."

"You're welcome anytime," Elly said with her warmest smile.

"Are you finding the answers you seek?" Fulbright asked.

"I've read the official reports, and so far, the interviews and physical evidence line up very well. I should have all finished by the time the next ship launches for home."

"That's very encouraging," Elly said, shooting a sly glance in my direction.

"Thank you," Westergaard replied. "I'll need to interview practically everyone who was at the Icehouse that night. They may have eyewitness accounts, and, more importantly, the witnesses can tell me what they saw when Ms. Duval died."

"Oh, no, no," Lilith said. "There shall be no work talk. We have office hours for that."

Elly chuckled, "You're right. So, tell us what you did on Earth, Lilith? What brought you to Mars?"

She shrugged. "My husband died some years ago, and I found I preferred adventure to a new marriage. The family business was well in hand, so I followed disease and misfortune, tending to those who required it. But such a life wore on me, and I wanted a different adventure. Mars needed a nurse. Voila! I am here."

"It's hard to imagine that working here is easier than a life chasing viruses," Jinae said. "But at least our Martian challenges are known and predictable."

"And, unlike viruses, there are fewer possibilities," Lilith added. "So far, I enjoy it here."

"What about you, Neils?" Jinae asked. "How were you chosen as an investigator?"

His brow added a furrow as he leaned over the table to reply. "There are many investigators on Earth who would qualify, but I was one of the few willing to take this journey."

"What was your reason for that?" Andy asked.

"My business associates persuaded me. Many of them are involved in propulsion or space colony sciences." He pointed to the dishes on the table, "And some are busy innovating food sources for Mars and future destinations. They are the ones who had me eat crickets," he said, shrugging. "And what about you, Spring?" he asked.

How much of my sad past did I care to share?

"My life on Earth had many unpleasant twists, and the final straw was that I found myself homeless with one opportunity—Mars. Being here has greatly improved my life. Sometimes I wish I had been born here," I said.

Elly tucked a loose tendril into her silvery upsweep. "There was nowhere besides Earth and its moon in those days. You arrived just when we needed you, and you needed us."

Neils cocked his head. "I see the rumors are true. You and Andy think of Spring as a daughter."

After that, the conversation shifted to comparing the recent voyage to Mars to the nine-month-long trips in the earlier days of the colony. Then, Milo Torres entered the room.

"Forgive me for intruding," Milo said. "I'm here to collect Maria, and I just wanted to welcome everyone to Mars. You must be Ms. Marchand," he said, bowing to Lilith. Then he turned to Neils. "Mr. Westergaard, you know where to find me if you have more questions. Feel free anytime."

Neils nodded, "I'll do so, Mr. Torres." Then he leaned back, studying Milo over his nose, as he added, "I do have one favor. I understand Beth Martin was close to Ginger Welsh. Could you allow her time from work to speak with me?"

What would Ginger or Beth have to do with the night Duval died?

Milo might have straightened his neck, but he hardly missed a beat as he replied, "Just let me know your time frame, and we'll work it out."

The line connecting Beth to Ginger led to Ross Hashimi and Ray.

Would an investigator of two unexpected deaths draw a conclusion leading to Ray? And would I become part of that chain?

Dr. Fulbright offered to escort me home when our party broke up, but Neils Westergaard stepped in instead. He leaned toward me, baring the first full smile I had seen on him, explaining, "Dr. Fulbright's Icehouse is in the opposite direction, but I live in the communications sector. Your home in the sciences pod is practically on my way. If you don't mind, Spring, I'd enjoy a short walk with you."

My friends were as surprised as I was at the offer, but they hid their curious glances. I couldn't get beyond that slick smile.

Fulbright spoke up first. "Ah, then my questions will hold until the meeting we scheduled."

"Of course, Dr. Fulbright," I said. "But let me know if you need anything before then."

Neils pulled the chair out for me and offered his arm. Then, looking around the table, he said, "There's no need to worry; Mr. Grant's quarters are quite near mine, and I may drop in on an old acquaintance in the Sciences Pod, Roderick Alexander."

Andy stood to give me a quick hug and turned to Westergaard. "Good night then, Neils. I'll see you in the office tomorrow."

"Good night to you all," he replied. "Lilith, thank you for a nice evening."

We were soon out the door and in the virtual falling leaves display of the station's Central Park. Westergaard walked with no more contact than a touch on the elbow to steer me toward the Sciences Sector. But his questions were more invasive.

"Collin works under the supervision of Dr. Alexander, doesn't he?" Neils asked.

"Yes, Roderick was his supervisor in the Geology department, and now Dr. Alexander is Secretary of Sciences. How do you know him?"

"He was one of the first Martian colonists Luis Kaneko introduced me to. He could answer my questions about exposure to the Martian terrain and why Duval and Craig may have been at Sanctuary Cave.

He's been quite helpful."

Something nagged at me. Neils droned on about Central Park's virtual scenery as I tried to ferret out what troubled me. He got my attention again when he mentioned Collin.

"I may cross paths with your partner this week, Dr. Graviston. That is still your name, isn't it? You haven't remarried, have you?" he asked.

That stopped me. It took a few ticks to put together a reply. "No. Collin and I are not married. Did you know my husband?" I asked.

"Only through his reputation with AI systems," he replied. "But some of my business associates knew him, and they speak of the genius of his work."

"Yes, he was well-respected."

"Did he influence your coming to Mars?"

"Only indirectly. But working with Edward's Martian simulations gave me experience that applies here."

"Ah. That explains it," he said.

The conversation was unnerving, and I was glad when we reached my living quarters.

"Thank you for your company, Dr. Graviston," Neils said. "I'm sure we will speak again soon."

Why did that sound like a threat? Then I realized that in that short walk from the restaurant to home, Neils confessed to talking to Collin's boss and planned to cross paths with us again. He even knew about Edward. He had been prying into our backgrounds and personal details.

Collin welcomed me home and immediately noticed my annoyed expression.

"What's up?" he asked. "Did you have too much tequila?"

"No tequila," I replied. "Too much Neils Westergaard. Watch out for him. He says he's likely to cross paths with you soon."

"Is that worrisome?" he asked.

I shook my head. "Something's wrong. I can't put my finger on it. He says he'll be talking with me again soon, too."

"You can handle him," Collin said.

"I think I'd rather stay out of his way," I replied.

Collin chuckled as he poured Martian strawberry wine to ease into the evening.

I let the sip flow through me, hoping it would ease the puzzle of Neils Westergaard.

5 The Council

Collin's hand slipped from mine as he went to meet his ride in the Transport Bay, and I turned toward Council Hall for our Friday wrap-up.

Jinae Kim eagerly beckoned by the Town Hall door. She still bubbled with as much excitement for her third Council Meeting as she had for the first. We had become more than friends but were nothing like Dexter Craig and Bernadette Duval, our predecessors in our new positions. We linked arms, confident we'd figure out how to fill their shoes as the new Council Secretary of Human Services and her assistant.

"I need to ask you about something before the meeting," Jinae whispered as she pulled a parcel from her satchel. "Look at this."

"Didn't those belong to Bernadette?" I asked as I examined the familiar paperweight and inkwell that had adorned Duval's desk.

Jinae pursed her lips, shrugging as she replied, "Yeah. They were left on my desk, and I don't know what to do with them. Lilith recognized them as priceless French antiques, maybe 18th-century."

"Does she want to send them back to Earth?" I asked.

"Maybe. Lilith thought they should occupy a special place here as they would have in France, and she asked if the memorial niches will ever contain real objects."

"That's not a bad idea. I'll speak to Luis and see what he says."

"Take these then," Jinae said as she passed the parcel to me. "I don't feel comfortable holding them."

"OK." I shrugged, "Maybe Luis has a vault."

Luis tapped his gavel for our attention, and the meeting began.

I had been a regular attendee at council meetings for several weeks and knew the Friday wrap-up routine. First, the Communications Secretary, Peter Ulikov, explained any new dispatches from Earthside and the lunar Threshold station. Then, each WayPoint secretary gave notes and entertained questions on updates from their division. That part of the meeting could take over an hour, as many divisions overlapped and discussions arose.

My division, Human Services, was primarily medical support, but that extended to human well-being, which involved nearly every other division. After all, the grand mission of WayPoint Station was our experiment on human survival on Mars.

Ulikov informed us that the hearing for Garrison Mathis was underway. The prospect of his return to Mars wouldn't be decided until the hearing and possible trial were completed.

"I'll act as the temporary fill-in for your Prime Two for a while longer," Westergaard said.

And since Neils had a slot on the agenda, Kaneko invited him to update us on his investigation.

"I've completed the review of the written reports and depositions, and I've just begun personal interviews, so I have a way to go before I can file my report," Neils said.

Secretary Alexander told us Collin Grant would lead an examination of every inch of the barrier lining Sanctuary Cave. Until that was completed and the cave proved contaminant-free, the space would be closed for events and other visits.

When it was my turn, I explained that Dr. Fulbright was settling back into his old position as Doctor of Psychiatric Sciences and making headway with the final hallucinatory patients, Giles Cardiff and Thaman Bakshi, and that Elly Petersen would host the next

Supper Club meeting on the following Friday night.

"Thank you, Dr. Graviston," Luis said, "If any division has newcomers that aren't settling in well, please point them toward the Supper Club." After waiting for questions, he added, "Spring, can you update us on your memorial room for lost colonists of WayPoint?"

I explained the general purpose and operation of the room and added that anyone may leave instructions on how they would like to be memorialized should that time come while they are on Mars. Luis followed my comments with his impression.

"I've seen the room, and I approve. So far, the comments are good. Spring. Do you plan any changes?" Kaneko asked.

"Today, I had a suggestion to make physical objects part of a person's memorial. But since the virtual display is intangible, we would have to add a new physical feature to the memorial."

Luis stroked his chin, then said, "Perhaps we can make a series of small niches along the ceiling in that room. That would give space for hundreds of receptacles for personal objects. And each could display a small label identifying the lost Martian. Perhaps in years to come, some of your relatives may come to Mars and want to touch something you touched. We can't go overboard with that, but we can make it so."

Roderick spoke from his remote screen. "I'll order a few samples for your approval, and then we can combine Martian soil with Earth clay to make the receptacles."

"Earth and Mars combined—perfect! Let's do that," Luis replied.

Some of the divisions had only material requisitions and production figures to report. Maria was last on the agenda, reminding everyone that now was a good time to eat chicken dishes as we had fresh supplies from Earth.

After the meeting, Jinae and I followed Maria's advice. We grabbed some chicken tacos and found a park bench to enjoy lunch.

"How do you like your new desk in the clinic?" I asked.

"It's OK. I offered my quarters to Lilith, and now I sleep in the nurse's overnight room. That way, I'm handy to fill in, and I still get to do some nursing."

"That's a lot of your life tied to business," I said.

"Listen to who's taking. You used to eat, sleep, and work in the clinic, not to mention the off-hours you devoted to the Supper Club. Besides, I like keeping my eye on things. Fulbright's good company, too. We play cards after hours, sometimes, *if* I can get him away from Lilith Marchand."

"Oh, Lilith is sticking to him, eh?"

"She is, but she seems more interested in his patients. They play cards, too, especially poker. Wolfgang says it's therapy for their weaknesses."

"Oh? In what way?"

She shrugged. "Fulbright says cards can build confidence in making independent decisions and spotting bluffs."

"I never thought of it that way."

"Dexter and Bernadette come up in conversation, too. When I'm the fourth player with Lilith, Giles, and Thaman, she always mentions Bernadette. Despite Duval's beauty, neither Giles nor Thaman cared much for her. But Thaman likes Lilith a lot. He always wants to be on her team if we play partners."

"What do you make of that?" I asked.

"Nothing, really," she said with a shrug. "By the way, don't forget, meeting Fulbright on Tuesday is on your calendar. He can explain how playing cards is part of his therapy."

Part of her duty was to remind me of things, but I had not forgotten Wolfgang. Collin and I were both weary of juggling our secret. Wolfgang Fulbright knew about Ray; perhaps he had an insight that Collin and I had missed. The eccentric doctor should be the first brought into our confidence. We needed wise counsel about our hidden friend. The sooner, the better.

6 The Blue Room

On Tuesday, the night we were to meet with Dr. Fulbright, Collin was late getting home.

"Sorry, hon. Rod wanted a complete walk-through of the areas we've used in Sanctuary Cave. He took his time looking them over, too."

"What did he expect to find?" I asked. "Not little green men, I hope."

Collin shook his head. "I don't think he had anything in mind, and it's not like he hasn't been in that cave enough times."

"Is he under pressure about something?" I asked.

"Maybe so. When I worked above ground, Rod didn't want anyone else analyzing samples until he knew what was in them. What was the point of that?"

"Do you think he was looking for Martian diamonds—something valuable?"

"I don't know; maybe he thought he was helping us. He could have been rushing; Neils Westergaard wants a tour as soon as possible."

"Well, clean up. Fulbright will finish his dinner date soon. I'll run out for taquitos to keep you from starving."

"Sounds like a plan."

***

While Collin was in the sonic shower, I hurried to Taco Marciano to grab the food and nearly bumped into Milo as I pushed through the door.

"Oops, sorry. Did I spill anything?" I asked, brushing Milo's sleeve.

"No, no. All is well, but I have news you may want to hear," he said. "Ginger was due to stop for rock samples today, and she messaged to let me know when she would arrive at the Phobos drop-off point."

"So, you're not worried something is wrong."

"Now, I'm not. I told Beth, and she was relieved, too. Ginger hasn't replied to her messages, but maybe that's what she wants now."

"When it comes to Ginger Welsh, who knows?" I replied.

"Neils Westergaard asked about her, too, and he seemed relieved that we don't have another Martian in trouble."

"Me too," I said, calling over my shoulder as I ran to grab my order.

***

Collin met me at the door. "Mmm. Smells yummy."

"I'll get these on a platter," I said, pushing his hand from the parcel. "You get ready for Wolfgang."

All was ready when Marvin announced Fulbright at the door, and we welcomed him inside. Wolfgang raised an eyebrow as Collin put Marvin in complete privacy mode.

"In case of a visitor," Collin said with a wink.

"Did you have a nice dinner?" I asked.

"I did. Lilith wanted to try the French Restaurant, so I got an early reservation. She asked why I wanted to end our evening so quickly, and I told her we planned to discuss our patients. She might notice if I return too late, though."

We spent a few moments chatting about the dinner and our two remaining patients, but finally, we reached the point of this meeting—Ray.

"How did you first meet Rayfarer, and how did you interact with him?" I asked.

"So, he has a name now," Wolfgang grinned.

Collin shrugged. "It was Spring's idea, but Ray doesn't seem to mind. How did you meet him?"

"When I found the blue charms on Hashimi's body, I began to have—I guess you'd call them daydreams—pictures in my mind that made no sense," Fulbright said. "But I noticed they happened more often when I held the charm. Eventually, I understood that the images were communication, but it was hard to match words to pictures. I finally understood: the being behind the images was in trouble. Sometimes, he showed me pictures like the ones my patients saw, but I couldn't decode the meaning."

"You didn't give me much to work with," I said.

"No, and it was even worse when his communications became fragmented. Anyway, what I shared with you must have been enough. Your Rayfarer is safe, and you understand him better than I did." Fulbright replied.

"Yes, and when I could speak to him better, he was able to repair some of our patients."

"So, may I meet him tonight?"

"Yes. At least, I hope it will work. We had to shield Ray with the charms, but Collin and I can still meet with him mentally. Since you had previous contact, we think we can include you in the group."

"I'm ready."

"OK. Let's see how this goes," Collin said, taking my hands in his.

In our minds, we went to our Blue Room, and the silvery vision of Ray appeared.

"Oh. So nice to see you both," Ray said. "Waking on this planet brought me the first real communication in ages. Now that I'm in hiding, I miss it."

"We have someone else here tonight. Someone you contacted before you met Spring. His name is Wolfgang Fulbright, and I hope you can bring him to our room," Collin said.

Collin reached a hand toward Fulbright, and I stretched to touch Ray's cool arm. After a moment, four of us were in the room.

When Fulbright gasped, I asked, "What do you see?"

"I see the visitor. He's silvery, thin, and tall. Is that what he looks like?" Fulbright asked.

"It's what he thinks we expect," I said.

"I don't look like much of anything now, but I hope to acquire a body soon," Ray said. "What you see is an image that Spring and Collin can accept. You seem to respond to it, too."

"Why couldn't you speak like this to me before?" Wolfgang asked.

"I could not use words before and damaged your patients when I tried to contact them with images. I learned more quickly with Spring. I began learning with her, then working with Collin expanded my understanding until we could cure some of those I damaged."

"Will you still be able to work with the remaining patients?" Wolfgang asked. "There are two more to cure."

"I will be happy to fix what I broke if I can. We had a mediary before, a way for me to interact with Collin and Sarah visually. Is that body still available?" Ray asked.

"Yes and no," I replied. "Ray can interact with electronic images, like our advanced AI teachers. The ones that generate sense effects, like smell, taste, and touch, allow Ray to carry on more realistic conversations."

"We didn't get to use that for long, though," Collin said. "After Bernadette discovered that Spring was using advanced AI to treat her patients, Eldredge Osgood, an AI psychologist program, was reduced to audio-only."

"Why would they do that?" Fulbright asked.

"Dexter Craig was my boss then, and he claimed weird stuff on Mars might discourage settlers. So, he forbade me to use extraordinary means to treat the hallucinations, including advanced AI."

Collin shrugged. "Spring fudged a bit, and Ray interacted with our patients through Vince, the boxing coach. We got into trouble for that, too."

"But Fulbright has access to the current audio-only AI Osgood. That should be useful," I said.

"Will that expose Ray?" Fulbright asked.

Collin shrugged. "I don't know. Ray, are you still shielded?"

"My shields are in place. I'm here through my strong links to you and Spring. But in some ways, I know the beings I broke even better than Fulbright. Those beings had a stronger ability to receive me even without the charm as an amplifier. Maybe I can reach them while shielded."

"Have you experienced any interference tonight?" Fulbright asked.

The silver man shook his head.

I turned to Wolfgang. "Then maybe you can meet with Giles while Ray interacts as audio Osgood and repair Giles that way," I said.

Ray liked the idea. "I'm willing to try it. I'd welcome the break in my solitude," he said.

Fulbright tapped his knee, thinking. "We'd need one of you as a relay. Communication through me alone might not be strong enough yet. And it won't rouse suspicion if Spring consults with me regarding her former patients."

"We should set up a trial run," I said.

"Perfect," Fulbright said. "And now that we have a plan for healing, I have other questions." Wolfgang turned to our alien. "How and why did you come here, Ray?"

Ray leaned forward but then began to flicker as he spoke. "This … thi … is plan …," he began.

"Oh, no, the stuttering," I said.

"Ray, are you being scanned? Is something interfering?" Collin asked.

Ray's head jerked, and then he vanished from the headroom.

"Collin, what's happening?" Fulbright asked.

Collin shrugged. "I don't know. Rod might have returned to the cave, but no one should be near enough to bother Ray."

I shook my head in disbelief. *How could this happen?*

"Is he gone?" Fulbright asked. "Have you seen this before?"

I nodded. "We believed someone was scanning for him. But how can anything breach the shield?"

"Maybe the seekers are trying something new," Fulbright said.

"Or maybe they are closer than we think," Collin added. "Spring, I'm going to the cave earlier tomorrow."

My eyes widened. "Don't wait. Go now."

"That might be too suspicious," Fulbright said.

"Tomorrow. First thing," Collin replied.

"Should I come with you?" I asked.

"No," Fulbright insisted. "Don't do anything out of the ordinary."

Collin nodded. "He's right."

Fulbright fidgeted as he prepared to leave. Finally, he said, "This is too much for you two alone. You should tell Kaneko about Ray."

"But we don't even know if he can reach Luis," Collin said. "He never held the charm."

"Do you know where the charm is now?" Fulbright asked.

"Yes. It's with Ray in the cave, but he won't be shielded if we move it. His enemies may find him."

"Then figure it out. It must be done. It's wrong to keep this secret from Kaneko; he should know we have an alien on the planet. Contact *both* Kanekos. It's too much to ask Luis to keep secrets from his wife. They should be added to the loop as soon as possible."

"We have a little wrinkle with the cave," Collin said. "Roderick Alexander oversees the cave right now. I'm there daily to help with the inspection Kaneko demanded after the incident."

"Will he get anywhere close to Ray?"

"I think I can keep him away from that part of the cave, but if he becomes comfortable there, he might explore when I'm not around to watch him."

Fulbright leaned forward. "My advice is to keep others away from Ray for now. You two work it out. I should return to the clinic."

After Wolfgang left for the Icehouse, Collin poured us a short glass of strawberry wine. "How can we get Kaneko and Michelle to the cave without piquing Rod's curiosity?" he asked.

We cuddled on the couch as we mulled over the evening.

"It felt good to be with Ray again," Collin said.

I agreed. "He feels like part of us."

"We've made progress with healing the others, but as for Ray's problem, we're no closer to finding his body."

I leaned on his shoulder. "We made one giant step when we found him—his container, anyway. And step two was shielding him to keep him safe."

Collin squeezed my hand. "At least there's that."

"Rod hasn't asked about the back tunnels, has he?"

"He hasn't mentioned them to me. So far, he is interested in the meeting room, storage room, work room, and transition chambers. He wants me to inspect the small tunnel that leads to raw terrain. He wants that portal sealed, for sure."

"Good, then Ray is safe for now. And if he is safe, we are safer, too."

Collin nodded. "I sure hope so. But who knows what can happen when we add two more to our secret club."

"We must tell Luis," I said.

"Would it be easier to go through Michelle?" Collin asked.

I leaned forward, "Luis will be upset when he finds out we didn't mention Ray before now."

Collin shook his head, adding, "You're right. The news won't go down any easier if he gets it secondhand from his wife."

"What do you think he'll do with us?" I asked.

Collin's face went stony. "We can't be bothered by what may happen to us. Our fate is secondary," he said. His fists were so tight I thought he would bleed. "Fulbright is right; we can't wait any longer."

"But when?" I asked.

"It must happen in the cave with us and the Kanekos."

"Friday, then. Luis wants me to escort Neils to the next Supper Club. I'll beg off and ask him to let Rod take Neils instead. That will clear the cave. You'll be there already, and I'll bring the Kanekos."

Collin shook his head, asking, "How can we ever convince them to go there?"

"We need good explanations for not telling them about Ray before and why they must know now," I said.

"They'd better be darn good reasons," Collin replied.

***

The Supper Club scenario worked like a charm. My excuse? Collin wanted to show me something unusual he found in the cave, and Michelle interpreted that as needing time alone.

On Thursday, Collin messaged Luis, inviting him to see a curiosity worthy of the leader of Mars. There were a few more questions about what could be so important, but vague answers sufficed, and the Kanekos made plans to take me to the cave on Friday.

That was enough to start, but I expected some pointed questions during that trip. The ride to the cave was too long for silence. It would be close quarters in the Prime Minister's rover, and the Kanekos were already curious about Collin's secret. If the conversation came too close to the truth, I'd face an inquisition during the entire trip to Sanctuary Cave, and it was bad form to lie to anyone—especially WayPoint's leader.

So, I planned to hint about alien artifacts on the ride toward the Sanctuary and save any mention of an actual alien until we were close enough to meet him, but sticking to that plan would be a struggle.

"Don't worry," Collin said. "Your best is always good enough."

How I wish that were true.

7 Worlds Collide

Neils Westergaard and Rod Alexander were occupied on Friday evening, as scheduled. So, when Kaneko finally escaped his office, Luis, Michelle, and I suited up and headed toward Sanctuary Cave. We rode silently until we were clear of the WayPoint perimeter, but questions were inevitable. I had a plan for that. Answer simply but true.

Michelle started the inquisition.

"So, what has Collin found in the cave?" she asked.

"You know how Collin loves to dig," I replied. "He found something strange while he was inspecting the cave."

That much was true.

"But why didn't he ask Roderick Alexander about it? He's a geologist, too."

"Collin says this specimen is unique; it might not be from this solar system. He thought Luis should handle it."

The truth was a bit tarnished around the edges in that statement, but still not a complete lie.

Luis was focused on driving around rocks, but he shrugged his shoulders. "Most of our craters are made by impact; surely some space debris is from outside our orbits."

"Oh? Are you aware of any samples like that?" I asked. When he shook his head, I added, "Collin hasn't seen anything like this either."

"He didn't find part of a spaceship from Alpha Centauri, did he, Spring?" Michelle asked, chuckling.

I wished she hadn't made that joke, but I tried to laugh it off. "Pfft. Alpha Centauri? Where did you get that idea?" I replied.

That was the wrong response. Luis looked over his shoulder. "Then where was it from?"

I shrugged again, trying to make the answer unimportant. "I c … can't s…say. Maybe it's not even alien."

Luis stopped the rover and spun his body to face me. "Are you saying that it *might* not be alien? Or does he *believe* it's alien?"

Michelle patted his shoulder. "Relax, mon cher. Spring must have been joking."

Luis was not in the mood for games. "Spring cleared everyone else from the cave and spirited us away from WayPoint. Such trouble must have a reason, and *alien* is the word *she* used." He turned to me. "Tell me. Have you found something alien?"

"Seriously, Luis, she's not on the witness stand. Don't interrogate her," Michelle begged.

But Luis was more determined than ever. "Answer my question, Spring."

It was a yes or no question.

"Yes," I whispered.

Michelle's blue eyes burned into me as she gasped. "Alien! Is it a machine? A ship? What has Collin found?"

I picked her first question, "No."

That was true. It wasn't a machine. At least, I was pretty sure it wasn't a machine … not by Earth's definition, anyway.

Luis stretched his throbbing neck over the barrier between our benches. "We will not move another inch until you answer. What has Collin found?"

Michelle raised her dropped jaw. "Is it … an *alien*?" she whispered.

I lowered my eyes, barely whispering, "It *might* be an alien."

Luis twisted to the front, engaged the hover drive, and sped over the rocks toward Sanctuary Cave. He made noises, but they sounded more like rocks in a tumbler than words.

I interrupted his growling, "It's not *exactly* an alien. It's more alien communication."

That didn't help.

Michelle tried to speak, but her words were lost in her gasps. "When did he find this? How do you know it's true? Is Collin hallucinating again?" she asked.

I shook my head no. "The alien accidentally gave him his hallucinations, but then he cured Collin of them. He tries to be helpful."

Luis banged the control screen as he swore in Japanese. I pressed my back deep into the seat support, sweating inside my helmet and wishing I could disappear.

"Spring … cherie …, tell us what this alien looks like. Will he frighten us?" Michelle asked.

I shook my head no. "You can't see him."

"No?" she asked.

"Only the container holding him."

Luis swore again. "An alien in a can. No more! Silence, please, both of you. We will find our answers in the cave."

***

Luis ran from the rover in full gear; Michelle and I followed more slowly. "Hurry," he said, beckoning us into the Gateway transition tube. Once the atmosphere was safe, he spun the hatch open and rushed into the cave.

Collin, in standard WayPoint attire, smiled as he beckoned us to sit at a meeting table.

"Should we stay in our gear?" Michelle asked. "And can we speak freely in here?"

"Only we are here, so speak as you wish. It's safe to remove your helmets and gloves for now," Collin said.

Luis banged his helmet onto the table, and once Michelle removed her gloves, she grabbed Collin's hand. "Is it truly an alien?" she whispered.

Collin's eyes darted to mine. I shrugged, replying, "I'm sorry. It came out in the ride here." Then I turned to Michelle. "I'm convinced he is an alien. At least, he's most of one. But he is in trouble." Then I turned to Luis. "He has messages for us, but we must help him first."

"*Most* of one." Luis shook his head again. "Where is this part of an alien?"

"He's divided. That's why he's in trouble," Collin replied.

Despite my previous failures, I tried to help. "We have his ... well, I think of it as his brain, but that's inaccurate. There is very little *matter* to him yet, but we have his *energy*, and that's the part speaking to us."

"How long have you known about this alien?" Luis demanded.

"Don't blame Collin," I said. "Ray ... that's what we named him. Ray approached me when I was new to Mars. All of Mars was strange, and I didn't know he was alien until he explained it to me."

"This sounds like an AI trick," Luis replied. "Are you sure of what you've seen? Could it be a deception?"

"I'm convinced it's real, too," Collin replied, "Spring helped him cure most of her hallucinating patients, too."

"The visions were Ray's fault, and he wanted to fix them," I said. "You've seen him at work, too."

"We have?" Luis shouted, wild-eyed. "When was that?"

"He can interact through electronic bodies, like our Virtual Boxing Instructor, Vince. We used him as Virtual Eldredge Osgood to cure the patients, and he appeared at my trial. Do you remember?"

Michelle nodded. "I remember. He was above and beyond any AI that I had seen. And Osgood gave me clues to win that trial."

"See. Ray means to be helpful." I said, not mentioning that he was more *above and beyond* than they guessed.

"Did you work with an alien to repair the minds of WayPoint citizens?" Luis asked.

"You said I should use any means possible to do my job, that I was the expert."

"Are you using my words against me?" Luis demanded.

"Here, here," Michelle said. "Tempers flaring will do no good. Calmer minds must prevail if we want the truth."

Luis, clearly losing his patience, scowled. "Convince me this is not a fraud. Produce this alien, and I'll see what I make of him." Then he turned his anger toward Collin and me. "I don't know what has gotten into you two, but this had better be good."

"We hope you will meet him tonight," Collin said.

Luis' face turned red. "Hope is not enough."

"Spring and I connect to him mentally, like meeting in a room in our heads," Collin said. "He didn't know how to communicate with us at first. That's where the hallucinations came from. But now he knows most of our words. Let's see if you can meet him the way we do."

"Very well," Luis jerked two chairs from the meeting table and motioned for Michelle to sit with him. Collin and I joined them at the table.

In a flash, I was in two places at once. Mentally, Collin and I met Ray in our headroom, but we were also in Sanctuary Cave with Michelle and Luis. I took a stab at the introductions in the Blue Room.

"Ray, our leader, Luis Kaneko, is here. Please explain your mission so that he can help us. Please try to reach him."

It was impossible to know what Ray did when he went silent, but emotion sometimes washed over the silver face; now, he looked puzzled. But once he had considered options, he focused on the mental ceiling.

"I'm trying," Ray said. "But it's like the others who came to the cave. I could reach some and not others. I cannot find your Luis."

"He's having trouble reaching you, Luis. Try opening your mind as if trying to hear voices in the wind or make a daydream real. See if you can meet him halfway."

Luis shook his head. "There's nothing there."

"What else can we try?" I shrugged.

"Wait," Michelle said. "I hear him." She beamed as she scanned her surroundings in the wonderous Blue Room, then turned to her husband in the cave. “I can see him, Luis.”

“What do you see?” he asked.

“I am in another room with blue chairs; Collin, Spring, and the alien are there, too. It’s like a shared dream. The silver man’s name is Rayfarer. I can communicate with them there. Whatever I speak in this cave, Spring, Collin, and Ray can hear in the Blue Room, but my voice comes from my mind, not my throat.”

Luis hurried to his wife. “This can’t be happening. Is my wife seeing things now? Is this what the hallucinations were all about? We can’t stay here. Michelle is in danger.”

She reached for her husband’s arm. “Sit, my love. I am fine. We will convince you. Please, sit.”

“How can we do that?” Collin asked.

“Take me to Michelle in this Blue Room. Then maybe I’ll believe this is real.” Luis said.

She took his hand. “mon cher, ask me a question only you and I know. I will *think* the answer to the others in the Blue Room, and then Spring or Collin can speak the answer here. At least that will prove that I have two ways of communicating with them.”

Luis squeezed her hand. “Very well. Collin, tell me the name of my first dog. Michelle knows the answer, but I’m sure neither of you does.”

She nodded and *thought* to us in the Blue Room.

“I heard it,” Collin said. “Your first dog was named Ninja.”

“This is a trick,” Luis said. “Maybe you told that to Spring sometime.”

“A better test, then; think of something she can’t know, and I’ll ask that,” Michelle said.

“Very well. Ask Collin the name of the first child you kissed after our wedding. You remember, don’t you?”

“Of course I do,” she replied.

Then she *thought* us the answer, and Cave Collin replied out loud. “It was the ring bearer. His name was Sosha. Michelle kissed his scraped knee after he tripped.”

Luis took a grudging step toward being convinced.

"We can do this all day," Michelle said. "But maybe we should get to the heart of the matter. Perhaps hearing how we can help Ray will convince you."

"I'd rather hear what our visitor *wants* from us," Luis said.

"We know the answer," Collin replied. "But in this case, Ray will tell Michelle, and she can relay what he says."

After listening in the Blue Room, Michelle spoke out loud. "Ray has been on Mars for a long time, waiting for the people to reach this planet, our doorway to space. He knows about civilizations beyond our reach. He means to be an ambassador to this solar system, but he needs his body, and it's missing."

Collin picked up the story. "He can't be a teacher until he can stand among our people face to face."

"How can he be missing a body?" Luis asked.

"As far as I understand, Ray's matter and energy were separated as part of his travel through the stars," I said. "But those two parts—you might call them his body and soul—were to be reunited when it was time to make contact."

"So, is there a dead alien body lying around somewhere?" Luis asked, eyes wide.

"No, it's not like that," I replied, and when Michelle heard Ray's answer, she explained to Luis.

"When his two parts are brought together, his energy will combine with matter from this planet to reconstitute into a complete being," she said.

Luis spread his hands, asking, "How can I know that's true? How can I believe he means good for Earth?"

"We believe him," I said. Collin nodded.

Michelle smiled, adding, "They are telling you what I heard, and I believe the visitor speaks the truth."

"But how can I risk my duties to Earth and Mars by believing something unproven? How can I have the same faith in him that you do?"

“There is a way that might work,” Collin said. “But it’s dangerous. We shielded him against interfering scans, but we can take you to him in the cave.”

“Please do it,” Luis said, reaching for his helmet.

“We can take you to the container holding his energy,” Collin replied.

Michelle grabbed her husband’s elbow. “If it’s so dangerous, can’t you bring him and his shields here?” she asked.

Collin shook his head. “That will put Ray at risk. If we remove the objects that shield him, those searching might find Ray.”

“Who is searching for him?” Michelle asked.

“We aren’t sure who or why, but we know Bernadette Duval, Dexter Craig, and Garrison Mathis were part of it,” I replied.

“Mathis … and Duval,” Luis said. “I see.”

“We talked with Ray before we knew where he was,” Collin said. “We found him the night Bernadette and Dexter died. We don’t know how important a part Craig, Duval, and Mathis played, but they were looking for something that had to do with Ray. That’s why Spring and I were here that night, and it’s why we are here now. We came to help protect him.”

I picked up the story. “Bernadette believed Wolfgang Fulbright knew where to find the prize she sought, and when she and Dexter could not find Fulbright, they found Collin and me at Sanctuary Cave and looked for Wolfgang here.”

“But Fulbright wasn’t on Mars that night,” Michelle said. “He was under treatment on Earth.”

Luis brushed that aside, interrupting. “Garrison Mathis and Bernadette Duval wanted nothing more than power. They lied to steal my authority; the coup proved that. If they were after Ray or some part of him, they meant to use it for their own gains, which means this thing you call an alien holds great power. Whoever was with them in the plot mustn’t find him. Take me to the alien.”

“Are you sure?” Spring asked.

Michelle touched her husband’s arm. “If this alien has power, he could be dangerous to you, mon cher. Please do not go."

"Michelle, if this is danger, it is upon us. And if I cannot survive it, neither can our WayPoint citizens. I must go."

"You'll need your full gear and an oxygen supply," Collin said.

Michelle stood as she replaced her gloves. "I'm coming, too."

Collin held up a hand to stop her. "More than two of us will make the path more difficult."

"Please, dear. I must go alone this time. No matter what's behind this, it affects our colony, and I'm sworn to protect WayPoint," Luis said before refitting his helmet.

I took Michelle's arm. "We will go as far as the raw tunnel entrance and guard against intruders."

"Very well, but my helmet stays with me, and if my husband is in danger, I'm going to him," she replied.

Collin geared up in the storage room and opened communication with Luis. Michelle and I were still present with Ray and Blue Room Collin; we could hear what was said there.

Collin pointed toward the Guardian transition portal in the storage room. "Past this door is raw Martian terrain. Full suits are required. Spring, seal both safety hatches once we're beyond the transition tunnel."

I nodded, and we watched as the safety protocol played out, and the two men entered a tunnel carved from raw Mars.

Collin took Luis down the path to the right; after a few more turns, they reached the lava tube cave-in and the pile of rubble that held Ray's cask at the top.

"You are here," Ray whispered.

"Do you see that white thing at the top, Luis?" Collin asked. "That holds Ray's energy. If you can climb up there, you will find two blue curved pieces fastened to the cask. Those are shielding him. Touch those, and you should be able to see Ray the way Michelle does."

Luis started up, but the rocks slipped beneath his feet.

"I'll go with you," Collin said. "I'll climb up the other side and help you find solid footholds."

They made better progress then, but Luis huffed as they reached the top.

"You are nearly within reach," Ray said.

"I see it. I see the blue pieces. Are these parts of Spring's heart pendant?" he asked.

"They are," Collin said. "They helped her learn to speak to Ray."

"Will one hand do?" Luis asked. "I need to hold on with the other."

"Try it," Collin replied, and within seconds, Luis appeared in our Blue Room.

"Voila! See, my love. We are not coo-coo."

"Perhaps we are *all* coo-coo," he muttered.

But soon, he spoke to Ray directly and finally grasped the gravity of Ray's mission.

"You are on the threshold of far more than space," Ray said. "In time, you will meet old civilizations that have learned and grown beyond the wisest on Earth. We need you. Life in the universe is common, but sentient life is far rarer. We welcome other beings such as yourselves. But I must prepare your people before our civilizations meet, and I need my full strength to do it."

"Why don't you have it then?" Luis asked. "What happened?"

"I can't be sure, but it would take great power to separate my controllers, the blue charms, from my cask. There must have been some catastrophe as I landed. Things were shifted from where they should have been. From inside this cask, I wasn't aware of the problem till your colonists arrived and awakened me, but now I must be able to do my duty."

"And I must do mine," Luis said. "You bring me tasks I never expected. We will shield you until we know more, but my first duty is to protect WayPoint."

"As it should be," Ray replied.

"Do you have any idea where your missing half is?" Luis asked.

"I do not know. The ambassador role is a once-in-a-lifetime task that usually continues till death. I have no experience with rejoining, but I was prepared for it. I expected the two casks to be close enough to start reconstitution when I signaled it, but my other half was not within range."

Luis turned to Collin. "Has anyone searched the rest of these tunnels?"

"Spring and I only saw the parts of the cave we passed while searching for Ray."

Luis turned back to his image of the silver man. "Will you be safe here?" he asked.

"I have been so far."

"But what happened the other night? Something interrupted you," I said.

"I can't explain it, but something reached me."

"I'll check my monitors and see what I can find," Collin said. "Maybe someone else holds a clue, too. For now, we will block this part of the cave. We need to keep searchers away."

In the Blue Room, Luis turned to Ray. "I have a million questions, but we must leave you now. But I hope our search will bring evidence for me and a resolution of status for you. In the meantime, I'll take measures to keep this site secure."

Ray's smile was not quite human, but it was friendly, even as we sealed him into his lonely tunnel again.

We walked back to the Sanctuary room with the Kanekos, and one of the last things Luis suggested was the highest possible security with night and day guards in the cave.

"Night and day for how long?" I asked, but no one replied.

Then, when we were all clear of the Blue Room, Luis asked, "Can he hear us now?"

Collin shook his head. "I can't feel him. How about you, Spring?"

"He isn't with me now," I replied.

Before the Kanekos entered the Gateway chamber to exit, Luis set the helmet comms to the four of us. "Guards night and day. No one else must find him, and he should not start communication with anyone else without my permission. For now, he must be safe from the threats he faces here and isolated from the rest of WayPoint."

"Do you not trust him yet, mon cher?" Michelle asked.

"I don't know what to think," Luis replied. "But I see why Collin and Spring are convinced. And I must apologize if my reaction was less than calm before." He turned to me. "I should never have questioned your professionalism, Dr. Graviston. For matters in your field, I bow to your expertise. For matters of WayPoint security, you must bow to mine."

"Apology accepted," I said. "I remember how hard it was for me to accept Ray initially. I thought I was going mad until calmer voices convinced me otherwise."

Luis nodded. "What do we know of the body this alien will inhabit? Will he be all-powerful? Will he destroy us?"

I shook my head. "I find that unlikely. Why would an ambassador mean harm to us?"

Luis turned to me, his eyes steely behind the helmet. "How do we know he truly means to be an ambassador? We should not let him become a complete being until we know his true purpose. We should find that second cask before anyone else does."

Collin tried to explain. "I was one of the first he tried to communicate with, and he damaged me to the point I couldn't do my job. But he was eager to repair that damage and set me right again. He worked with Spring and me to cure the other patients and helped us locate his position in the cave."

I added, "We've known him for months, and after we recovered from the initial disbelief, we became convinced of his purpose. Since then, he's never given us a minute of doubt or concern. We trust him."

Luis nodded, "And I imagine that fits in with his plans." Then Luis' face turned grim. "Why didn't you tell me before?"

"No excuse is good enough," I said, "But in those first days, everything in WayPoint was new to me, and I didn't know that Ray was … unusual. Then, there were patients to cure and a trial. Bernadette was constantly hammering me, and then the coup came. It was a lot to process, and take no offense, but I didn't know whom to trust."

"Spring was alone in this secret until Duval imprisoned her in 407. That's when I finally learned about Ray. Soon after that, Bernadette and Dexter died, and we were under investigation from Earth."

"Here's another answer I must have," Luis said. "Did Ray have anything to do with the deaths of Dexter and Duval?"

"Bernadette wanted power," I said. "She found it when she picked up the blue charms and saw Ray for the first time. She ranted with delusions of invincibility, and she must have thought Mars couldn't hurt her when she ripped off her helmet."

"And did the alien plant these delusions in her head the same way he caused hallucinations in Collin and the others?"

"Ray says he didn't kill her," I replied. *But was I right?* None of us knew the depths of this alien mind nor what secrets were hidden there. And Bernadette's behavior was a mystery long before we met Ray.

"All we know is that she craved power, and meeting Rayfarer amplified that," Collin said.

I added, "But it may have been her narcissism finding a new place to take root, nothing malicious on Ray's part."

"What happened to Dexter?" Michelle asked.

"Duval left him trapped in the exit chamber with no helmet," Collin said. "Ray had nothing to do with that."

"Even so, I will know more about this body he plans before anyone else hears of this genie in a bottle or for him to be removed from the cave. We have nowhere safer to keep him than here. Guards must watch here night and day. Those are my orders."

"For how long?" I asked again. How long did Luis plan to take Collin from me?

"As long as it takes to be sure WayPoint and Earth are safe from this new entity. He may be a benevolent ambassador, as you say, but there is a chance that his mission is less friendly. He will not destroy us on my watch. Will you stand with this alien or me?"

"We believe in Ray," I said.

Collin interrupted, adding, "We believe in him, but I will follow your orders until you believe as strongly as we do. You are right. Earth chose you to call the shots for WayPoint. I will respect that."

I agreed.

"Then respect this," Kaneko said. "After we leave, make sure no one can follow our trail to Ray's location. Then, when you are alone here, search for that cask. As far as I know, only those who prepared this site have been in the lava tubes beyond the barrier. Maybe his body is still here."

I trusted that Luis would soon realize that the chance of danger was slim compared to the opportunity for a deeper understanding of the universe.

Soon after Luis and Michelle left, Collin checked a monitor he had planted, a camera watching the bio-glass transition tunnel leading to the raw Martian terrain.

"I found something," he said. "Roderick Alexander and Neils Westergaard were in this room after hours Wednesday night. They entered the transition tunnel in full gear but did not go beyond it."

"Wednesday was the day after Ray stuttered. I thought you checked the monitors that day."

He nodded. "I did, but that was early in the day; this image was made after I left."

"So, Rod and Neils being here had nothing to do with the interference, right?" I asked.

"What they did here on Wednesday didn't cause interference on the day before. But that doesn't mean the two events aren't connected. I'll check again; I bet one or both tried that tunnel on Tuesday."

I nodded, "But we don't know what they are doing."

"That's true, but it's worth watching."

***

We left Sanctuary Cave soon after the monitor was secured. We were silent driving over the rough road toward WayPoint, but Collin finally said, "Telling Luis was the right thing."

I nodded, adding, "Luis has always been on our side. Perhaps he trusts us less now that he knows the situation."

Doing the right things meant that now we had five beings on Mars to keep safe, four possible ways to leak our secret, and an unknown number of seekers trying to solve the puzzle from the other side.

I shook my head and sighed, pondering the mess we were in.

Collin turned to me. "What's the problem now?"

With a wrinkled forehead, I asked, "Who are these seekers, and what do they already know?"

He grinned. "I reckon we'd better find out." Then he squeezed my hand. "Hon, maybe I should be the cave guard during nights and days."

"Must it be you?" I asked.

"It's me, or we add someone else to our inner circle."

"Let's find another way."

"We can try," he said. "At least I'll be home with you tonight."

I felt the bands of fear tightening until Collin put the rover on auto-drive and slipped an arm around me. Things felt better then—at least for a moment.

Part II: Together Apart

8 Not Forever

Raw nerves rode home with us, and tension built as we neared WayPoint Station. The Kanekos had met our resident alien, and naturally, they were shaken by the revelation. If word of an alien reached the wrong ears, WayPoint would be in flames, but the chaos wouldn't stop with Luis. Every life on two plants would be upended.

Who would they tell? And would they know before we reached WayPoint? During the rest of the ride home, the snippets of conversation between Collin and me were different ways of asking the same question: *What had we done?*

When Collin gripped my fingers to help me out of the rover, I found my anchor to get through the storm.

"Kaneko will come around," Collin said as we disembarked.

"I'm sure he will," I said, but the word *sure* was an overstatement.

After we stowed our terrain gear, Collin took my hand as we walked home. Even though we were doubly bound by purpose and love, we made a grim picture with sullen eyes focused more on those around us than each other. At least WayPoint wasn't in a panic yet. The Kanekos had kept the secret so far, but for how long?

Once we were in our home and Marvin was in privacy mode, Collin met me in the bed, and I cuddled against his shoulder.

"When will you start the 24-hour guard?" I asked.

"It will have to be soon, hon. We have already seen signs of a breach."

"Tomorrow?" I asked.

He nodded. "I must be there."

"What will become of us?"

"We will do our work as always, but with a more urgent focus. I'll take care of the cave by protecting Ray and completing my inspection. You will have to handle everything outside the cave."

"That sounds fair," I said.

"There's no other way to split up the job. With luck, I'll find his body cask in the tunnels. However, sealing the tunnels will be a magnet for the seekers, and those monitors will cause trouble for us if the wrong person finds them. I'll remove them the first chance I get."

"What should I do?" I asked.

"Use your new Earthside contacts; maybe you can find out who is scanning for Ray," he said.

I set my jaw. "The *seekers,*" I replied, realizing we had named the mysterious group searching for Ray. "I'll fish for answers with Jefferson Stafford, my counterpart on the moon. We've exchanged a few messages, but we're set to communicate regularly."

"Maybe you can find out more about Neils Westergaard. Where did he come from anyway? If he's one of the seekers, it would be useful to know who sent him here."

When we were silent again, I caressed his forearm, thinking how lonely life would be without him. Then, I hit a practical thought. "Where will you sleep?"

"There must be fifty sleeping pads in the storage room, preparations for when WayPoint needs a real sanctuary. But I think I'll bring a cot; cave floors aren't that comfortable."

"Take your pillow and my favorite quilt," I said.

Then he turned to me, grinning. "It won't be all that bad, not for us. We can meet with Ray in our Blue Room. No one will know."

"That's a happy thought," I said, smiling for the first time in hours.

"Yeah," he said. "We won't miss a beat. It will be like we're still together."

"Do you promise?" I asked.

"I sure do. Anyway, it won't be forever. Maybe they'll let you cook for me," he said. "I have to eat something."

"No one will be that cruel to you," I replied. "I'll volunteer to be the takeaway driver."

"We'll work it out. And once things are secure enough, we'll find another night guard."

I smiled brighter. "That sounds good. Oh. And when Luis is more confident about Ray, maybe he won't insist on around-the-clock guards."

"There you go, Sugar Spring. Think positive thoughts."

"It won't be forever," I said, snuggling close.

"No. And we can travel like we did to Maui. It might be fun."

"Maybe," I said, grinning. "Our first honeymoon can continue in a way."

"Yes, and when this is over, we can figure out how to take a real honeymoon."

"A trip around the world?" I asked, resting my hand on his chest.

"Maybe two worlds," he replied, covering my hand with his.

I grinned. "Maybe more than two if Ray is a part of it."

Collin soon fell asleep, and I relished the feel of his palm over my fingers as I listened to him breathe.

Every day away from Collin would feel like an eternity, but I rested easier knowing we wouldn't be parted in every way. Not forever.

After Saturday coffee, he packed the necessary clothes and tools, and I tucked in the quilt and pillow and asked if he needed snacks.

"There's plenty of emergency food stored in the sanctuary, but some of that has been there for years, so I'll requisition some of my favorites and a cot for better sleeping. Maybe the delivery man will let you come along for the ride," he said.

***

Unfortunately, the delivery man turned out to be Roderick Alexander. Luis didn't want anyone new in the cave, and Rod visited there most days. But when I met him at the transport, I realized I couldn't recall meeting him in person. He had always contacted our home via Marvin and was usually on a remote screen during Council Meetings.

I knew the wiry, brown hair that stood up as if always at attention, but I hadn't noticed his deep-set, black eyes or ruddy complexion. The few broken veins around his nose suggested overindulgence with alcohol or perhaps an explosive temper.

The body was a complete surprise. I did not expect a short-legged man with muscular arms and a bulging belly. But he settled me into the rover, grinning as we headed out the dock door.

I hoped he wouldn't say much to me during the ride to Sanctuary Cave, but he had a million questions about Bernadette. How did we get along? Did she ever share secrets with me?

I dodged his questions, claiming they might impact the ongoing investigation, but it was clear he was curious about where she went and what she knew. But he stopped the inquisition when I turned the tables and asked him about the times I saw him with Bernadette. Then he added a final remark that sounded friendly at first.

"It's a shame you and Collin are being separated so soon. But don't worry, I'll look after Collin, and I'm practically outside your door if you ever need me," he said.

Perhaps I was too hard on Rod. But even if he meant well, Rod on my doorstep was not a comforting thought.

We finally reached the cave, and once we were cleared to enter, we unloaded the equipment and ration containers. Collin set up his cot in a dark corner of the main room and showed me the familiar bio-glass lining, explaining how it worked.

I had heard all that before, and Collin knew it. But he touched my elbow as he directed me from point to point, allowing us a few more moments while touching was possible.

Rod was my ride to the cave and back, so Collin and I weren't alone for even a moment. As Rod and I prepared to return to WayPoint, Collin kissed me on the cheek, whispering, "*Tomorrow night, Iceland.*"

I'd hold him to that promise.

9 The New Normal

I was annoyed when Roderick Alexander asked to be my dinner companion on my first night alone. Collin and I had planned a virtual trip to Iceland, so my excuse was that I needed a night at home to settle into the new normal. That wasn't a lie. Iceland didn't require leaving home, and being with Collin virtually was my new normal.

Work was a big distraction from loneliness, and I made contact at least weekly with my Moon-side work buddy, Jefferson Stafford. If we had questions from our sister station, we were instructed to ask each other first, but Moon-to-Mars communication was complicated.

Even though scientists used quantum relays to push communication speeds by a bit, we either had to message through recorded presentations or endure minutes of lag between each line of conversation. And since our daylight hours were rarely the same, at least one of us spoke outside of regular work hours. When it was my night and Jeff's day, I had a built-in excuse to work from home and munch on Mar's best version of comfort food while I waited for his responses.

Stafford didn't often have news that Council meetings hadn't covered. Still, he had the latest on the moon's Threshold Station launch times, arrivals, and passenger lists, including times for sample drops and experimental results from our Phobos Station. When we became impatient with the message lag, we ended the conversation, understanding a reply would be forthcoming.

On my first Monday alone, I asked, "Anything new on Mathis?"

We sent fewer messages with more questions in each one to save transmission time. So, I sent my first set of questions, started on my burrito, and ate half of it before the reply came.

> *"There was a new witness today, Benjamin Hessling of Earth's Forward Shot Aeronautics. He knew Mathis from the astronomy team at Sol Moons, a company where they had both worked. Hessling claimed that Mathis had done cutting-edge work on how gravity, orbits, and space forces might improve space travel. He was part of the peer review on one of Mathis' papers. He also claimed to know Ross Hashimi but had little to say about him."*

Hm. Neils Westergaard said he met Ross Hashimi. Could there be a connection between Mathis and Westergaard? That was my next question. I had finished my burrito when my reply arrived.

> *"I found no connection between Mathis and Westergaard. There was no other mention of Hashimi in today's transcript, but the CVs of Hashimi and Hessling show them working on the moon at the same time—Hashimi in Geology and Hessling on launch sites. Scientific circles are small, I imagine, especially on the moon."*

I signed off after that and recorded a few notes. Mathis, a suspected conspirator, worked on Mars when Hashimi was there. Hessling knew Mathis and Hashimi from the moon base. That made a neat three-way connection among Mathis, Hessling, and Hashimi on the moon, but how did Westergaard know Hashimi on Earth?

Hashimi had once visited my house to meet with Edward, and Westergaard had asked me about Edward. But that wasn't much of a connection.

Oh well, digging sometimes comes up empty-handed. That's what Collin said.

Thinking of Collin reminded me I should say good night. So, I connected with him in Ray's mental Blue Room. Ray's presence made the meeting possible, so when I saw him, I asked if he had experienced more interference.

"No," he replied. "My loneliness is spent seeking my other half, but there isn't enough data yet to do much about that. Occasionally, Collin rescues me from the gloom with a conversation."

After polite exchanges, Ray disappeared from the room. He was still there, of course. Ray was the generous enabler of our meeting, but the love between Collin and me did not extend to a group of three. So, Ray stepped away when the loving phrases started. In that way, he was rather like Marvin going into privacy mode.

It wasn't all sweet nothings, of course. We both worked on how to fix Ray, but we were on different ends of the problem. When Collin asked if I had anything new, I mentioned the name Hessling, but it meant nothing to Collin. And when I mentioned that Rod Alexander seemed eager to keep me company, Collin's reply surprised me.

"Take him up on it sometime," Collin said.

"Are you serious?"

"Yes, maybe you can find out what he's up to, and we can compare notes to see if he's telling us different stories or zeroing in on the same questions."

"OK. That makes sense. The next time I feel like living a lie, I'll try that," I said with a wink. But that reminded me of the two patients who needed a cure. I planned to meet with Dr. Fulbright and Giles the next day, so I asked Rayfarer to return to the conversation.

"Greetings again," he said. "How may I help you."

"Stay safe. That's the main thing," I replied. "But you may be able to avoid solitude in a new way tomorrow if you wish. Dr. Fulbright has a meeting with Giles Cardiff, and he wants me to patch you in. Since you planted Giles' hallucinations, you may have insight on how to fix him."

"Oh, I'd love to get back to that problem," he said.

"You'll have the words of Dr. Osgood to work with, but hologram won't be part of it. He will not be able to see you, only hear you."

"What was Giles' issue?" Collin asked. "In what way was he broken?"

"He was bullied in his youth," I replied. Then I turned to Rayfarer. "Ray, do you understand bullying?"

Our friend took longer than expected to reply. "Such a concept is not part of my people's current culture. But it is deep in our history. Is a *bully* one who demands obedience or surrender, even when there is no reason for compliance? A show of dominance?"

"That's about right," I replied.

"No wonder I broke him," Ray said. "I searched for faces that evoked a response. I hoped such a face would reach him and stimulate conversation. Now I see he did not respect that face but felt a duty to appease the man behind it. That was quite a mistake on my part."

"Giles says someone accused him of stealing."

"Yes," Ray said. "I chose a face from his past, a lanky red-haired man, who asked for something to be returned."

"So, you chose someone who accused him unjustly?" Collin asked.

"Right. It wasn't helpful for me to reproduce that face," Ray said. "I didn't consider that the memory might be a bully, as most sentient races move quickly past that behavior state."

"Can you fix that?" Collin asked.

"What was Giles' job again?" Ray asked. "Why was he in the cave?"

"He was part of development and engineering, and he first saw his hallucinations when he delivered equipment to the laboratory in the cave near your section in the lava tubes."

"Yes, that sounds like when I approached him. But I wasn't aggressive," Ray said.

"No, but you pressed his bully buttons."

"His what?"

Collin leaned in. "You triggered memories of bullies from his past, and now he replays those thoughts when he's in the tunnels."

"I can't meet him in the tunnels right now, but if he triggers the memories, perhaps I can affect those."

"Then, let's go for that," I replied.

"And I wish you good luck," Collin said. "You two should discuss strategy, so I'll turn in now."

His virtual kiss was almost as real as a natural one, but when Collin left us, Ray and I discussed how we might use audio-Osgood to help him solve Giles' visions.

10 Giles Meets Audio-Osgood

"It's nice to see you, Giles," Dr. Fulbright said. "I hope you won't mind Dr. Spring joining us today."

Giles pushed the straggly blond tresses from his face. "Not at all. Hey, Dr. Spring."

"Hey to you," I replied, smiling.

Fulbright continued, "Today, we are going to try something new. Eldredge Osgood was an Earthside friend of Dr. Spring's. He is a famous psychologist, and we are lucky to have access to a version of him that can speak to us."

"An artificial man?" Giles asked.

"Audio only," Fulbright replied. "He will speak to you, but you won't see him."

"Sounds OK," Giles said.

"Then say hello, and we can hear what he has to say," Fulbright said.

"Hello, Dr. Osgood. I'm Giles Cardiff."

Then Osgood replied with the scholarly voice so familiar to me. "Greetings, young man. I hear you've seen things in our caves. Is that right?"

"I see people—bad ones. I can't work in the caves while they are there."

"So, is that what you wish to remedy?" Osgood asked.

"Yes, Sir, I do. I didn't expect to find bullies on Mars."

"Quite right. Bullies are common among Earth's young people, and a few continue that behavior to adulthood, but most eventually understand that bullying is not good for anyone."

"Can't see how it would be," Giles said.

Osgood spoke in his scholarly voice again. "Let's try an experiment. Close your eyes and imagine being in that cave where you first met your cave bully."

Giles saw him right away. Since Ray, now acting as Osgood, was the source of Giles' hallucination, he knew exactly what images to reproduce in the young man's mind.

"What does he look like?" Osgood asked.

"Hair like mine, but orangey-red. Bigger shoulders. Taller. And bossy."

"How old do you think he is?"

"Younger than I am, maybe. Eighteen."

"Still a little old for a bully, isn't it?"

"I'd say so."

"Now, since this man is from your imagination, you can control him. Make him stand still. You can do that with people born of your mind."

Giles nodded. "He's still."

"Now, see if you can make him look older. He'd have saggier skin, maybe."

"His hair has receded some, and his eyes are sadder."

"Good job. You have a good imagination, Giles. While he's quiet, tell him what you'd like to say."

"It's what I always say."

"Yes, but now you have him quiet. He'll have to hear you."

I watched my patient's face as he addressed Ray's image of the hallucinated bully. Giles vowed again that he didn't steal anything and told the bully to look elsewhere for whatever he lost.

"Is he listening?" Fulbright asked.

Giles nodded. "I think he is."

"How do you know?" I asked.

"He's nodding, and he looks sad."

Fulbright directed the next step. "When you are ready to hear what he has to say, let him speak. Remember, you control this man in your mind, so nothing he says can hurt you unless you allow it."

"He says he's sorry," Giles said. Then he shrugged, "Maybe he knows where to look for his gadget. But he's just standing there."

"That's because you have power over him and haven't released him yet," Fulbright said.

Giles shooed the bully away. "Go on with you. Go look somewhere else."

I watched silently as Fulbright brought the scene to an end.

"What's happening now?" Fulbright asked.

"He's leaving. And he waved goodbye."

"OK, are you alone in the cave now?"

"I am."

"How do you feel?"

"OK."

"Are you in a rush to leave the cave?"

"Not really. I have work to finish."

"Leave the imaginary cave now, Giles," Fulbright said. "Let's talk in this room for a while. If you had the chance, would you return to the cave today … to finish your work?"

"Maybe. Maybe not. I feel more in control but can't say what might happen in a cave. Maybe the Bully would be there again."

"Probably not. Have you met any real bullies on Mars?"

"No. Not even in the gyms."

"Then let's take a few more sessions of imagining bullies in the caves, and when you are ready, we'll go to a real cave and see what happens. I'll be with you, so you won't have anything to worry about. I can be something of a bully myself when I must. Just ask Dr. Spring."

I snickered. "You were scary enough the first time we met, Dr.

Fulbright, but you are far less of a bully now."

"Exactly," Fulbright said. "Bullies usually grow up, and if they don't, they are the ones who need help."

Giles smiled at that, and I sensed less nervousness in his movement. I spoke to encourage him. "Giles, you're making great progress; you're on the mend."

He grinned. "I hope so, Dr. Spring."

"Would you feel comfortable going a step farther?" Fulbright asked.

"How?" Giles asked, twisting his hair.

"We have a virtual version of Sanctuary Cave. Will you allow me to change this room to the cave?"

"I don't know. I don't like the cave," Giles said, nibbling his nails.

I had an idea, so I turned to Fulbright. "May I ask a few questions?"

"Of course, please do, Dr. Spring," he replied.

"Do you mind, Giles?"

"No. You turned out to be a good egg, even though you haven't cured Thaman and me yet. I don't mind. Ask away, Dr. Spring."

"What would your life be like if the bully had never come and you had continued your work?" I asked.

"Well, the most important thing is I wouldn't feel different from everyone else, and the second-best thing is I could do the job I came here to do. I'd be back on the promotion list. Maybe I could learn and do new things. That's how it should be, right, Dr. Spring?"

I nodded. "Weren't you in development and engineering?" I asked.

"Yes. But I was doing more delivery and parts preparation than true engineering. I liked both, though, but I expected to advance. And sure, I'd be happy to work at anything and not be stuck here. No offense, Dr. Fulbright."

"None taken," Fulbright replied. "Everyone wants to be as free as they can be. But first, you must be free of this bully. The cave I want you to visit is virtual, not real, and I promise the program will have no bullies. If you see one, it will be from your mind, not this fake cave. Shall we try?"

"If I don't like it, can we end it?" Giles asked.

Fulbright nodded. "I promise I will end it as soon as you say."

Giles wiped his palms on his thighs. "Let's do it then."

"Fulbright and I will be right here," I said. "But Osgood was a master at scaring bullies away, so his voice will guide you in the experiment. Is that OK with you?"

Giles nodded.

Fulbright spoke to start the simulation. "Marvin, show us Sanctuary Cave."

First, Giles squeezed his eyelids shut, but then he opened his eyes wide and held his breath as cave walls rendered, replacing those in the conservatory. "I see it," he said.

Osgood's voice was loud but calm. "Look around. Find something you can pick up."

Giles jerked his head to one side. "Will someone accuse me of stealing?"

"Let's see what happens," Osgood replied.

Giles stood, taking tiny steps toward a sample table in the middle of the room. Then he stopped and kept his hands at his side as he scanned the table. "Some pretty rocks," he said.

"Choose one," Osgood said. "Which do you like best?"

Giles sidled to the right. "That one," he replied, pointing to a ruby-colored specimen. He reached his hand toward the stone but was reluctant to touch it. Finally, his fingers brushed the edge, and a figure appeared from the corner of the room.

Giles caught his breath and pulled away from the stone as he stepped from the table.

"Wh … who …?" he stuttered. "You said no one would be here."

"It's only me," Osgood said, and the figure stepped forward. I had seen him when Dexter introduced me to advanced AI. Osgood was working inside the body of the virtual geology instructor.

Giles pursed his lips. "You surprised me. They said you were only a voice."

"I found this guy in the program." The virtual man did a complete turn. "How do I look?" he asked.

"OK, I guess," Giles muttered as he stepped backward toward Fulbright.

"I used to look like this," Osgood said as the geology teacher morphed into my friend, Eldredge Osgood. "Did you ever see me?"

"I am not sure. You look familiar."

"They used to let me look like Earth Osgood," he said. "But now they only trust me to speak."

"Are you being bullied?" Giles asked.

"No. Not bullied. I'm only a program," Osgood replied. "But what if I looked like this?" My old friend's physique changed to a figure I hadn't seen, but Giles knew the red-haired man.

He sucked in his breath. "It's you from the cave. I … I didn't take anything. But I'm sorry if you lost something."

"It's all right," he said, and the scrawny, auburn-haired man picked up the red sample and passed it to Giles. "Here, take this. I don't need it."

Giles drew back.

"It's all right," the former bully said. "Open your hand. I'll give this to you."

Giles, eyes still wide and unsure, reached out a palm, and the virtual man placed the red stone there and folded Giles' fingers around it.

"I'm sorry," the former bully said. "I misunderstood what you were doing, and I should have known better than to accuse you falsely. I remember bullies from long ago, and I should never have behaved like one."

"Can I keep this rock?" Giles asked.

The figure shrugged. "I think it's only virtual, like me. But maybe we can find one for you."

I knew where to find one, so I spoke up. "I know someone who has a stone just like that. I'll get it to you, Giles."

"Thank you," he said, smiling.

"May I show you another face?" the virtual bully asked.

The bully stood straight when Giles nodded, and a friendly smile spread over the ruddy face. "I'm sorry I was so immature that day," he said. "I was wrong. We never know what another person may be going through, and sometimes, even well-meant words leave scars. Don't be afraid if you see me again. And if you see me on a bad day, please remind me to act my age."

Giles giggled. "OK, then." He smiled as he reached to shake the virtual man's hand.

"Marvin, remove the cave and end the Osgood program," Fulbright said. Sanctuary Cave vanished along with Osgood and Ray, leaving Fulbright, Giles, and me in the conservatory.

"What do you say, Giles? Would you like a few more sessions?"

"Maybe," he replied. "And maybe we can try the real cave soon."

I nodded. "Maybe *some* cave," I said. "Right now, Sanctuary Cave is closed for maintenance."

"Due to what happened to Ms. Duval?" he asked.

"Yes."

"I reckon she saw stuff, too. Too bad you didn't get a chance to fix her, Dr. Fulbright."

"It's too late for Ms. Duval, but I'm glad we can work with you, Giles," Fulbright said.

"Dr. Fulbright, I want to be sure I can pass the test of being in a cave again," Giles said. "But maybe I'd like to do something different when I'm all better. Maybe I can work above ground, but still in my division. Do you think that's possible?"

It pleased me to see Giles doing so well. "I'd say everything is possible, Giles. Keep working, and you'll be wherever you want to be in WayPoint," I said. Then, I left Fulbright to continue his session without Ray.

Ray must have spoken to Collin once our session ended because Rod Alexander appeared at my door that night with a gift.

"Collin asked me to drop this off," he said, handing me a fist-sized sample of red jasper-like rock.

"It's just what I needed," I said, smiling.

"Great. Don't forget. I'm always around for dinner if you'd like company."

"Soon then," I replied.

After he left, I juggled the stone in one hand as I walked to the bedroom.

Oops. *Ouch.* My throbbing toe proved I needed practice before juggling in lower gravity. Luckily, my toe wasn't broken, but this rock, a tiny piece of the Martian surface, would help Giles break through his problem. I was sure of it.

11 Games With Lilith

The following day, Elly asked if I could cover the clinic welcome desk for Jinae while she attended a Supper Club planning session. That worked for me. I'd do anything for Elly, and I'd have a chance to deliver the red rock to Giles.

Promptly at 1800, I started toward WayPoint clinic, practicing my juggling as I strolled. I pushed through the Ring Street entry portal and headed straight for Jinae's Welcome Desk, where I had clear views of the street portal to the right and the central nurse's station straight ahead. The hall was empty except for a nurse delivering night medicines, but I followed a soft French accent and found Lilith in the nearby patient's lounge. Giles was there, too, so I had the perfect opportunity to deliver his red rock.

"Hello, Dr. Graviston," Lilith said. "Welcome to our party."

"This looks fun. Please excuse the disturbance; I have something for Giles," I said, smiling as I presented the red jasper.

"Oh, wow, thank you," he grinned. "Now I have something to bean Thaman with if he calls me a cheater again."

I chuckled, "He isn't bullying you, is he?"

"Naa. I can handle that one," Giles replied.

"Hm. You think so," Thaman said. Then he turned to me. "Didn't you bring a gift for me, Dr. Spring?"

"I need to find the right thing," I replied. "This rock is a souvenir from Giles' last therapy session. How is your treatment going, Thaman?"

"OK, I guess. Giles tells me he had help from the Osgood files. I can't wait to see how it works."

Giles swept the hair from his eyes and tested low gravity by rocking back on two chair legs. Then, with arms locked behind his head and grinning like a Cheshire cat, he said, "Between the two doctors and Virtual Osgood, it's working for me. That's all I know."

I checked out the game table. "What game are you playing?"

"Poker," Thaman said, frowning, "It's not my favorite. I can't read their bluffs, and I can't play partners. I want a new game."

"Are you saying Giles has a poker face? I would never have guessed it," I said.

Giles opened his mouth to protest, but when he braced his hands on the table's edge, the back chair legs slid forward, and the seat crashed to the floor with Giles in it. He looked up from his undignified position, yelling, "Hey! I can bluff when I need to."

"Maybe try partners. Then bluffing will help you and someone else, too. What partner games do you play?" I asked.

"None yet tonight," Giles grimaced. "It isn't fair when he plays with Lilith, and I get the artificially intelligent partner."

Nurse Marchand pointed to the empty seat. "Come join us, Spring. Dr. Fulbright is in the meeting with Nurse Kim, and if you play, Giles will have a human partner, too."

"He has a point about AI," I said. "They're aces at calculations but behind the curve at predicting human behavior."

Giles, now upright again, grinned as he whispered, "You'll hurt Marvin's feelings."

"Don't worry about Marvin," I replied. "If any version of him has skin, it's very thick, and he follows protocol. Besides, I'll keep him busy; he can help me man the welcome desk. What partner games are on this table?"

"Do you know Spades?" Lilith asked. I hadn't played in years, so they agreed to let me use the AI hint for the first round. "You will catch up quickly with a few reminders."

The table was already in card-playing mode, with a private screen for each player. Due to my AI assistance, the first round did not count in scoring. When I selected *hint*, the best choice flashed, and a pop-up told me why that card was a good choice. Lilith was right. The hints helped me remember.

Fulbright was right about the game, too—successful bidding required logical choices. Watching how opponents worked together helped to spot bluffs, too. After one round, I removed the hint option, and the assisted player alert icon vanished from all screens. We were ready for regular play.

After three rounds, Giles said, "I like playing with a human. We lose some, and we win some. You're a much better partner than AI, Dr. Spring."

"Thanks. I'm surprised it was so easy to catch on again."

As we played, the conversation shifted to other topics.

"Have you ever played Milles Bornes?" Lillith asked. "I played that as a child in France. It's another fun game."

"Oh, I remember that one," I said.

"Bernadette Duval mentioned it," Thaman said, "but I didn't enjoy playing with her, and from what she said, her sister didn't like to play with her either. Besides, it's hard to relate to flat tires, running out of gas, and speed limits here on Mars."

"She was too busy to bother with us, anyway," Giles replied. "Even at the card table, she took messages or primped for a date; she'd leave the game early without finishing a round."

Thaman grimaced. "Yeah. Sorry I mentioned her."

"You fellows didn't care for Bernadette, and I wonder why," Lilith said. "Her image in the memorial room was quite beautiful."

"She wanted to keep us in here. She had Dr. Fulbright sent away when he was close to curing us, and she didn't like Dr. Spring," Giles said. "She's more heartburn than a heartthrob, and Heartburn Bernadette was a bully. That's what she was."

"She said Dr. Fulbright got hallucinating sickness, too," Thaman said. "That's why he was locked away."

Giles frowned, "Yeah, but he was the doctor, then. Who else could say if he was sick or not?"

"It's hard to know who to believe," Thaman said. "And when Dr. Spring came, they kept Fulbright locked up and wouldn't let her meet him."

Giles added, "None of us could visit him, even those already seeing things."

Lilith shrugged. "Someone must have believed Ms. Duval. Otherwise, they wouldn't have taken such strong actions against the doctor."

"You know Dr. Fulbright," Giles said. "Does he look sick to you?"

"No, but I am not a doctor," she replied, "and Fulbright has just returned from treatment. What's your opinion, Dr. Spring?"

I tilted my head, wondering how to answer without mentioning Bernadette. Finally, I replied, "Dr. Fulbright is quite reasonable and capable. If he were not, I wouldn't put my patients in his hands."

"So, do you and Fulbright side against Ms. Duval?" Lilith asked.

She didn't buy my side-step. I studied Lilith's face for a gambler's tell, but there was no sign of deception. "Dr. Fulbright and I share the goal of curing WayPoint's hallucinating patients," I replied. "As for Ms. Duval, she is beyond our care. Neither Dr. Fulbright nor I are *against* her, and it's too late to be *for* her."

"She put you in prison, Dr. Spring. She'd win no medals for that," Giles added.

"And she helped others throw Dr. Kaneko out of his office," Thaman said. "Bernadette Duval never showed any care toward me or the others. She was all about herself."

"You are from France like she was, Lilith," Giles said. "Is such behavior normal in France? Have you seen it in others there?"

Nurse Marchand sighed, "Sadly, selfishness is everywhere, but it's nothing to be proud of. I believe people struggle to rise above it and that someday it will be a rare behavior."

"We are still in prison here, Dr. Spring. When can we get out?" Thaman asked.

I patted his hand. "You're in care, not behind bars. Your release is no longer up to me, but Giles' session with Dr. Fulbright went brilliantly. If it works as well for you, you should both be back at work soon."

"I hope so," he replied.

Giles nodded vigorously. "But for now, let's keep playing. Are you ready to swap partners, Tham?" Giles asked.

"No," Thaman said, smiling. "I'll keep Nurse Lil. She's one human I can read, and I want her on my side."

When I returned to my card screen, I noticed a hint flashing to help me bid. "Did one of you turn hints back on for me?" I asked.

The dealer had such controls, but none admitted to changing the settings and couldn't see that they had changed.

"How odd," I said.

"Maybe the game needs a reset," Lilith said.

I shrugged. "There must be a glitch, but Nurse Kim will return soon. You should reset the table and start over with her. I'll put Marvin on desk duty and monitor his alerts until she arrives."

As I left the portal and started down the street between the clinic and DownTown, I met Dr. Fulbright and Nurse Kim, who were still chatting about their meeting. The Supper Club was a project close to my heart, and it was gratifying to hear them speak so highly of it. They were excited about innovations in the works.

"I'm so pleased the project is still successful. Thank you for helping, and I'll tell Elly what a good job she's doing."

Jinae chuckled. "We do your work while you do ours. It's only fair."

"Oh, it was a quiet night at the clinic, and I only played cards. It was fun, and I saw your strategies in action, Dr. Fulbright. Thaman is learning to trust a partner, and Giles' self-confidence is growing."

"They are progressing, especially Giles, but they need work to catch up to where they should be. Card games reinforce facets of that."

"Will they be able to return to work soon?" Jinae asked.

Wolfgang nodded, "Giles is on the fast track." Then he turned to me. "Did the topic of Bernadette Duval come up while you played?"

"Yes, it did. Giles and Thaman explained why they didn't like Duval, and even when Lilith brought up her beauty, they stuck to their dislike."

"Marchand is always prodding the topic of Bernadette, fishing for something. I can't figure it out yet."

"Do they ever discuss Neils Westergaard?" I asked. "I wonder about *his* background."

"No, Lilith still sees him socially but doesn't mention him. As for Giles and Thaman, they are on his interview list, so maybe they'll have more to say about him after that."

"Was he in the Supper Club meeting?" I asked.

Kim shook her head. "No. He wasn't in the meeting, but we saw him."

"Neils and Rod were outside Bistro sur Mars when we left our meeting. They paused in the park to finish a discussion," Fulbright said.

Jinae shrugged. "There's not much else to tell about that."

So, after a round of good night wishes, Jinae and Wolfgang continued to the clinic, and I came home to Collin's shadow in Ray's Blue Room, where we shared our day's events.

"Any luck on your treasure hunt?" I asked.

"None," Collin replied. "But Ray had an idea. He linked with me mentally while I wandered through the lava tubes to see if he could detect his matter cask if I came close enough. But, so far, no luck."

Ray spoke up. "But Collin says there are dozens of tunnels to explore. Perhaps we will find it."

I nodded. "Have you had any more interference, Ray?"

"Nothing strong. But I feel weak attempts sometimes."

"Collin, do you have any ideas what that may be?" I asked. "Could it be a probe generated from the second cask, the one you're trying to find?"

He shrugged, "There's no clue as to how that technology works. But we'll keep trying. If anything is in the cave, we'll find it."

"With you and Ray working together, I'm sure of it," I said.

Collin winked at me, saying, "I'm glad you had a little fun tonight. We haven't played cards much. Maybe when I get home, we can do that."

"Sure," I replied. "I'll look forward to that."

But after I left the Blue Room, I couldn't stop replaying the evening. Why would Lilith be so interested in Bernadette? Where could Ray's cask be? Who else searched for it? And why would the card table give me hints after I turned off that option? Glitches were a part of technology, but finding them in an AI machine, especially one on WayPoint Station, was unusual.

I started the day juggling stones, but now I wondered. *Who was playing games with whom?*

12 Dinner with the Enemy

Rod Alexander called me three times during my first week alone and at least twice a week after that. So, when he asked to be my dinner companion again, I took Collin's advice and agreed to meet him. Rod chose Bistro sur Mars, a restaurant I hadn't visited since I met Michelle Kaneko when I pitched the Supper Club plan.

At least tonight, I wasn't starting a new program. There was a different purpose. Rod Alexander had promised to keep me from feeling lonely while Collin was in Sanctuary Cave. I questioned that motive, but I had an agenda, too. I was to protect our big secret by steering Rod away while Collin searched the lava tubes for anything that might help Ray.

As Collin suggested, "Keep him busy, and I'll have more time to explore here alone without Rod popping in for a visit."

OK. I could drag out the evening, even if I didn't want to be with Rod a minute longer than necessary.

Besides the choice of restaurant, there was a second surprise. As Rod led me past the Bistro's elegant, filigreed chairs and damask tablecloths, I noticed Neils Westergaard with Lilith Marchand at a dark corner table. Unlike Rod, who had not given much attention to dressing for dinner, Westergaard had shifted from his grey and beige tweed suit, choosing Martian garments with a similar effect. A perfectly fitted tan jacket hung open, revealing a black body-suit tee clinging to his slim chest. Lilith wore a lavender shirt, probably brought from Earth, with vest and slacks in Martian white.

Finding them sharing dinner wasn't entirely unexpected; Fulbright said they kept company. The surprise was Thaman Bakshi sitting in a third chair in the same corner. Had he been released so quickly?

Westergaard spotted Rod and beckoned us to his table. Rod escorted me to join the others. Dinner with the three newcomers wasn't the most comfortable situation, but I'd have an opportunity to see how Thaman was doing. Besides, with a larger party to share the conversation, it would be easier to stretch out the evening and give Collin more time alone in the cave.

Thaman grinned as he helped me with my chair. "I bet you're shocked to see me, Dr. Spring."

"You didn't crack the clinic's portal code, did you?" I asked.

He chuckled. "No, that's not it."

Neils explained, saying, "Nurse Marchand raved about Thaman as a card partner, so I asked her to bring him along; a clever fellow always livens a party."

"It's good to be here," Thaman added.

"Well, it's very nice to see you all," I said, smiling. "Lilith and Thaman were more than a match for me at Spades. Their bidding and playing styles matched. Now I'd see if the same was true with menu choices."

Neils lit the menu screen. "Let's see what looks good this evening. Oh, I hear the French have wonderful wine. I hope that is true on Mars as well as Earth."

"Bien sur," Lilith replied. "Mars is limited on grape varieties, but I've enjoyed their version of Pinot Noir."

Neils smiled, "Is there anything in it besides grapes?"

"I do not know, and I shall not ask," Lilith replied, tapping the side of her nose.

I nodded. "On this planet, that's the best thing to do when it comes to food and drink."

While we worked our way through appetizers and our first beverages, I steered the conversation toward Thaman.

"Have you had more sessions with Dr. Fulbright, Thaman? How is your treatment going?"

Lilith touched my arm with lavender-tipped fingers. "My dear, we should leave work behind us while we have dinner company."

Thaman replied despite her reminder. "My sessions are going well. Dr. Fulbright thinks I'll be working soon, and Mr. Westergaard agrees. He has plans for me."

Neils touched his lips with the napkin and replied, "In addition to Lilith's glowing recommendation, I've talked to Thaman, and I believe he can help me with my investigation."

Thaman grinned. "Mr. Westergaard wants me to show him around."

"Is your sense of direction improving?" Rod asked.

"If it's not good enough yet, it soon should be," Thaman replied, shrugging.

I turned to Neils. "We have a transportation division, you know. It would be easy to find a seasoned driver."

"True enough," Neils replied, "but Thaman has been to the sites I'll visit. His inside knowledge could be critical."

"But if Ms. Duval and Mr. Craig died on the open terrain and in the cave's gateway tunnel, what more do you need to see?" Lilith asked. She made a good point.

Neils cleared his throat. "Explaining how the transition tunnels work would be helpful to an off-worlder like me."

I turned to my escort. "Don't you have instructions prepared, Rod?"

"Perhaps it may be easier to understand when explained by someone other than an engineer," Lilith replied.

"True," I said, "Even I know how they work," I said.

"But they can't use you, Dr. Spring," Thaman said. "You have a history with Ms. Duval and Mr. Craig."

"Oh?" Neils asked, turning toward me. "What history is that?"

No one else replied, so Tham continued. "When Dr. Spring first arrived, she and Dexter Craig kept company for a while. Ms. Duval was jealous; everyone saw it. And even after they stopped seeing each other, Bernadette still said unkind things about Spring."

Neils raised his eyebrows. "Did Spring and Dexter Craig have a relationship that ended badly? That usually involves hard feelings."

I wrung my napkin under the table as I replied. "Ms. Duval and I were not best friends, but my break with Dexter had nothing to do with that—not from my perspective, anyway. Our relationship had run its course, as many do."

"It's no wonder Dexter yearned for Bernadette's attention; she was charming and beautiful," Rod said. "Pardon my saying so, Dr. Spring, but you seem much better matched with Collin Grant."

"I certainly hope so," I muttered.

Lilith rapped the edge of her plate. "I must insist. No work talk and no personal talk."

The expressions varied from surprise to annoyance, but we agreed.

Our entrees were soon delivered, so we compared dishes and how our entrees measured up to other meals. Lilith schooled us on which wine was best with our chosen entrees, and we shared sips and bites with those nearest us.

When we had finished our dinners, Thaman spoke again. "I apologize if this is too much work talk, but I'm thrilled I might be working again. Mr. Westergaard has promised to speak to Fulbright about a job I will be able to do for him, and the sooner, the better."

"Take your time, Thaman," I replied, smiling. "Be sure you're ready."

"Oh, I'm ready. I've missed working long enough, and being away from the clinic tonight makes me feel it more than ever. It's like a breath of fresh air."

"I'll be happy to see you out and about soon," I replied. "But be cautious. If you leave treatment too quickly, you may have to begin again."

"I'll be careful, Dr. Spring," he said. "And neither Dr. Fulbright nor Neils will push me too far."

"Here, here," Neils said, raising a glass to the table. "This calls for dessert. Let's light up the menu again." Then, after checking the pastry list, Neils announced his choice. "Caramel-topped cheesecake, that's it. That's my favorite back home. What do you say, Rod?"

He shook his head. "Mars food engineers are making marvels, but creamy cheese isn't their best so far."

"I'll take a risk. Is it cheesecake for two, Thaman?" Neils asked.

Lilith wasn't sure. "What do you think, Spring? You've been here for a while."

"Strawberry mousse for me. We grow strawberries on Mars now."

Neils turned to the lady at his side. "And you, Lilith?" he asked.

She studied the menu before tapping her choice. "Apple tart," she announced. "As talented as our cooks are, I'd bet apples wrapped in Martian pastry will be divine. Perhaps they'll add a touch of caramel sauce on top."

Rod seconded the apple tart and turned to Thaman. "Your turn, Tham. What will it be?"

He looked at Rod, turned to Lilith, and then back to Rod. "I'll be an adventurer like you, Mr. Westergaard. Cheesecake it is."

Was Tham becoming attached to Neils?

After dessert, Lilith insisted on a final coffee, and then Rod escorted me home. On the way, he repeated parts of our conversation from the restaurant, often focusing on Thaman and prodding for what happened to separate Dexter and me. I dodged those conversational bullets, but a moment at my door rattled me.

When I pressed my finger against the lock sensor, Rod grabbed my elbow, holding me at the threshold. "You seem quite interested in Thaman," he said, eyes narrowed. "Are you friends? Is he privy to your secrets?"

I jerked my arm to free it from his chubby fingers, but he held firm. "He was my patient, and I care about his welfare."

Rod nodded. "Fair enough. But he *was* your patient, and *now* Dr.

Fulbright decides about his condition. Isn't it out of your lane to get in the way of Neils working with Tham?" Dr. Alexander stood quite close, so I stepped back, but he held tight to my arm.

"Dr. Fulbright asked me to consult on my two former patients, Giles and Thaman. He'll let me know if I overstep, but I can't see how your opinion matters. You barely know Tham at all, and you have no medical expertise." This time, a quick downward pull freed my arm from his grasp, and I opened the door a crack, ready to rush inside.

Rod raised his hands in surrender. "Don't be alarmed," he said. "And don't misunderstand me, but these answers matter to Neils."

Then he turned toward his quarters, and I watched long enough to be sure he was gone.

Once safe inside, I checked in with Collin, but he had only one small discovery in the cave—a discarded box in the storeroom. The label said it was for Garrison Mathis from Dr. Benjamin Hessling. "Is that the Hessling you asked about before?"

"It was, but what can an empty box tell me?"

"Hmm. The label has no shipment date, but I'd guess it was opened recently. It was on top of the recycling bin."

"Let's tuck that clue into the might-mean-something-someday hopper," I said.

Collin was amused by our dinner conversation, especially the dessert choices. He agreed that Thaman might shift his allegiance from Lilith to Neils Westergaard.

13 Wednesday with the Girls

My friends insisted on a girl's night out every Wednesday while Collin was away. Sometimes, it was a local talent show or a Ring Street marathon, but we often met for dinner. Since Maria couldn't escape her café this Wednesday and Jinae was trapped at the welcome desk, Elly and Maria waited for me in the backroom of Taco Marciano.

We waved greetings as I pulled out my chair, but—w*hy were they grinning?*

I spun toward a soft tap on my shoulder to find Alissa Arvani draped in her signature bright headscarf. "What a pleasant surprise," I said, gently hugging Alissa.

"Oh, Elly twisted my arm, and Bashir convinced me he could handle the night shift alone. So, I am free," she said, spreading her arms as she smiled. "How are you, my dear?"

"Well enough," I replied, "and even better with this lovely company tonight. How is Bashir?"

"He is well, and he sends his greetings. Plus, he asked me to say you may take AdMon back anytime you like."

"Oh, I'll let him keep that bit of trouble with my blessing," I replied, and we chuckled as she took the chair beside me. "AdMon has probably rarely been used since the restrictions increased."

"It's probably better that way," Alissa replied. "There's more security for privacy, and the program is no longer used to find out where a person was at any time, nor with whom they shared their evenings."

She was right about that. Unlike Dexter Craig, Bashir would never abuse this technology to spy on anyone.

"You know how Bashir is," Alissa continued, "He's a stickler for protocol, and we've been lucky. Marvin's health alerts are enough for emergencies. So far, anyway."

I patted her arm. "AdMon couldn't be in better hands." But then, after a pause, I turned to her. "But what about Giles and Thaman? When they are released, will anyone watch to be sure they're settling back into their old routines? Is that a condition AdMon can monitor?"

Maria wagged her finger. "We don't need AdMon for that. Giles works for Milo now. He monitors his employees and their vehicles. Nothing unusual has happened; no alerts have sounded."

She flipped on a screen to keep an eye on the shop. When our appetizer was delivered, she assigned café monitoring to Marvin and asked him to notify her of anything unusual. Then, she focused on our group and started the evening agenda.

"OK, ladies. Time to dish. What's new with everyone?"

Elly shoved my shoulder. "Spring, you go first. What keeps you busy since they trapped Collin in the dungeon?"

I shrugged. "Just work. It's tedious sometimes, but it keeps me occupied. The most interesting Earthside information comes from Jefferson Stafford. He said there was a recent moon-to-moon delivery, Phobos to Threshold Station."

"What's unusual about that?" Alissa asked. "They toss rock samples to Earth all the time."

"Jeff said an encrypted message was routed along with the samples. Benjamin Hessling picked it up personally. It must have been a special request for the moon branch of Forward Shot Aeronautics."

"Who is Hessling?" Elly asked.

"Ah, sorry," I said. "I heard about him from the Earth-Link.

Hessling knew Ross Hashimi on Earth."

If the Ross-to-Hessling connection registered with anyone, they didn't mention it. How important was Ross anyway? He had died in the Martian wilderness carrying the odd blue charms that later connected Fulbright and me to Rayfarer. Maybe Ross was no more than a victim of the trinket and the hallucinations that Ray accidentally induced.

Before I could ask for opinions about Hessling, Maria tapped her screen and turned to us, grinning. "Oh, here's something you'll enjoy, Spring." She switched our table viewers so all of us could see. It was Giles and Beth, giggling over a Pina No-Lada.

"I see Giles has more than Milo to watch him," I said.

"Yes," Maria nodded. "Milo says he's doing well. His engineering background makes him ideal for equipment transfer, and he assists in setup, too. His new coworkers enjoy his sense of humor."

Elly chucked. "I can see he gets along with Beth; she's happier than I've ever seen her."

"Go figure," Maria said. "I would never have pegged those two as friends. Beth has always been solemn and worried, and Giles is a joker."

I nodded. "Beth was under Ginger's thumb when I knew her. She spent so much time worrying about Ginger that I wasn't sure she knew how to have fun."

"She's learning," Elly said, beaming at Beth's happy face.

Alissa's smile faded. "Why would Beth care about her so much anyway? The trial we endured was Ginger's fault, and she wasn't even there to testify."

"True," Elly added. "And she started it all with her outrageous accusations. Ginger was up to her knees in the mud with some bad actors, including her lawyer, Mr. Treason, himself, Garrison Mathis."

"To be fair, he hasn't been proven treasonous yet," I said.

"Pfft," Elly replied. "We all know he's guilty."

I nodded. "Well, at least *I* wasn't found guilty."

"True," Maria replied, "But you lost the Supper Club,"

"And you designed it, Spring. Its success depended on you," Elly added.

I smiled. "Such good friends. But the Supper Club lives, Elly. You do a wonderful job with it, too. You make me very proud."

"Argh, Ginger!" Elly growled. "Let's change the subject."

"I saw Thaman Bakshi at Bistro sur Mars with Lilith and Westergaard," I said. "Has he been released for work, too?"

Elly shook her head. "Not as far as I know. Andy would have said. That young man is progressing but is not out the door yet."

"His old job was with materials and delivery. Will he work with Milo, like Giles does?"

Maria shrugged. "Milo hasn't said, so I assume he hasn't been released, not to his old job, anyway."

"At the Bistro, Westergaard suggested he wants Tham as a guide," I said.

"Hmm. Milo hasn't said anything about that," Maria said. "But Thaman made deliveries to many of the caves. He might save Neils some time researching."

Alissa tapped a spoon against her water glass. "Back to important matters. How is our Spring doing without her Collin?"

It was my turn to shrug. "We speak every day, so it's not so bad. Besides, Collin hopes to get a reprieve from the cave soon. If Rod Alexander can find a suitable guard, he'll give Collin a break. Duty comes first on WayPoint."

Ellie sighed. "Sad but true."

The mood darkened. Everyone returned to eating, and I wondered how to reshape the conversation. Collin wanted a break, but he'd never leave that cave without safeguards for Ray. The potential peril was far greater than even our relationship. WayPoint, Earth, and perhaps interstellar relations were at risk.

Luckily, Elly found the right topic to cheer us up. We all loved food, so she turned to Maria. "I hear they are making strides with powdered dairy products. Any chance of real cheesecake soon?"

"Or ice cream?" Alissa asked, hand on her tummy as her eyes rolled in ecstasy.

"Oh, can you imagine real chocolate ice cream?" I added.

"I dream of it," Elly replied. "Or mousse—creamy, luscious, chocolate mousse."

Maria frowned. "Well, if they're researching chocolate, I hope they get on with it quickly. I'll turn Taco Marciano into Big Dipper Chocolates. Until then, the best I can offer is coffee with a dash of dried cream and chocolate liqueur. Anyone for that?"

We all nodded happily and cooed over our coffee as we talked through the rest of the evening.

Then, while Maria took care of shift changes in her shop, I walked with Alissa and Elly until our paths forked and they headed toward the clinic. But when I turned around, I nearly bumped into Giles and Beth, giggling at my surprise.

"We wanted to sneak up on you," Beth said. It was a pleasure to see her face aglow.

"You're surprised, aren't you, Dr. Spring," Giles asked. "I'm a free man now, with a new job and all."

"Does the work suit you?" I asked.

"Aye," he replied. "I'm sharing a room in the transportation pod, and Beth is a close neighbor." He put an arm around her waist and pulled her closer.

"Close in more than one way, I see."

Beth giggled again. "He's a nut, but he's fun."

I smiled as I shook my head. "He was never a nut, but he was always fun." Then I placed a hand on each of their shoulders, adding, "I saw a fun-loving spirit in each of you."

Giles giggled again, "Yeah, Beth just hides hers better."

As we walked toward the spoke roads, I had another question for Beth. "I hate to bring up a sad topic, but has Kaneko found answers about Ginger?"

Her brows dipped. "No, nothing more than that she was still on the roster. No one on Mars has answers for me."

Giles patted her arm. "You'll hear from Ginger when she's ready."

Then he grinned, adding, "Until then, you've got me to talk to."

She chuckled. "Yeah. Good company and a good friend."

"So, how's the new job, Giles?" I asked.

"It's great. It's mostly above-ground—driving, but I'm OK in caves, too. Things are perfect, Dr. Spring. Thank you for all you did for me."

"You've had all of WayPoint on your side, Giles," I replied.

"Maybe not all, but close enough," he replied. "I hope things work out for Thaman as well."

"Is he ready to leave the clinic?" I asked.

Beth spoke up. "Mr. Torres tells me that Tham's sense of direction needs honing; he's not ready for assignments like the ones we get. Not yet."

Giles nodded. "She's right. But he's coming along. Tham thinks he'll be working soon. Maybe he's found something where his sense of direction doesn't matter. Will they release him for other duty if he can't judge direction?"

"I don't know," I replied. "I guess it depends on how Fulbright sees it and what kind of support Tham has in a new position."

Beth crooked her elbow through her companion's arm. "Giles wants his friend to be as free as he is," she said.

Giles turned to her. "But Tham can't be free on WayPoint until he stops hallucinating. He must regain all his skills to recover completely, including knowing which way is which."

"Yes," I said. "Tham should stay in treatment until he regains everything he lost, including his direction."

"It will be soon, though. Don't you think so, Dr. Spring?" Beth asked.

"As soon as can be," I replied.

Then they left for the transportation pod, and I returned to Collin's dark apartment. Thank goodness I had my second Wednesday date to enjoy—one I yearned for even more than a night out with my friends. The meeting was brief, but even so, time with Collin via our Rayfarer connection brightened my night.

***

"Good evening, Spring," Ray said. "I'll be in my corner counting pebbles. You two feel free to talk."

Our meeting and his corner were all imaginary, but despite that, I appreciated Ray's consideration for our privacy.

"So, how's my girl?" Collin asked, squeezing our interlocked fingers as they rested on the arm of his blue chair. "Were the ladies full of secrets?"

"Secrets, news, and fun," I replied. "The big news was improved chocolate ice cream coming soon."

"I'm with you there," he replied. "Better ice cream would be fantastic. But how was the Mexican food?"

"Great, as usual. Maria keeps outdoing herself. How did you know we met at Taco Marciano? Was it a lucky guess, or did Ray tell you?"

"No," he replied, "According to Marvin, Ray doesn't know where we are unless we tell him."

"Yes, Marvin knows everything," I replied. Then I thought of more news. "Oh. Giles and Beth have become friends. He's working with transportation now."

Collin chuckled. "I never thought of it before, but those two have the same sweetness. Good for them; Beth needs more friends."

"They seem happy, both giggly. Giles' giggle is still nervous, but it's a move in the right direction. I'm glad the girls have someone to focus on besides me. Maybe I'm finally convincing them I will not fall apart just because you're stuck in this cave."

"You aren't falling apart?" he asked, faking astonishment. "How could you possibly be holding together without me?"

My smile faded. "It's only temporary. You promised it won't be forever."

"And I'll keep that promise. Rod is looking for another gatekeeper for the cave. I hope it's soon."

"Me too."

He interlocked our fingers and kissed our joined fists. "As soon as possible, hon." Then, returning our hands to the chair arm, he added, "Who was there tonight?"

"Only Maria, Elly. Oh, and Alissa surprised me by joining us. She says Bashir wants to give AdMon back to me."

"Is Bashir finding any secrets that might help us with Ray?" he asked.

"Bashir isn't looking. He uses AdMon when he needs an answer he can't get otherwise. That rarely happens, if ever. How about you? Any luck searching the tubes?"

"Nothing so far. Ray hasn't had much interference lately, though."

"Then, hopefully, no one is searching for him now," I said.

"Maybe not. But I don't want to risk the world on that bet. What's the rest of your week like?"

"Not much excitement, as far as I know. I expect a dispatch from Jefferson tomorrow night, and Friday is wrap-up day, so I'll be in the Council Meeting and then sending memos to division heads. Meetings and paperwork, that's it. You?"

"Dragging out the barrier inspection and searching tubes when I get the chance. Boring work."

"Then, tell me where we should travel the next time you're home."

"What planet do you prefer?" he asked. "Something on Earth? Or maybe Ray can take us to his planet."

"Wow. I never thought of that. I wonder what his planet is like."

Collin shrugged with his free hand. "He and I talk about it some. After his long trip here, Ray doesn't notice the solitude, but I get lonely, so we talk. We tried cards, but he always wins. He can read my mind, you know."

"He's *in* your mind, don't you mean?"

"Only when I allow it."

"How about a place on Mars?" I said. "I've never been to the top of Olympus Mons. I hear you can see stars from there. Is it possible?"

"Sounds cool," Collin replied. "It's a date. We can probably find a simulation."

Then we stood, holding each other. And since the embrace was built from our shared memories, it was as natural and comforting as a real one. Our lips didn't physically touch, but our spirits did, and the kiss was as deep, passionate, and nearly as fulfilling as the last time we were skin-to-skin. When we pulled apart, I whispered, "Till forever."

And he replied. "It won't be long now."

Then our Blue Room dissolved, and I was alone in our quarters with memories of that kiss.

14 Protocol Rules

Maybe it was my loneliness or that Beth was on my mind, but I woke up thinking about Ginger Welsh. So, while I conferred with Marvin about the news and WayPoint's agenda, I asked him about Ginger, specifically for her supervisor's name and new job title.

"Ginger Welsh is a Special Transportation Operator assigned to the Phobos project," he replied. "All Phobos research personnel are under the supervision of the Project Director Morsey."

"Has Ginger had any medical alerts in the past months?" I asked.

"I'm sorry, Dr. Spring, Phobos personnel are not under the care of WayPoint medic. Protocol prohibits me from replying to your query."

That's the first I had heard of a project director on Phobos or that they had separate medical operatives, but it seemed logical. Phobos wasn't far away, but in any field site, emergency care was needed closer than WayPoint Clinic.

"No offense taken, Marvin. I respect your protocol. We'd all be in trouble if you didn't respect our privacy, wouldn't we?"

"Is that a rhetorical question, Dr. Spring?"

I chuckled as I replied, "Yes, Marvin, but wouldn't any Martian medical personnel be under my watch as Secretary of Human Services?"

"You aren't fully installed in that position, are you, Dr. Spring? Is there anything else? If so, please state your query."

Marvin was unlikely to tell me Thaman's release status and location, so I rephrased my question. "Who is Thaman Bakshi's current supervisor?"

Protocol allowed Marvin to release public information, so this time, he replied. "Thaman Bakshi is currently assigned as a personal guide to Neils Westergaard."

Marvin's reply raised more questions, so I made a mental note to speak to Dr. Fulbright immediately. He'd have the answers I wanted.

***

Immediately wasn't right away; first, I checked for unannounced but mandatory meetings. But as soon as possible, I headed for WayPoint Clinic. Jinae was at the welcome desk, as usual.

"Good morning, Dr. Spring. I was sorry to miss last night's gabfest, but I was stuck here."

"I heard. I don't suppose you have time for coffee now, do you?"

Nurse Kim looked around the floor and the portal corridor. "It's not busy. I can let Marvin watch the door. Follow me." Then, she led me to the nurses' lounge and the closest coffee maker. Since Jinae gave her old quarters to Lilith, the lounge also served as Nurse Kim's bedroom.

"Isn't sleeping here like being on duty all the time?" I asked.

"No," she said. "Lilith is new to Mars, and I figured she could use the comfort of a private room. And, truthfully, I'd rather be here than in the pod next door worrying about what's happening with the patients. It's quiet without Giles and Thaman, though. Everyone else is in and out after an injury or a bit of respiratory distress, and there's no one to play cards with except Lilith."

"How did Thaman get his release so quickly?"

"Here's the man who can tell you," she said, pointing toward the hall as Dr. Fulbright walked in.

Wolfgang brought his coffee and pulled out a chair to join us.

"Did you come to check on Thaman?" he asked. "I guessed you'd be curious."

"You're right about the curiosity, but I'd never second-guess your decisions. I'm glad he has improved."

"He isn't as well as he might be, but Westergaard pulled a few strings, and he convinced me Thaman wouldn't need a sense of direction for this job. He promised to look after him."

"Did you let him take responsibility for your patient?" I asked, astonished Fulbright would allow such a thing.

"I know, I know. It doesn't sit right with me, either. But Neils had the paperwork claiming Tham had unique qualifications to assist with Neil's investigation."

"Unique qualifications, my eye," Jinae said. "Milo has a dozen people on his team with as much knowledge as Thaman has about these cave sites. I don't know why Kaneko let him get away with that."

Fulbright shrugged. "Neils' paperwork was signed by Kaneko's earthside supervisor, Harvey Cross. On Mars, only Kaneko, with Andy's consent, can overturn decisions about my patients, but Cross is above them in the chain of command. Besides that, Neils acknowledged in writing that he understood Thaman's condition and promised to exercise the necessary cautions."

"Does that satisfy you?" I asked.

"Partly," he replied. "I insisted on impromptu visits, and Neils agreed that Thaman would return here to sleep. I can evaluate him at the end of each day." Then he shrugged. "I don't know. Maybe time in the field will complete his treatment."

"Where are they now? Thaman and Westergaard, I mean."

"When Neils and Thaman left here, they headed toward DownTown. I assume they went to sign out a robotic vehicle. Tham is to be his tour guide."

When Marvin called Jinae to the welcome desk to greet a guest, Wolfgang led me to his office to talk out of earshot of visitors. Once we were behind his closed door, I spilled my first question.

"So, do you think Tham is up to this task?"

"He's made progress, but I think he needs more exposure to caves.

Tham is clever, and he doesn't fully trust many people. When we run trials underground, I'm never sure he's being honest with me about what he sees. My choice would have been to keep him in the clinic longer."

"Then why did you let him go?"

"Protocol. Chain of command, as I said. But Westergaard promised that Tham would never be alone underground. Tham trusts Neils, and Neils knows what to watch out for. He says Thaman's issues won't affect the job he has for him."

I sighed. "You're keeping notes about all of this, aren't you?" I asked.

He nodded. "I am. Are *you*? Do you plan to put me on report?"

"Of course not. Making medical decisions is no longer my job. But human resource matters will be my responsibility when I'm released from in-training status. I'm making notes, too."

"Is that why you came here today?" he asked. "Are you here to investigate Tham's release?"

I shook my head. "I was curious about it, but you've answered my questions. There was another matter, though. Are we in private mode here?"

"Let's be sure," Wolfgang said. "Marvin, privacy mode, please,"

The flashing red button on my wrist turned dark as it did whenever Marvin stopped listening. It was safe to speak, so I asked, "Can you tell me about the day you found Ross Hashimi?"

"Why Ross?" he asked. "Has something new been uncovered?"

"No. But I never heard the details from you. Ginger was with you, and she has been on my mind."

Fulbright leaned back with fingers pointing under his chin as he tried to recall the day.

"I was in the office, and a medical alert came through on Ross. We arranged a car, and Ginger drove me to the spot far from WayPoint Station, near the south crater wall. Hashimi was on the ground, and sensors indicated no heartbeat."

"Do you know why he was there?"

Fulbright's wild hair wiggled as he shook his head. "There was no sign that anyone had been there. It was just Ross lying in the pebbles."

"Was his suit functioning?"

"Yes, that's how we got the alert, and the suit is programmed to perform limited resuscitation. But Ross was far from WayPoint; he must have walked some distance. His oxygen was nearly gone, and the suit couldn't fix him."

I leaned forward to whisper. "You examined him. Is that when you found the blue charm on his body?"

He nodded. "And soon after that, Ray tried to contact me, but you know all that. Why is this important now?"

"Because Beth thinks Ginger Welsh is missing, I can't say she's wrong. Ginger was with you when you found Ross dead, and now we can't find her. I hoped for answers, but there's nothing so far," I said.

"I'll see what I can remember about Ross," he said. "But, concerning our patient, will you join me for one of the impromptu meetings with Tham?"

I grinned. "If we meet him in Sanctuary Cave, I can have a moment with Collin. I'd love that."

"I figured you would," he said. Then he spoke to the air, "Marvin, normal mode, please."

I looked at my wrist and found an unusual grayish-mauve light turn to flash red. Odd. I'd never noticed the light indicating silent mode being anything other than black before. Perhaps we'd had a system upgrade.

This was one of the rare times I wished for access to AdMon. I'd find out instantly where Neils investigated with Thaman. But maybe it was a good thing I couldn't. The last time I used it, I ended up in the crosshairs of a Council investigation.

I spent the rest of the afternoon checking with division heads and reading their reports to spot anything needing the attention of Human Services. And the evening was filled with sporadic communication from Jeff Stafford. It was odd how much trouble we took asking questions and waiting to learn nearly nothing new in the staggeringly slow reply. But this time, he had news worth waiting for. Garrison Mathis' hearing was delayed. Mathis was in the clinic after suffering an acute respiratory issue. Jefferson had no details, but he said such attacks were not unheard of when Martian colonists returned to Earth. According to his reports, Mathis expected a full recovery, and the trial would resume when he was well.

***

When I had my short good-night chat with Collin, he was curious about Mathis but more concerned about Thaman. "You don't suppose Neils wants Thaman to be my replacement, do you?" he asked.

"I hope not. He isn't entirely out of the woods with his direction problems yet. The last thing he needs is to spend a night alone in Sanctuary Cave."

Collin agreed. Thaman might get in the way of the hunt for Ray's other half, but that wasn't Collin's only complaint.

"If Thaman isn't ready for the caves, I'll spend all my time sorting him out, and who knows when I'll get a night off," he said. "I promised you Olympus Mons."

"Then I hope Thaman isn't your roommate in the cave. Find someone who can handle the job without you so you can get out of there."

Collin grinned. "I'll try. It can't be just anyone, though. We need a good gatekeeper."

I agreed. "Maybe I'll get clues during tomorrow's wrap-up."

We both hoped it would happen. We were ready for some good news.

15 Neils Steps up the Pace

I shouldn't have been surprised, but even before the meeting started, the Council Hall was buzzing with news of Garrison Mathis' condition. Of course, they knew. My Earth-link, Jefferson Stafford, had told me about Mathis. Everyone on Mars had Earth connections, some official, others not, and Neils Westergaard had more than most.

When Luis and Secretary Ulikov entered the room, Neils rushed to join them in their stroll toward the podium. His animated gestures contrasted the stayed demeanor of the two executives.

Nurse Kim took her seat beside me. "What's going on there?" she asked, "Neils looks like a puppy yapping at two guard dogs."

"It might have to do with Garrison Mathis," I whispered. "I hear he's fallen ill, and his trial has stopped."

"Why would that upset Neils?" she asked.

Neils' whispers became loud enough to hear as he told Luis, "Of course I know what happened. Now I want to know how that impacts *me*."

Luis banged his gavel, but he spoke softly. "Have a seat, Neils; it's time to begin." Then he turned toward the room. "We'd better start with Earth news."

Ulikov took the podium. "I am sorry to report that Garrison Mathis is under care on Earth for apparent lung distress. His court proceedings have been paused, but he has the attention of the best physicians on Earth. Your good wishes for Mathis and this important WayPoint matter are appreciated."

"Important, indeed," Jinae muttered. "That rascal and his cronies tried to oust Kaneko. Hmm. I wonder if someone is trying to oust *him*."

Neils Westergaard had the first question. "How long till his trial resumes?"

"We won't know that until they have a treatment plan."

Rod Alexander, on his remote screen, had the next question. "Was foul play involved?"

Ulikov responded with what felt like a standard answer, saying he didn't know what caused Mathis' illness and that foul play had not been ruled out, but neither was it likely. Then Rod's screen went dark as he dropped out of the meeting, and Ulikov returned the floor to Kaneko.

"Garrison Mathis' behavior impacted me more than any other on WayPoint, but please don't speculate about the cause of his health issues or the trial. Carry on as usual, and expect reports when we have more news. Does anyone have a question about that?"

Neils was recognized. "Will my work be held up until we hear more? And what about my role here as acting Vice Prime? Will I be here longer than expected?"

Luis looked miffed, but he responded as eloquently as ever. "Mr. Westergaard, I see no reason why you should not proceed at a reasonable pace. Regarding your time as WayPoint's second minister, I'm sure we can find another placeholder for Garrison should you wish it."

After Earth news, the rest of the meeting consisted of division head reports and questions, and the topics varied from news of better ice cream to a commendation to Dr. Fulbright for his work in curing Thaman Bakshi and Giles Cardiff so they could return to free society in WayPoint.

The wrap-up ended earlier than usual, so Jinae and I had a quick lunch at Deimos Pizza and caught up on personal news. After lunch, we ordered tea and compared notes from the meeting. Then, once we decided which points were critical to which departments, she was ready to prepare memos for each department head.

After that, we took a long walk around the outer ring street and ended up at the clinic. I followed her inside to congratulate Fulbright on his commendation.

Lilith stood as she yielded the welcome desk to Nurse Kim but rolled her eyes toward the end of the clinic's central corridor. Even though the voices were muffled from that distance, it was clear that the discussion in Fulbright's office was heated.

"It's Neils and Wolfgang," Lilith whispered.

"Sounds like Neils is bringing the council news here. Shall I go with you?" Jinae asked.

"No. I've got this. You carry on." Then I tucked my screen under my arm and found Fulbright in a nose-to-nose conversation with Neils. Thaman was seated between them, his eyes shifting from one loud voice to another.

"I don't have enough data, Neils. Thaman shouldn't be left in that cave until I have more information."

"But I need to finish this before Mathis' trial ends, Wolfgang," Neils said. "Even in Bakshi's current state, I need his assistance. I'll send you my notes on his behavior this evening. He'll be sleeping here, so interview him; follow up with him if you need to. Then, observe Tham over the weekend. By Monday, I need him at full service."

"I can't promise," Fulbright replied.

"And I can't promise to accept your decision if you don't comply," Neils replied before storming up the hall.

Fulbright was rattled. "Wait here," he said, pointing to Thaman. "I'll be right back. I need a minute." Then he added, "Spring, can you stay long enough to meet with us for a while? Your opinion may balance mine."

"Of course," I replied. "Jinae is taking care of my memos. I'm here as long as you need me."

Fulbright's only patient was Thaman, and Marvin was set to call me if I was needed elsewhere, so Tham had my full attention.

"How's it going?" I asked.

"Great, Dr. Spring. I don't know why Dr. Fulbright is so upset. Everything Neils asked me to do was easy as pie."

"What did he ask you to do?" I asked.

"Yesterday, he had me ride with him to most of our cave facilities. We went to both underground farms, a new archaeological excavation, and a water pumping station. I spent most of this morning in Sanctuary Cave."

I nodded. "Did you have any odd feelings or see anything unusual?" I asked.

"No. Everything was just like before the hallucinations. I was underground most of both days. Yesterday, I spoke to the other cave workers and explained a few things to Mr. Westergaard. Nothing was out of the ordinary."

"Do you think you were underground long enough to trigger those old visions? Did you need to use your sense of direction?" I asked.

"We had a robotic car, so neither of us drove. But when Neils asked me where we were, I could answer and point out the route. It was like old times."

"And today?"

"Rod Alexander drove me to the cave after he left the meeting. He asked me about safety protocol and showed me where the extra terrain gear was located. He asked me to remove my helmet and gloves and left me alone in the room for a little while. Nothing happened."

"Did he give you any jobs to do?" I asked.

"No, but Collin was there," he said, beaming. "He misses you. Rod had me follow him around to see the boundaries, the storage room, and the bolted passage to no-mans-land."

"No-mans-land? Do you mean the passage to the raw tunnels that aren't glassed in?"

"Yes. That's the one. Collin called it the Guardian tunnel and told me how dangerous it was there, even with gear on."

"Did Neils mention any other cave you might visit? Anywhere else he wants to investigate?"

"Well, while we were touring yesterday, he had a list of coordinates, and we paused at one spot out in the flats near the crater wall, but Neils didn't want to stop there. As soon as we slowed down, Neils directed the car to the next destination. Other than that, we stopped at caves, and at each one, he asked me about the purpose, the security protocol, and how to get in and out safely. I think I passed his tests."

"So, what happens now?" I asked.

"They test me, and if I can do all Westergaard asks of me, they'll grant me a full work release. I want that, Dr. Spring. I like being able to go where I want to."

"I understand, Thaman. It sounds as if you might be close to doing that."

"I hope Dr. Fulbright thinks so."

"Thinks what?" Fulbright asked, returning with fresh reports on his screen.

Thaman ambushed him with his burning question. "I've answered all Dr. Spring's questions. She thinks I'm OK. You trust her opinion, don't you, Dr. Fulbright?"

Fulbright grunted. "Hm. Is that right, Spring? Do you think Thaman is ready for release?"

"We only had a short time to chat. Thaman seems to have adjusted to his adventures very well. But the deep questions are up to you. See what you think. But so far, I didn't find any red flags."

"Then let me see what Osgood and I can find out," he said.

"If you need me to help with Osgood, I'll ask Jinae to cover for me."

"No. Audio-Osgood is sufficient this time," Fulbright said. "If you have time tomorrow, perhaps you can join me at the cave. We can watch Thaman in the dark and see how he does."

"I'd love to," I grinned.

***

When I returned home, I contacted Collin via Ray. We were thrilled that we might meet in Sanctuary Cave. As for his visit with Thaman, Collin thought the young man did fine. He saw no definite signs of hallucination, but he had one moment of doubt.

"I met Thaman in the main room, where Rod left him. Tham had removed his hat and gloves and wandered along the walls, studying his reflection in the glass. I thought he might be hallucinating, but when he turned, he collected himself, and nothing else odd happened."

"Did you speak to Ray? Did he try to reach Thaman?"

Ray turned from his pebble-counting corner. "Ahem. I'm here, you know. You can ask me directly."

"Then answer, please," Collin said.

"I could *see* Tham, and I can *see* the one you call Rod Alexander, too. However, I felt it was too risky to attempt communication. I sensed Alexander had motives below the surface. I was better off quiet."

Collin had doubts about Tham's readiness, but we hoped Collin could get a reprieve from the cave so we could complete our honeymoon.

"Honeymoon, eh?" Ray said, researching the term. "Oh, I see. Yes, I think you should leave me out of that meeting."

"Don't worry," Collin said, grinning from his blue chair. "We can handle that trip alone."

Before Ray noticed my blush, we said goodnight and ended the meeting.

16 Return to Sanctuary Cave

The following day, Wolfgang appeared on my screen. He was more rattled than usual and hadn't attempted to comb Einstein out of his hair.

"Neils is taking Tham to Sanctuary Cave today, and I will meet them there. Will you come with me?"

"Is this one of your impromptu meetings?" I asked.

"Well, it won't be a surprise, but he's given me only two days to decide about Tham."

"Two days to agree with *his* call, you mean," I replied.

"If I can't agree with him, it will be in the hands of Luis and the Earth Liaison Committee. If they won't listen to me, at least I can make a thorough report, and your input will strengthen it. Besides, wouldn't you like to see Collin?"

"You know I would. Tell me when and where to meet you."

Within an hour, we were inside a robotic rover. Wolfgang was crabby all the way there, but the thought of meeting Collin kept me as happy as butterflies in summer. My smile faded when we approached the cave entrance, and I saw the windows of the Gateway chamber.

I hadn't paid attention to the chamber when we brought the

Kanekos to meet Ray. And on my last visit. I had been loaded with boxes for Collin. But this time, I recalled Dexter panting for his last breaths, scratching at the door as he begged for help from Bernadette. But when we were cleared to enter the Sanctuary, Collin rushed to hug me. When he saw the tears through my helmet, he helped me lift the glass visor and wipe my eyes.

"It's all right," he whispered. "It's behind us now."

Neils Westergaard entered, witnessing our tender scene. "Are you experiencing regrets about Dexter and Duval?" he asked.

"I have had sessions with Spring and Collin about the trauma they experienced," Fulbright replied. "No witness can escape upset from such a sight."

"I'm fine," I whispered. "Where is Thaman?"

"Rod is showing him equipment storage in the back room. You can meet him there if you like."

I released Collin's hand, and he followed me and Fulbright through the little passageway connecting the large sanctuary room to the storeroom behind it.

The storage room was more untidy than usual, with drawers and cupboards opened as Thaman became acquainted with the contents. He was taking inventory of the safety gear, and Rod reminded him that the Gateway tunnel had spare emergency equipment. He found food rations, heat and light sources, and a stack of sleeping pads with built-in bedding.

"You may find these useful if you are ever assigned to sleep here overnight," Rod said.

Collin chimed in. "Don't worry. It's not as bad as it looks. I've been sleeping on this one," he said, pointing to a deployed cot in the corner. "It's comfortable enough."

"Do they all come with a yellow quilt?" Tham asked.

"No," I replied. "That's my quilt. I insisted Collin bring it."

"Tham shouldn't sleep here alone," Fulbright interrupted. "He isn't cleared for that."

"Not yet," Neils replied. "But the weekend isn't over."

Thaman grimaced. "How can I get clearance for work here or anywhere? My life has been on hold long enough. I can't find happiness while stuck in the clinic. Let me move among other WayPointers. Help me get there, Dr. Fulbright."

"Very well then. I'll observe for a time. Just go about your business for now. I may prescribe tasks later."

"I'm ready," Tham said, following Rod Alexander to continue the storage room tour. Collin needed to check the Guardian portal between the safe habitat and raw Martian tunnels, so Wolfgang and I returned to the large sanctuary chamber.

I sat at the table with Wolfgang, asking, "What shall we look for?"

He shrugged. "We will know it when we see it."

After a few moments, Thaman joined us in the main room and positioned his sleeping cot. Once the bed suited him, he made a few trips to the storage room, bringing back a lantern, hammer, knife, water bottle, ration pack, and an electronic compass.

"Are you planning to leave here at night, Tham?" I asked. "Why do you need a compass?"

He shrugged. "Underground, I only have tunnels to direct me. There are no landmarks, and Mars doesn't have the same magnetic field as Earth, so only a Martian electronic compass can help."

"But aren't the tunnels enough?" I asked. "You only have this room, the exit tunnel, and the storage room. Where could you need a compass?"

"It's in case of emergency. If I need terrain gear, I might need a compass to get me somewhere on the surface."

"Always good to be prepared for the unexpected, Tham," Fulbright said. "But the hammer and knife?"

"I just like having them handy. As you said, prepare for the unexpected." Then, he returned to his tour of the storage room.

After an hour or so, Collin returned to me and leaned in to whisper, "I finished checking security in the back tunnel. That's it for the tasks Rod gave me. I'm running out of reasons to stay here."

Fulbright said, "But your real purpose, the one Kaneko gave you, isn't accomplished."

Collin nodded. "I'll move my sleeping set up next to Tham's. That will take some time."

I squeezed his hand, wishing he would not stay there even one more night, but I understood why he must.

Thaman returned to us with Westergaard at his heels.

"I've checked out the storage room," Tham said. "There are enough rations here to live for months. Somebody put a lot of thought in to planning this Sanctuary."

"That was the idea," Wolfgang replied. "Luckily, we haven't had to use this space for emergencies yet."

Westergaard pointed to the characters scrolling over the top edge of the barrier wall. "Those are the conditions of the room, Tham. If they flash green, the environment here is safe, and you won't need your terrain gear."

"Collin had his on in the storage room," Tham said.

Collin nodded. "Yes, but I was in the Guardian tunnel and needed to be safe from Martian toxins while I checked for leaks or problems."

Neils watched as Rod ran Bakshi through the safety drills. Tham knew where to find terrain gear and understood how to enter and exit between the cave and the exterior terrain.

Next, Rod gave orders with the cave lights turned to dim, and Tham followed them with no problem. Then Rod put Thaman through his paces with more disorienting tests, but Bakshi met the challenge on each one.

"He checks out," Rod announced. "No problems so far."

Fulbright wanted to see more. "Let's try that without any terrain gear and with no one else in the room."

So Tham stowed his terrain suit in the storage closet, and once he was standing by the table, we left Tham alone in the room. The lights were dimmed to a minimum, and Marvin relayed instructions.

"Sit in the chair until you're told to move," Marvin said nothing else for 20 minutes, but he reported to us that Thaman fidgeted in the chair, and once, he called out to see if anyone was there.

I found that odd since we couldn't exit without him knowing.

Then, Marvin ordered Tham to walk to the wall to his left and focus on a particular rock behind the glass barrier. After five minutes, he was told to make several paths going left, right, back, and forth as directed, and then he was to find the original rock he focused on.

Fulbright and I peeked from the storage corridor as Tham executed his orders. Tham completed his test but continued staring at the focus wall as if searching for something else. When I asked what he was doing, Tham explained that he was trying to see someone giving him false directions, as he had witnessed before. But it didn't happen. There were no signs of confusion, fear, or visions.

"What do you think, Fulbright?" Neils asked. "Does he pass your tests? Can you release him from the clinic?"

"It's not enough," Wolfgang replied. "One day won't be enough. If we release him too soon, we'll have all his treatment to do again."

"But you know my reasons for speed. We need him back on the job soon."

"Let him stay with me tonight," Collin said. "That will be a longer test, and I can watch him. I know how the hallucinations affected me; that should be helpful."

Fulbright wasn't convinced, but he agreed Collin could watch him. "I'll pick him up in the morning and put him through some tests in the office. Then we can see how things look."

All parties agreed.

Collin and I had had no time alone, but at least we held hands, and he pulled me into the storage room for a private kiss when we had an opportunity.

"I'll be home soon," he said.

"Be quick about it," I said and kissed him again.

Then, the rest of us left Collin and Tham to make dinner from the Sanctuary rations, and I rode home with Fulbright.

17 More Ginger

I woke up hungry on Sunday, ready for a big breakfast. Powdered eggs were better with a bit of spice, so I headed to Taco Marciano, where I found Beth Martin waiting for takeout.

"Late breakfast for you, too, Beth?" I asked.

"Nope. Early lunch," she replied. "Milo says I should give Giles a look at some of the routes he hasn't run yet."

With a wink and a grin, I replied, "Oh, that sounds more like fun than work."

She beamed back. "I think so, too."

"Where will you go?" I asked.

"Milo programmed routes usually assigned to other teams, so I'm not sure where we will end up."

"Well, you should have a good day together, anyway. Have fun."

As she picked up her order, I found a table and ordered my breakfast, a Mexican omelet with powdered almost-eggs, soy cheese, soy sausage, and real peppers. It tasted better than it sounded, and there was a helping of fresh Martian-grown strawberries on the side.

Milo came in to pick up his lunch, and while he waited for his order, he sat with me to chat.

"I hear Collin may get a break from that cave soon," he said. "You must be thrilled about that."

"I sure am. But I hope Rod has someone besides Thaman to take over for him. Tham's still a little shaky underground."

"Oh, isn't that settled? I thought he'd be digging up some answers for Neils. That's why they are touring together."

"I guess that's up to Dr. Fulbright and Neils. It's not my call, but I hope they are sure before they stick Tham in a cave alone."

"Other than the Sanctuary, every cave has a working team. He won't be alone. They have staff around the clock."

"Then maybe he can sleep somewhere besides the Sanctuary. From what I hear, he can get from place to place on the surface without much trouble, and that's where his problem was before."

Milo shrugged, "Then maybe you'll get Collin back sooner than you think."

"I hope so," I said, then asked, "Have you discovered more about Ginger?"

"Nothing more than she's on the payroll and at the same job she had when she left us."

"But she hasn't contacted Beth, has she?" I asked.

He shook his head. "Ginger was always interested in herself more than anyone else. I hate to say it, but maybe she doesn't think about Beth anymore."

"Does Ginger ever land on Mars these days?"

"I'd guess so. The drops from Phobos don't require landing, but there is a drop-off point near the crater's north rim. Ginger must land to pick up supplies, mostly food, for Phobos. She assists with the landing, but the transfer can be purely robotic. Ginger wouldn't have to set foot on Mars, but she might if needed."

"Is that the only touch point with Phobos?" I asked.

"Most of their equipment and supplies come from robotic craft from Earth. New shifts of scientists come through on the satellite. The lander comes here to pick up food or the occasional passenger, and it ferries dead bodies to Phobos for their last trip. I only heard of the food stop, and that's because of Maria."

"Is that the place where Ross Hashimi was found? Do you think he was trying to get to Phobos?"

"No, I can't see why he'd do that, and it wasn't at the Phobos food drop. It was nowhere that made sense. It was just south of the road against a tall regolith dune but nowhere near our regular stops. We think he was just lost or out of his mind."

"That's so sad," I replied.

"It is. But thanks to you and Fulbright, all our hallucinators are cured. There are no more odd wanderers in the wilderness. That's a relief."

After breakfast, I visited the Rim of Forever in Destiny Temple, admiring the fantastic dance of galaxies, constellations, and pulsing stars. The view always relaxed me. Strangeness and wonder were everywhere, and I was a part of it. I had never fit in on Earth, but a late-night visit to the Rim made me feel at home. That night, I thought I saw Elly there, but now I know it was Ray, trying to explain himself to me in the guise of someone I trusted.

Ray.

From my first day on Mars, Ray came to me using the friendly faces of my first love, my father, and even Elly, wearing Edward's wire-rimmed glasses. Things had not turned out well between me and my former husband, but I had loved Edward once, too. Ray had done his best to appeal to me with faces of love before he approached me to reveal his real identity.

The thought of Ray trapped in the tunnel bothered me. His existence depended on the help that Luis, Michelle, Collin, and I could give him, and so far, we hadn't been much help. Luis still had doubts about our resident alien, but Collin and I had agreed to help him. Somewhere, there were parts for a body so he could walk among us. Helping Ray complete that mission was worth being parted from Collin, but I still prayed it wouldn't be for long.

After meditation, I took a few laps around Ring Street, stopping to visit with friends. The exercise and the fellowship were invigorating, and in the early evening, I found Beth and Giles in Central Park. I asked them how their day trip had gone.

"The trip was great but confusing," Giles replied.

"Did you lose your way on the route?" I asked.

He shook his head. "No, it wasn't that. We had programmed stops to check out. We were on the route Neils and Thaman followed. Everywhere else was a working site, but one stop seemed nowhere special. Beth didn't know it, and it wasn't near anywhere I had been before."

"But we made the most of it," Beth said. "After we ate lunch in the rover, we put our helmets back on to walk around. We expected to find something important, but it was just Martian sand and tall, stony ridges. Nothing more."

"We had a good day anyway," Beth said.

"Yeah, we did," Giles agreed, "I marked the coordinates. Maybe that spot can be a special place for Beth and me," he added, taking her hand.

Beth smiled, adding, "Next, we visited the food drop site and saw a path the rover could follow that went up the slope toward the taller compound wall. Since we were exploring without a timetable, we decided to see how high the rover could climb, but then the dust started kicking up." Beth turned to Giles. "I'll admit it if you won't," she said. Then she turned to me. "We saw something odd, and we weren't hallucinating."

"I'm positive you were not," I replied. "What did you see?"

Giles started the story. "I was busy navigating through the dust, so Beth saw it first."

Beth nodded. "It was something in the sky. I thought it was a shuttle, and maybe Ginger was the pilot."

"I only got a glimpse; navigation was too treacherous to keep locked onto it," Giles said.

Beth touched his arm to interrupt. "But I was looking straight at it. We were near the north edge of the crater, and the flyer swooped up from the south. I thought it would pass right over us. I kept staring, hoping it would get close enough to see Ginger through the window. Or even better, she might land."

"What was it?" I asked.

"We don't know," Giles shrugged. "A UFO on Mars, maybe."

"It got lost in the thick dust, and we didn't see it again," Beth said. "It didn't appear to be landing, though. It was climbing when it passed over the food drop."

"The dust was whirling by then, so it might have been our imaginations," Giles said.

I grinned, "Well, I'm glad you don't think it was a hallucination."

"Naa. I'm good with that now," he said.

"At least you had a good trip," I said. "But it's time for me to head home. Have a nice evening, guys."

That night, Collin contacted me via Marvin instead of via Ray.

"Just wanted to say goodnight, Sweety," he said. "Thaman will be here again tonight, and Neils and Rod are reviewing his instructions. I'm unsure how long they'll be here, so I figured I'd better let you get to bed."

Odd. But at least we got to share a *goodnight* and an *I love you*. It was better than nothing.

18 Uneasy Rest

Collin video-messaged me before lunch the following day, and I saw how tired he was, but beyond the fatigue, he was stressed.

"Brace yourself," he said. "I'll be home sooner than expected, but it's not exactly on my terms."

"No matter how it happens, I'd love to have you home. Did Rod find a different replacement guard?" I asked.

"No. Neils and Rod say Thaman can do it, but I'm not sure he's ready. I told Dr. Fulbright why I was worried, and he tried to talk Neils out of it, but Westergaard is not one to be convinced easily. He believes he's right, regardless of what Fulbright says."

"I can't imagine Tham's ready either, not after such a short treatment, but did you notice something? Is he seeing things or failing at directions?"

"No. But I caught him walking through the cave rooms—sleepwalking, I guess. He didn't have his terrain suit on, but he wore his helmet and gloves and walked along the same wall he stared at for so long the day before."

"The one where he said he was trying to force seeing things?" I asked.

"Yes, that one." This time, he touched the wall as if reaching for something, trying to grab whatever was on the other side. Finally, he gave up and went back to bed.

"I helped him stow his gloves and helmet, but when I jumped into the cot beside his, he asked me if I heard someone giving him directions by the wall."

"Wow, what could that be? Was it Ray?"

"I asked him if it was like the visions he had before—someone trying to mislead him, but he said it was a different voice asking him to look for something out of place."

"That doesn't sound like Ray or anyone else we know," I said.

"Tham agreed it would be easier to find after we had more sleep, so he rolled over, and I thought that was it. But I took precautions for Marvin to wake me if Tham started walking around again."

"Did Marvin wake you?" I asked.

"No, and he should have. Tham had his helmet and full terrain suit on. He had to have been up for a while. I'm not sure, but I think Tham tried to pass through the barrier in the interior tunnel that leads to the raw Martian caves. Luckily, there was no sign he passed through. When I asked him about it, he said he had roused in the night, and the words across the glass wall had turned red. The gases were out of balance. So, he went to the storage room to get his gear and tried to see if the Guardian tunnel was secure, but he couldn't enter. His rattling at the hatch woke me."

"Did you tell Fulbright and the others? Didn't they think that flagged Tham as having underground issues?"

"Fulbright and I argued that point, but Neils and Rod said everything was fine. They wanted me to take a few days away and leave Rod to watch him. They suspected I upset Thaman because he was always fine with Rod."

"Are you coming home tonight, then?" I asked.

"No. Not tonight. I convinced Rod and Neils I should check that internal tunnel to be sure nothing had happened with it and that I needed hours to run the safety tests. But I think they won't let me stay beyond tonight. I'll be home tomorrow."

"Do you think our traveling friend tried to contact Thaman again?"

I asked.

"While Fulbright was examining Tham, I found a moment to connect with Ray mentally, and he said no. He tries to stay shut down except when you and I try to reach him. He didn't cause this."

"No one else could have done that, could they? So, it's either a dream, as he said, or a hallucination. From what you've told me, I can't say which."

"Neither could Fulbright. He's run all the simulations he can and doesn't see signs of Tham's former problem. But even though he isn't sure, Neils pressures him to confirm that Tham is fit to be his assistant. Westergaard is our acting Second Prime and has authority over Fulbright."

"But will Tham be fit?" I asked.

"It's a hard call, but if Rod watches him at night, he might be OK."

"So, will you be home tomorrow?" I asked, and I felt my smile broaden despite my worry.

Collin grinned first, then he broke into a chuckle. "I'll be there, Hon. Maybe we shouldn't postpone that trip to Olympus Mons. I have a feeling my nights in the cave aren't over."

I smiled, wishing I could touch his hand. "I'll clear my calendar," I said. "At least we will have tomorrow."

19 Starry Mountain

It was midafternoon when Collin arrived, and even before Marvin announced him, I flung the door open and pulled him inside, oblivious to the dust, smell, and scruffiness from cave grooming.

"Glad to see me, are you?"

Then, he grinned as he dropped his belongings, and we locked in an embrace that neither of us wanted to end. After long moments of holding each other, we parted long enough to breathe, but neither of us let go. His hand rested on my waist as my fingers brushed his cheek.

Tears flowed, and since there was barely any breath to speak, I squeaked out my confession.

"I … uh … baked a … cake. Sort of."

"You did?" He smiled, but his eyes shifted as if scanning for a trap. "Er … let me clean up first."

So, I laid the kitchen table and set the cake on a wobbly plate where it reminded me of Phobos, lumpy and out of round. I didn't expect it to be good, and since I baked it, neither did Collin. Still, it felt right to celebrate his homecoming.

After we choked down a few bites, he placed a parcel beside the cake. "For you."

I studied the little box and looked at him, puzzled. "For me? The label says it's for Garrison Mathis at Sanctuary Cave."

"It's for you; trust me. That's the only box I could find, the one Benjamin Hessling shipped."

After fumbling till it opened, I found my old blue question-mark-looking charms inside. I had seen them last in Sanctuary Cave, where they shielded Ray since Bernadette died.

Shocked, my questions tumbled out. "Why did you bring these from the cave? Doesn't our friend need these? Is he safe?"

"Don't fret. These aren't Ray's. His shields are in place. I carved these from my labradorite samples in the cave. The tools were there, and making these gave me something to do on lonely nights."

"I thought you played cards with Ray."

"He tired of winning, so he directed my carving to make sure these were as accurate as possible. Of course, they are stone and don't have the heft of his alien alloy, but they look the same. Ray wanted you to have them, too. They won't help you communicate with him, but if your friends ask why you never wear your pendant anymore, you can show them this."

"Can I twist these into different shapes?"

"Maybe a few, but not so many as before. These are fastened into a heart by magnetic bits I drilled into each half. You may be able to create some of your old shapes but not all of them. The alien charms seem to connect anywhere, while these only connect with magnets."

I beamed. "I'll keep the heart," I said. "What else could I possibly need?"

"Oh, there might be something else," he said, eyes twinkling. "But for now, do what you must for our trip to Olympus Mons."

"What should I prepare? We're traveling virtually, aren't we? We're on Mars, but that mountain is over a thousand kilometers away."

He chuckled. "Yes, of course, we're going virtually. Martian virtual is close to real."

"You know, on my first night on Mars, I missed a starry view. Tonight, I hope I'll see Martian stars at last."

"We'll meet Martian stars up close and personal tonight. I promise."

***

Collin had planned for our night under the stars to be a campout, and it took a while for him to set the scene. After shifting our sitting room furniture aside, he set up the fluffiest camping bed I had ever seen. Then, he searched for a few more special touches to add to our evening.

Around 20:00, Marvin announced the deliveries Collin had ordered. I arranged Maria's best finger food and chilled champagne from Bistro sur Mars on our campsite table.

"Who knew a rockhound from Arizona could be so romantic?" I asked as he returned from our bedroom, carrying our quilt.

He shrugged, grinning. "Who'd know better than you?" he asked, tossing the quilt onto the fluffy bed. Then he reached toward me. "Come here. Let's get this show started."

I took his hand, and Collin ordered Marvin to start the Olympus Mons simulation. The room dimmed until our walls faded, and the only light was from the barely glowing embers of our campsite. But then the darkness deepened, and without much atmosphere or dust from the Martian surface, the stars blazed. My mouth dropped as the Milky Way lit up, streaming from heaven to the horizon.

"Ooooh," I sighed, squeezing his hand tighter.

Collin chuckled. "Is that all you have to say?"

I turned to his face, serene, like the man on Earth's moon, gleaming in reflected light. Collin, the only love I had ever known, was fair competition for the magnificent spectacle in the sky.

I turned back to the stars, lost, dazzled by the display of actual stellar majesty that exceeded even Destiny Temple's cosmic show. Air whisked across my skin, and while the climate of Olympus Mons would have flash-frozen me, Collin, Marvin, or maybe the programmer had left me with nothing more severe than an icy tingle on my cheek.

The sounds reminded me of movies with a dancer moving to jazz beats on a city street. Stiff breezes whispering over the rocks were shoes brushing a sidewalk, and when the wind shrieked through tall fissures, I heard the outrageous screams of blaring brass instruments. And then the view captured me again. The Milky Way dropped like a shower of fiery sparks as stars shifted and dipped below the horizon.

Why did Olympus Mons taste like salt? Until the tears crossed my open lips, I had no idea I was crying as I smiled.

Collin beamed at my tears as he shifted his hands to my shoulders. "Was it worth leaving Earth for this?" he asked.

Even without the atmosphere wavering between Mars and the sky, the stars shimmered like dancing bits of rainbow colors. I scanned the heavens, but my eyes locked on the one thing brighter than the universe: Collin's luminous face.

"Yes," I whispered, "this is worth leaving Earth." I pressed my head to his shoulder as we watched the great river of stars slip into the horizon.

Then he sat on the cushions and pulled me to face him, eye-to-eye. "Do you like it?"

"It's perfect," I said, touching his chest.

He smiled as he reached into the pillows. "There's one more thing."

"It's not bad news, is it? Please. No bad news."

He chuckled again. "Of course not. I have something for you."

"Another present?" I asked. "And all I did was bake a cake."

This time, he laughed out loud. "Well, let's forget that cake. Open this."

This parcel had a ribbon and pretty paper; he must have hidden it before he left. I took my time unwrapping it.

"Don't be so slow," he said. "Show me what's inside."

It was a gold ring, and deep red ant-hill garnets flashed around a large peridot crystal in the center, blazing in the starlight.

"It's magnificent. Did you mine these?"

"I did. I made this for my oldest sister, who insisted I bring it to Mars. She told me I'd need it. She was right."

"Why would you need this beautiful ring here?"

He took the ring and leaned close to my ear, whispering, "Because

I want you to marry me." When I said nothing, he slipped it on my finger. "Will you?"

I caught my breath, inhaling but not exhaling. Gasping, I grabbed the hand that had just given me the ring and shook my head slightly. Collin misunderstood my slow reply.

"Is that a *no*?" he asked. Now, *he* was blithering.

I shook my head more rapidly. "No. Not no."

"What?" he asked, clutching my shoulders.

"Not no .... Yes." The word was finally spoken, but I repeated it to be sure I had said it out loud. "Yes." I wrapped my arms around him, pulling him tight, and whispered again, "Yes."

"You're sure?" he asked.

I nodded my head, holding him tightly. The words cracked as I said, "I love you."

Then he pulled me into the pillows, and we found ways other than words to show our love. After convincing each other several times, Collin commanded Marvin to turn back the stars, and we cuddled under the Milky Way and watched it slip under the horizon again.

"When?" I whispered.

"I'm a bit spent at the moment, but as soon as I'm able," he replied.

I elbowed him. "You know what I mean."

He sighed, "When we return to Earth," he replied.

"Why? That won't be soon." I was shocked he wanted to wait so long.

"Because I want children, and our children should be born on Earth."

"Children?" We had never discussed kids. "Children aren't allowed on Mars," I replied. "We'd either spend a lifetime away from them or the rest of our lives off Mars."

"I know," he replied. "And I know we can't leave till we settle Ray to help him do what he came here for. Does that break our deal? Will you still marry me considering all that?"

I pulled him closer. "I'd marry you anytime, anywhere, and under any circumstances. You saved me, Collin."

"You'd be perfect with or without me," he replied. "But maybe I was unfair. We never spoke of children. What do you say about that?"

"That's a new thought for me, but I love the idea of bringing another Collin to the solar system. The universe should be so blessed."

His lips brushed the back of my neck. "Maybe we marry first and decide on kids when we can move back to Earth. Would that work?"

I breathed easier. "Yes, that works. Ray first, Earth later, then kids if we want that." I turned to face him, pushing the blonde curls from his face. Then I pressed against him, brushing my lips over his cheeks, relishing the feel of his body against mine.

He caressed me gently, but he was quiet for a time, and then he asked, "Why would you say I saved you? You are the one who cured *me*. I was the patient; you were the one who helped chase my hallucinations. You gave Mars back to me, and I found you. You are the healer here. Not I."

How could he not know? We had discussed Edward, but did I dump the pain on Elly and Maria while hiding it from Collin? He deserved to know the truth about me, even if I hated to admit it.

"From everything you've told me, you had an ideal life---four sisters who adored you, loving parents. From rodeos to rock climbing, you relished your life on Earth. I had none of that," I whispered.

"How can you say that? You were married to a man still revered for his work on AI, and you were his partner, helping him with his success."

"My parents were lovely, but I was rarely part of their plan. Nannies and boarding school employees raised me. In those circumstances, friends came and left like fruit flies. Edward was renowned, and I was honored to marry him, but it became clear that our marriage was no more than a practical solution for him. I did his bidding, and he appreciated that. But he didn't love me. The obedient service he demanded, my hunger for love, and his refusal to give it destroyed my fragile self-esteem."

"Then he wasn't as smart as people believed. He should have nurtured you, cherished you."

I shrugged. "Maybe. But I considered *myself* lacking. I had no value to Edward; that was no new revelation about myself. All Earth had found me worthless, even my parents and friends."

He touched my cheek, smiling. "You are worth a gold mine, and it's a shame that circumstances convinced you otherwise."

"Well, it has been a slow discovery. I took my first steps toward self-worth while working with Dr. Osgood at Coulton University. He encouraged me to take my chances on Mars."

"And you did great here. You healed me. That proves it."

"How could I know my friends and family were waiting for me here? They helped me find my feet—the ability to stand—for the first time. But then there was you. You healed the scars and stopped the bleeding that sapped my spirit. You made me whole after I was broken."

He held me tighter as he kissed my forehead. I shivered as his hands moved down my torso.

***

It must have been near midnight when Marvin sounded through Collin's wristband.

"Ending simulation. Thaman Bakshi needs assistance at Sanctuary Cave. He requests assistance from Collin Grant."

"Is the medical team on alert?" I asked.

Marvin replied, "No medical assistance is requested."

Collin threw the quilt aside as he hurried to our room. "Don't worry, Sweety. I'll take care of it and return as soon as possible."

He was out the door in five minutes.

After moving the camping setup back to storage, I arranged our room. Then I sipped champagne and nibbled taquitos, studying the ring on my hand. The halo of brilliant stones, redder than the red planet, orbited the pale green peridot that sparkled in the simulated candlelight. Entranced by that Martian fantasy in stone, I imagined life on Earth with Collin—and children. Would we marry on Earth? Would his family be there? Would they like me?

When that became too much to believe, I settled for safer dreams—Collin as the partner who loved me—my husband. I imagined us in the roles of Elly and Andy—the Petersens. We'd be the Grants, the Grants on Mars. It was a comforting thought.

The hour was late, and the champagne bottle was empty when Marvin announced someone at the door.

This time, it was Michelle Kaneko.

20 The Sky Goes Dark

"What's happened? Is Collin all right?" I asked.

Michelle noticed the empty champagne bottle. "Is Collin here?"

"No, he left over an hour ago."

"Do you have any tequila? Never mind, Maria is coming; she'll think of it." But to be sure, she sent a message via Marvin.

My body was paralyzed, but my mind raced. By then, it was the wee hours, nearly 02:00, and our Prime Minister's wife was in our house while Collin was not. The situation reeked of catastrophe. My jaw loosened just enough to repeat my question.

"What happened?"

Michelle was busy fielding messages and did not reply. Then she ran to answer the door. Maria entered, passing the tequila to Michelle as she rushed to join me on the sofa.

I gripped her hands. "Who's hurt?"

"Milo got an emergency alert. Thaman needs help in the cave."

"Then why are you both here? Shouldn't I go to Thaman?"

Michelle set the tequila and glasses on the coffee table. "You're not medical staff now," Michelle said, her fists piling onto ours. "Milo is taking Luis and Andy there. It's covered."

"Luis? Why would Luis go to a medical emergency?" Then it hit me. "Is Ray safe?"

"They aren't there yet," Maria replied. "We'll know more soon."

"Why are you here? Is it Collin?" I turned frantically to Michelle. "He had a message that Tham needed him, but that was over an hour ago. Did an alert go out about Collin?"

Michelle tilted her head. "Was there an alert an hour ago?"

"Yes. Collin left shortly after midnight. Do you need him?"

Michelle shook her head. "We didn't know Collin was home. We thought maybe you could tell if Ray is safe."

I glanced from Michelle to Maria and then back to Michelle, asking a silent question. *What was the protocol here?*

"Speak freely. Maria has clearance, and what Milo knows, she will know soon."

"I'll see if I can reach him."

The first try didn't go through. Then success. There was no Blue Room, but I heard Ray.

"Collin is here. I am vul … able. I … sh…"

Ray was stuttering. That had not happened in a while. But then Collin spoke to me. *Collin could speak. Collin was OK.*

"Ray is secure for now, but I must break contact. I love you."

And he was silent, but I held onto those last words like a velvet rope … a lifeline.

"Can he tell you more?" Michelle asked.

I shook my head, "He seemed rushed, and then he broke contact."

"Is that unusual?" Michelle asked.

"Everything tonight is unusual. Maybe Ray's in trouble." Then, after reaching for other possibilities, I added, "Or maybe he's occupied with whatever catastrophe is in the cave."

"Milo is on do-not-disturb mode. He's probably on limited channels from his terrain helmet," Maria said.

Michelle nodded. "It's the same with Luis. You said you got an alert from Marvin. Maybe he knows what's going on." She asked Marvin, but he didn't reply, either.

Maria was shocked. "How can that possibly be? Marvin is everywhere at every time."

Terror crept through my diaphragm, breathing was labored, and speaking was next to impossible. My mouth hung open, gasping for relief as I sobbed, tears flowing down my face. My friends huddled around me, offering drinks and spouting commiserations.

"Maybe it's no more than some glitch in communications," Maria said.

"Luis is always connected," Michelle said. "If he's incommunicado, something is wrong."

"Did anyone try to reach Neils?" Maria asked. "Maybe some override shifted alerts to him instead of Luis."

No one knew, and no one figured Neils would be much help.

My friends drank.

I sobbed.

We worried.

What had happened?

It was nearly 03:00 when Elly came to us. She whispered at the door with Michelle, who was crying as she led my surrogate mother to our huddle.

None of us spoke until Elly was ready to share her answers.

"Thaman is injured, and Andy has called Dr. Fulbright to assist in his treatment."

"Is he hallucinating again?" I asked.

She shook her head. "We don't know. He can't speak yet."

The heaviness of her movements and her stony expression said more than she would tell. Michelle was as petrified as Elly, and the paralysis passed to Maria before Elly spoke again.

"Rod Alexander found Thaman and Collin in the storage room." Then she thawed enough to cry, and her sobs kept swallowing the words.

I did not go to the Blue Room, but I felt Ray's steely hand underneath the human pile of palms on mine. His hand was next to mine when she spoke the words.

"Collin did not survive."

My world went black.

Part III: Through the Veil

21 Somewhere, Somewhen

There was only pitch in the pit, but the sticky, heavy tar held me together when I could not do it alone.

It was only when my chest began to hurt that I noticed there was no air, and I didn't know how to remedy that. So, I struggled, gasping, until I slowly rose and emerged, floating in a sea of pitch darkness.

Fragile bubbles popped against my back and brushed my ankles. But the bubbles vanished, and I was left with nothing to feel, nothing to see. I did not know if my eyes were open—or if I had eyes.

I was nothing, in a world of nothing, until the monotony of emptiness took me to nowhere again, or maybe it was nowhen—a place with neither to nor fro, here nor yon, sooner nor later.

I did not care.

My body was still, but my forehead twitched. Was I frowning? Fretting? No. In this place, there was nothing to fret over.

Then there was something. It might have been flat once. It pushed like a sail twisting in several impossible directions at once. I was immersed but tangled and tumbling through an endless ocean. I was dead or slowly drowning, waiting to sink back to the pitch, where darkness would eat me, and I'd be gone.

If I had had control of eyelids, I would have closed them, or maybe opened them first and then closed them again. But I could do nothing, so I drifted through small eternities of absolute darkness amid flashes of wondering when I would reach the bottom.

Darkness swallowed me again, and for an eternity, all was still. Then, something flitted around me like a swarm of minnows. They touched my face, and I felt tiny lips, as light as the birth of an idea, as soft as the last press of a fading kiss. They whispered words too faint to understand, then swam away in the darkness.

I couldn't move, so I couldn't catch them, but it didn't matter. I was dead—or dying.

Then the dark whispers kited, and the words cycloned around me. Three of them squeezed my hand. One blew into my left ear, one to my right. Two brushed my chin.

What did they whisper?

The three words on my hand spoke. "You're. Not. Dead."

One tickled inside my right ear while the other tickled my left, and together they spoke. "I. Am."

Not another riddle. There'd be no more riddles for me.

Then, a pail full of bodiless, voiceless words poured over me, floating in the bubbles until they enveloped me, squeezing tightly. Somehow, I felt better, but that was impossible. How does one go from nothing to relief? There must be something between.

I couldn't speak, but I might have been frowning again.

"Stop puzzling," I commanded. "Let go."

The minnow words squeezed me tighter.

"Don't."

"Let."

"Go."

"But I want to."

They squeezed tighter and then spoke in a chorus, "No," as they lifted me into the crushing cyclone and released me, floating in the midnight air.

The two words that had rested on my chin spoke, and even though the voice was faint, crackling, and far away, I recognized Collin. Blood rushed as the two words spoke, "You can't."

Then, all the words squeezed around me, pushing my air out, and when they released me, I inhaled the midnight.

My fingers twitched against a hand that held mine, then clung to it as if the puppy-soft palm were a lifeline.

My eyes opened to darkness and shut to a dream. Collin was with me, and I could rest.

"I love you," he whispered. He lowered me to a bed of clouds, and I smiled before I fell asleep, our fingers entwined in the black, silent, deep.

***

When I roused, there was no comforting hand within my fingers. *How long had I slept? Seconds? Days?* I tossed, trying to throw off the blanket that smothered me. The heat inside me built to a fever. I shifted, longing to find the warm puppy again, but then another set of fingers settled against the back of my hand. The touch was light, but the fingers dense, and their coolness drained the stifling heat.

"Shh," someone whispered. "Dream."

I didn't know how, and I was afraid. Dreams might bring something I'd rather fight than face. Hope was dangerous.

Then, something tickled my nose.

"Wake up, buttercup. We've been here too long."

I opened my eyes to Collin's silhouette backlit by a setting Milky Way. The shadowy fingers brushed straw across my cheek.

"Good morning, Cowboy," I said, beaming as I snuggled against him under the covers. "Let's stay here."

"Not possible," he replied. "We have much to do."

"Someone else can do it."

He shook his head, and the starlight in his eye masked a deeper sadness.

"You are the only one for the job this time," he said, brushing the hair curling on my pillow.

Then he lifted my hand and kissed the peridot stone. "Don't forget Olympus Mons," he said, "and don't forget how strong you are."

I drifted back to sleep, but as he withdrew to the shadows, he whispered, "Rest a little longer. You'll soon be ready for your future."

It was a good idea, so I fell asleep again.

***

Someone tucked the quilt under my chin, and small, soft hands brushed against my brow. "She's coming around." It was Dr. Mama Elly.

I wasn't ready to open my eyes, but Elly bumped around the room, occasionally pausing to check my pulse or temperature. She made tea and put a cup on the table near me—orange spice. *No cookies?*

Marvin announced someone at the door, but when Elly went to open it, Marvin whispered. "Wake up. I need you. This is why you're here. Save us both."

His voice had changed. It was familiar but not dronish, like Marvin. Was he reprogrammed? *Dreaming again, I guessed.*

Elly returned, and she and Jinae Kim stood by my bed. Through my closed eyelids, I sensed them staring at me. I wanted them to stop, but instead of *"Why won't you let me sleep?"* I grumbled gibberish.

"Get some rest," Jinae said, but she wasn't talking to me.

"I can't leave her like this," Elly replied.

Jinae picked up my cup. "I'll warm the tea and find the cinnamon biscuits."

I rested in the twilight between waking and sleeping while they sipped silently to the rhythm of cups brushing against saucers.

The gibberish rose to the level of muttering. "Go home. Let me sleep."

Elly gasped. The cup clattered. "I'll call Michelle; you get Fulbright," she said.

Oh, drat. Were they having a party? Should I get dressed?

I kicked at the covers, and Elly hurried me to the air shower.

"What's happening?" I asked, but Elly was on the phone with Michelle.

"She's up. Hurry."

Once I was dressed, Elly planted me on the sofa. "I'll get your breakfast."

Jinae wasn't in the room either. I guessed she was calling Fulbright. If this was a party, Collin should be here.

"Marvin, message Collin Grant," I said.

Why wasn't he complying? Then Marvin spoke. "Collin Grant is not available. His communication unit has been disabled."

Then memories poured onto my head like buckets of melted bullets.

Collin didn't make it. I lay stone still under the weight of an avalanche.

Collin wasn't coming.

Collin didn't make it.

Tears rained faster than the water recovery system could collect them, but that was OK. It would suck them out of my suit, too—the suit, the sofa, the carpet, the teacup. No water would be lost.

Only my Collin was lost.

22 Rising to the Cause

I gagged on the first sip of cold orange spice tea. Elly chased me as I sprinted to the toilet, retching.

Like the good surrogate mother she was, Elly washed my face and stood by me until I could sit in a chair for two minutes without another outburst of sobs or another toilet dash.

"I can't … I … can't …" I sobbed, finding that I couldn't even finish the sentence.

"It has been a woeful night, my girl, but others have seen worse, and you can get through it, too. You're not alone. We've been standing by you, and we're here now."

I nodded. I heard her. But then Elly's voice faded as Collin's words pierced the pain. "I love you," then more softly, "We all do."

Collin's greatest gift to me was love beyond doubt; according to him, giving love was its own reward. I couldn't repay him, but I owed him his due. There were arrangements to see to. That would fall to me, and I wouldn't let him down.

So, I closed my eyes, nodding sadly. "I can do this."

Elly helped me to the sofa, and while one of them walked here or there to open a shutter or fill a cup, the silence raged like a river, drowning all other sounds.

Then Marvin sounded an alert that visitors had arrived. No one asked my opinion. What I wanted didn't matter. For whatever reason,

Michelle Kaneko and Wolfgang Fullbright were here. Jinae escorted them to the room.

"I'm so sorry, Spring," Fulbright said, but he didn't seem to care that I had no reply.

"It's coffee for Fulbright and tea for Michelle, right?" Jinae asked.

"Black," Fulbright replied. Michelle took two sugars. Jinae played hostess; she collected my cold cup before her trip to the galley.

Michelle sat by my right on the sofa, but Fulbright pulled Elly toward the entry to confer. He may have thought I was dazed, unaware, but I heard them.

"What does she understand?" he asked.

Elly's voice was barely louder than a sigh. "She knows he's gone and is still navigating her way back from the shock."

They moved cautiously back to the sitting area. Elly chose the sofa seat left of me, but at a comfortable distance, Wolfgang chose an armchair across the table. Elly rested an arm along the sofa back. Wolfgang tapped his knee.

When Jinae returned with her tray, the others leaned forward to take a cup, and Nurse Kim placed my mug on the coffee table and then carried her cup to the settee. I felt their eyes on me, so when everyone else raised a cup to their lips, there was a collective gasp when I followed suit.

"Spring, are you ready to speak with us?" Fulbright asked.

I finished my sip before replying, emotionless, "Yes. I must."

The shock of Michelle placing a hand on my knee shook the mug, and I steadied it with both hands.

"*Cherie*, do you have wishes as to how we should remember your dear Collin?"

I swallowed the sip near my throat. "No. I never …."

"*D'accord*. Why would you? There is no rush."

Then, while the others chatted, keeping a distance from that topic, I remembered my project, the WayPoint memorials. Collin would be there for me to visit as often as I cared to. *But what did I want to see?* He'd never speak to me again, so what phrase would I want him to repeat to every visitor? *Could anything offer comfort?*

I felt my back stiffen, and light, firm fingers gently massaged.

"Do you have any questions, Spring?" Wolfgang asked.

"What happened? How did he ...?"

Michelle leaned forward. "*Bien sur, cherie.* I know only a little, but he struggled to rescue Thaman in Sanctuary Cave. Your Collin was a hero; he died saving his friend."

"But why? That cave is well-stocked. Why would Thaman need rescuing?"

Wolfgang replied. "He and Collin were in terrain gear, so we think they either went outside or perhaps to the raw tunnels."

The raw tunnels? What had Thaman found there? *Was Ray safe?*

"I'm fine," a familiar voice whispered.

If those tunnels were breached, he might not be safe for long.

I sat my cup down with a moderate thump on the table.

"Spring, I'm so sorry if I've disturbed you," Wolfgang said. "We will tell you all we can, but wait till you're ready."

I nodded. "His terrain suit," I said.

"Yes, Collin was in his terrain suit, too. That's how he rescued Thaman," Jinae said.

I shook my head. "No. I mean, he should be memorialized in his terrain suit. He loved being among the rocks and cliffs."

"As you wish, cherie," Michelle said.

"And ... put him against the background of the Milky Way."

Michelle nodded. "Was it special to him?"

"It was special to us. He set that scene when he proposed yesterday. We were to marr ... marry." The sobs erased my words. *So much is lost.*

"Oh dear," Elly said, reaching to rescue my cup and grab my hand. "I'm so sorry," she said, tears streaming.

My face was wet, too, but they had sounded too many alarms. I had to pull away from the grief wallow; it was my job to finish the rescue now. I held Elly's hand to my cheek and kissed it lightly before twisting toward Michelle and grabbing her arm.

She saw the fire in my eyes but could not quiet the clanging while others were in the room.

My head spun as I found each face around me. "I … I need to …"

"You need to eat," Elly said. She turned to the others. "Please, she's with us again but needs food and rest. Let's give her space for now."

I dug nails into Michelle's arm as she said. "I must stay for a bit longer. There are official questions."

"Can't it wait?" Elly asked.

"For a bit, perhaps," Michelle replied. "I'll sit with her while you find supper."

"Tomorrow. I promise I'll speak with each of you tomorrow," I said.

Jinae brushed my face with her hand, and Wolfgang patted my shoulder. "Tomorrow, then," he said. Then, the two of them left for the clinic.

While Elly rattled a few dry wrappers to make soup, Michelle bent close, whispering, "Where is Ray?"

"Isn't he where we both saw him last?" I asked.

Her eyes were wide as she shook her head.

"Then, I don't know."

"Luis will come tomorrow. We must speak," she said.

I agreed.

She patted my arm and rose to leave as Elly brought soup. "Eat this, dear. Oh, wait. I think I saw something fruity. And bread. You need bread." Then she hurried back to the galley.

"Can you find him?" Michelle asked.

"I'll try," I replied.

Michell left, but Elly shared supper with me and stayed as long as she could keep me talking. But once she had me tucked in bed, she gave Marvin an order.

"Monitor her. Speak to her if she rouses, and contact me immediately if she's in distress."

The AI servant sounded like a proper butler. "At your service as usual," Marvin replied. "Complying."

23 Taking Action

Luis and Michelle Kaneko were WayPoint's staunch guardians of good manners, but I had barely finished my first coffee when they were at my door.

"My goodness. Welcome. I'll get the coffee," I said.

"No, no, Dr. Graviston," Luis replied.

Michelle stepped forward. "I must apologize for our early arrival, cherie. Luis insisted we arrive before you are covered with well-wishers. But, please, have your breakfast first."

Fate had ripped through my life, and I was hardly more than walking dead, but my guests had come with a purpose. So, I pointed them to the sofa while I warmed a few cups and filled a cozy pot. Then, after a moment of staring blindly out the window, I tossed several breakfast bars onto a self-serve tray and carried it to my sitting room.

The Kanekos accepted the cups politely and used them as hand warmers as we sat civilly, waiting for the burning questions to begin. They started simply, asking how I slept.

"Fine," I replied. The truth wouldn't please them. They understood my pain. But try as they might, they could not join me in peeking through the shreds left of my life.

Next, they asked if they could help in any way.

The Kanekos didn't need to be in my house to share condolences when a message would do. There was another agenda, and I was uneasy, waiting for them to drop the other shoe.

Michelle, ever diplomatic, was the first to get to the point. "As you must know, we have questions for you, cherie. But first, is there anything you want to ask us?"

I nodded, almost happy to put words to the question that haunted me each time I reached for Collin's pillow. "Where is he?"

Michelle smiled sweetly, saying, "I am sure Collin is with the angels, but his body is at the clinic with your friends. Dr. Fulbright and the Bashirs are examining him."

"How did he die?" I asked.

Luis handled the more technical questions. "There is more to learn, but it appears he had catastrophic system distress due to the failure of his suit."

"Thaman had similar injuries," Michelle added. "But his damage has not yet proved fatal. How can it be that two of our remarkably reliable terrain suits failed at the same time? WayPoint boots must touch Martian soil thousands of times daily. That's millions of opportunities for failure, yet this is the first time it has happened."

"We shall find the answers," Luis replied. Then he turned to me, "You can see Collin later today if you like."

See him? Today? Was he alive somewhere? Could I go to him? Hope flashed for half a second until reality smothered the flame.

"What will become of him? Has his family requested he be sent home?" I asked.

Luis leaned in to reply. "Soon after I take possession of Collin's chip, he will be shuttled to Phobos to await the next launch from our moon to Threshold Station on Earth's moon, and then he'll be shipped home."

Michelle touched my arm. "But you must prepare his memorial here so no one on WayPoint can ever forget him. And as for his home on Earth, I hope it was right—we sent word to the Grant family that you and Collin intended to marry. Will you speak with them should they ask to meet you?"

"Of course. I feel as if I know his family, especially his oldest sister." Then I turned to Michelle. "I've changed my mind about Collin's memorial. The setting should be Earth, not Mars. He wanted to return home someday. Let his hologram show him in Arizona. I'll work with Marvin to create the image and send it to you. The memory of Olympus Mons is my treasure."

"As you wish, my dear," Luis replied, "So we have settled one point."

He was interrupted when Marvin announced two more visitors. My nerves knotted upon hearing the names Neils Westergaard and Roderick Alexander. It may have been my imagination, but Luis and Michelle stiffened, too.

After greeting the Kanekos, the two visitors approached me with their heads slightly bowed. Rod rested a heavy hand on my shoulder, saying, "Your sorrow is too great for me to lift, but I'm ten steps away if you need anything. I'll arrange to have Collin's belongings in Sanctuary Cave delivered here."

"Yes, we can see to that. Whatever was his is yours now," Luis said.

It wasn't a smile, but the corners of my lips twitched. "Thank you. It's kind of you to offer."

Neils' brow wrinkled a bit more as he added, "Dr. Graviston, no one could guess that Sanctuary Cave would be the site of two tragedies so close together. I came here to investigate the deaths in the cave those months ago, and now we've had two more casualties. Please, grieve as you should; I'll be here when you feel more up to an interview."

Had Neils not asked all his questions of me by now? There was an agenda behind his condolences, but I summoned the same weak smile and replied, "Thank you. I appreciate your understanding."

When the two moved to the sofa, Luis sat straighter to address Rod. "Dr. Fulbright suggested that seeing where Collin was during his last moments might put Dr. Graviston's grief into perspective. Michelle and I are here to escort her to the cave today."

Michelle patted my knee. "*Oui*, my dear, you shouldn't be alone for that. Luis and I will walk beside you, and we can help transport his belongings if needed."

"Perhaps I should join you," Rod said. "I know the cave as well as anyone other than Collin. I'd be happy to attend."

"What do you say, Spring?" Luis asked. "Will my wife and I suffice to hold your hand, or would you prefer Rod be there?" Then he turned to Rod again, "Michelle and Spring have become confidants; my wife hopes to be a comfort today."

"Yes," Michelle added. "Luis will get us in and out of the shadows of death as efficiently as possible. Do you agree, cherie?"

I nodded, happy to avoid the company of a man who had occasionally made me uneasy. So, I turned to Rod, "I need to be with my friend today. And, as you say, you are just down the way should I have questions."

Michelle offered to pour coffee, but the two men declined and left soon after.

"Shall I make arrangements, then?" Luis asked.

My head bobbed. "Yes, please take me there. The sooner, the better."

Within the hour, we had donned our terrain gear and approached the transport Luis ordered from Emilio Torres. The news of Collin's passing had spread through WayPoint, and Milo and Maria were there to see us off, as were Giles Cardiff and Beth Martin.

Words had little meaning, but warm hugs and silent tears meant everything. Even wise-cracking Giles couldn't stop a few drops from slipping over his cheeks.

"We love you, my dear," Marie said. "Almost as much as Collin did."

Every such encounter refreshed my pain, but, like pressing into a bandaged wound, every new jab hurt a little less than the one before.

"I can drive for you if you like," Giles said. And his laughter was contagious as he giggled. "I hardly ever get lost these days."

Luis chuckled, replying, "Electronic assistance is sufficient, Giles, but thank you for the offer."

24 What Happened Here?

Without Giles, the drive might have been silent, but Michelle asked how Collin proposed, and I was happy to tell that story. Perhaps I shouldn't have said we discussed children and considered raising them on Earth, but it didn't rattle my friends. The Kanekos let me talk, gush, and cry, and when we arrived, the veils of grief were lighter.

The first transition tunnel, Sanctuary's Gateway, evoked sad memories of Dexter and Bernadette. But then came the main room, the sanctuary. Collin had rushed to greet me the last time I was there, and now I hurried through to learn what happened to him.

We had been together in that massive room the night we found Ray and confronted Bernadette. And the Kanekos were with us the night we introduced them to our alien visitor. It was fitting that Collin's final destiny came in Sanctuary Cave, and he hadn't been alone. Ray was there.

Luis hurried us along. "This way, my dear," he said, directing us to the workroom with its supply closet and Guardian Portal.

"Is this where you found him?" I asked.

Luis pointed to his right. "Tham was there, near the storage closet. His suit had a rip near the chest pocket, and his original helmet had rolled across the floor. We found him unconscious but with a fresh oxygen supply from the emergency closet."

"But Thaman wasn't injured when he called Collin to the cave," I said.

"Then, the medical alert sounded while Collin was en route, and he arrived before the crew. He must have found Tham injured and rendered aid," Michelle said.

"OK, Tham was short of oxygen, and Collin saved him, but what happened to my fiancé?" I asked.

This time, Luis pointed toward his left. "Collin's foot was just clear of the Guardian Portal when he fell. He was reaching toward Thaman, who was likely unconscious by then."

"If Collin had stayed with Tham, he would have fallen near him. He must have gone into the raw tunnels and fallen when he returned," I said. "How was Collin injured?"

"He had the same gash in his terrain suit pocket and another slash along the glove. But he was too far from the oxygen, and there was no one here to help him."

Michelle took my arm. "If it is any comfort, he died trying to save himself, and that was after he saved Thaman's life."

I nodded, "So, Collin helped save Tham but left him to go beyond the Guardian Portal."

Luis sighed. "From the position of the victims, that makes sense."

"And you can guess why Collin went there," Michelle added.

Luis nodded. "He was searching. That's why we wanted to be here with you alone. The situation is dire, and we must act quickly while the others are not here." Then he added, "Marvin, privacy mode, please."

"Complying," Marvin replied, and the light on my wristband dimmed to a blackened plum color.

"Is your *friend* still here? Is he safe?" Luis asked.

"I believe so," I said.

"Then we should find him," Luis replied.

Michelle turned to me. "Can Ray speak to you?"

I closed my eyes and found the Blue Room in my head. Ray was there, expressionless, and the image he projected was more pale than usual, probably a sign of his sympathy.

"I feel your pain," he said. "We've both lost a magnificent friend."

I pulled back to reality and turned to Luis. "He's speaking to me," I said.

Michelle tapped my shoulder. "What has he told you, Spring? Can he reach me?" Michelle asked.

In a flash, she was in the alien's Blue Room. "I see him," she said.

I leaned to touch Ray's arm as I asked, "May I come to you in the cave?"

"I sense no danger, but I do not know *where* I am," he replied.

"Aren't you where I first saw you?"

"Collin was here. He said he would move me somewhere safer."

"What happened?" Michelle asked.

"Thaman—the one who can't tell what is true—he found me first."

"But how? We didn't tell anyone about you," I said.

"Perhaps Tham searched for me or some sign of me as you and Collin did. But, this time, he interfered with me somehow. That didn't happen when I encountered him before. Either Tham changed, or there was some new external force at work."

"We are coming. Give us as much help as you can," I said. Then we lost the Blue Room, but Ray could still speak to us. Only Luis was out of communication, so Michelle explained.

"Collin moved Ray to a new location," she said. "There was interference … static."

"Someone, possibly Thaman, scanned for Ray," I added.

"What scanner did Tham have?" Michelle asked.

"I don't know," I replied. "That depends on what he searched for."

"We should hurry to find him," Luis said.

Then, we triple-checked our terrain gear, grabbed a few induction torches, and headed through the transition chamber. Luis opened the Guardian tunnel hatch, but I paused at the empty spot where Collin's body had been. Just a day ago—or was it two—he lay there dying.

"Don't dwell on that," Ray whispered. "Remember him in better ways."

"Spring? Are you coming?" Luis asked.

"A moment please. Ray is speaking to me," I said, then turned my thoughts to Ray. "Thank goodness you were near. Was Collin in pain? Was he afraid?" I asked.

"*Afraid* ...." Ray paused, pondering the word. "Oh, I understand. First, he was afraid for Thaman, then for me. Then, after another static explosion, Collin was momentarily afraid for himself. But when he realized he wouldn't survive, he became calm. He hoped help for Thaman would arrive quickly. But more of his thoughts were for you —and even a little for me."

"That sounds like Collin," I said. "He was determined to help you finish your mission. We're coming to you, Ray. We will start from where we last saw you."

I knew the trail, and while it was rocky in most spots, a few sandy places revealed Thaman's footprints, pointing in several directions, with some walking over the others as if he had been exploring alone. He had wandered through several passes before standing at the foot of the rubble pile where we had left Ray shielded in his orb.

"The cask isn't here," Luis said.

"No, Collin moved it, but he wasn't the first person here," I replied.

"Thaman," Luis said.

"Ray calls Thaman *the one who can't tell the truth from lies.* He was here, probably excited that he had found something important. That must be why he called Collin."

"He still wasn't sure who told the truth. That's a good sign, isn't it?" Michelle asked. "Tham had doubts about Rod and Neils, but he called Collin because he trusted him more. Did Tham take Ray away from here?"

"According to Ray, it was Collin, not Tham, who moved him," I said. "And from his description of events, Thaman was injured first, but Ray was close enough to experience a disturbance."

"So Thaman was injured here, near Ray's cask." He examined the tunnel floor. "The footprints are blurred here, and they turn back, moving more slowly than when they came. There is no sign of a fight, but there are signs of a man alone, staggering."

"Thaman, struggling back to the storeroom," Michelle said.

"That's when Collin arrived," Luis said. "He found Thaman unconscious and saved him with the oxygen mask."

I nodded, "But then Collin returned to these tunnels to help Ray. Ray said Collin feared for Thaman first and then Ray. It fits. Collin wanted to protect Ray's secret by moving him."

Luis agreed. "If Ray can contact Michelle, he must be hidden nearby."

"There should be more prints here," Michelle said. "Luis was here with Collin recently, and Spring was here the night they found Ray."

"Collin slept in this cave alone for days. He told me he searched for Ray's missing cask during the nights when he was alone, but he must have cleared his tracks to Ray after he explored," I said.

"But look," Luis said, pointing to the solid walls. "There are fresh partial prints near the rocks. Collin wanted to hide his new tracks, too."

"Right. And over there," Michelle added, pointing to the wall across the tunnel. "There are similar partial tracks there, but sometimes they slip. They are less hidden."

"Perhaps he was in a hurry when he left," Luis said. "But where could Ray be now?"

I had it!

"I know a place," I said. "There is a hidden tunnel on the other side of this pile. We can't get past the rubble, but I know the way to the other side. I was there the night Collin found Ray. Follow me."

We retraced our steps to the storeroom tunnel, but I led them beyond the Guardian Portal, following the raw tunnels I used months ago.

The Kanekos followed me into a cave so cluttered with obstacles that no one would expect a treasure inside. Fallen rocks, broken lava tube walls, and dusty piles made it seem impassable, but I had squeezed through before, and we could do it again.

We wiggled through much of the debris until Ray said we were near.

"Did Collin explore here?" Michelle asked.

"Not with me," I said, "He found Ray first at the rubble pile we led you to. I was on this side when he found Ray, so I backtracked to join him there."

Then Ray whispered from the Blue Room. "Come. You are quite near."

Encouraged, we wiggled through the darkness. We were so far from the induced power operating this cave that even our induction torches were dim. But deep in the farthest corner, Ray's white cask gleamed in our lamplight.

"You found me," Ray said.

"And you're still shielded," I said, flashing my torch toward the blue charms on the cask.

"Now I am," Ray replied. "Tell Luis to join us."

Luis touched the blue charms and joined us in the Blue Room, where Ray explained what happened.

"I wasn't fully shielded, not all the time. The static interfered with my processing and communication. It was strong before Thaman found me and excruciating when he touched me. Thaman was hurt, and when he left, my shielding was weaker than before. Then Collin came and put the shielding in place. But the noise returned, roaring louder this time. When it subsided, I was safe, but Collin had left me here. There have been no interference problems since then."

"Then this is where Collin was injured," Luis said.

"But why was there no medical alert for Collin?" I asked.

Luis sighed, resting a hand on my shoulder. "The damages didn't allow it. His sleeve was ripped and burned, and his chip was damaged, too."

"So no one came for him?" I asked.

"You are here, cherie," Michelle said. "But is this tunnel safe?"

Ray replied, "It has been. Collin told me they didn't bother with this part when exploring this area. There were easier paths without so much debris."

"But when Thaman recovers, he might remember things that will make Ray's seekers more thorough. We need to extract Ray and cover our tracks," Luis said.

"Might we be hurt like Thaman and Collin?" Michelle asked.

"I felt nothing when I touched his blue shield," Luis replied.

"Something else caused the static, and I don't hear it near any of you," Ray said.

"But how will we get Ray out of here safely?" Michelle asked.

Luis had the answer. "Our public reason for coming here was to help Spring collect Collin's things. Let's make Ray's cask one of those."

"Are we going to take it home?" I asked.

Michelle grinned. "Let's take it to our house. No one has better security than we do, and Rod Alexander is familiar with Spring's place. We can decide the next step after we move Ray to WayPoint."

"Let's box Ray's cask and mark it for the memorial room," I said. "If we can get home without much notice, we'll be safe for a while."

Once in the storeroom, Michelle and I searched for Collin's things while Luis used a rock duster on the lowest setting to obscure our tracks beyond the Guardian Portal. I found Collin's rock hammer and collected that for his niche. Other carving tools lay beside the scraps of labradorite from the charms he had made for me. I took those and any other instrument with his name on it. We sealed those in a box labeled *Collin Grant*. Then, we wrapped Ray's cask and stuffed it into a crate half-filled with rock samples for shipment to Threshold Station.

We were grateful for those precautions.

When we returned to WayPoint Station, I kept the box of Collin's things tucked under my arm, and when Luis returned the rover, he passed the rock samples to Milo for safekeeping. So, when Rod Alexander met us at the docking bay, he saw only one box carried from Sanctuary Cave. He was curious about Collin's things, but they were mine now, and he had no excuse to examine the box.

Rod had another reason for meeting us, though. The clinic had found a clue to what happened.

"No one is terribly excited," he said, shrugging. "It's a technical tidbit that can keep till morning." That meant one more sleepless night for me.

***

I was glad to arrive home. It was still our place, Collin's and mine, but without Collin. I sat in my chair for hours, remembering. Then I put his box beside the bed. I needed Collin close, so I climbed into bed and fell asleep watching his parcel.

There were still so many questions.

What happened? Did a scanner cause the interference? Where was it? Who had it?

But it wasn't just puzzling over the clues that kept me awake till the wee hours. Almost as soon as my eyes closed, a man with my father's dark, curly hair sat by the bed, holding my warm hand in his cool one.

"My dear, Spring," he said. "I am so sorry I was not with you when you needed me. The depth of your suffering did not occur to me, and I might have eased your pain."

"All is fine, Father. Or it was until now. I've found friends as close as family." I drew breath to tell him about Collin but realized they had never met, which made his reply more surprising.

"I know, daughter," he said. "You have lost someone again."

"Did you come to be sad with me, Father?" I asked. "Will you take the pain away?"

He shook his head. "Loss and life are two sides of the same coin, my love. But here I am with you again, and Collin is closer than I am. He will always be part of you."

"Did you come to tell me that?"

He smiled, revealing the dimples I had loved as a child. "I came to tell you that after you cross this rough path, you have a future not yet imagined, and all the love you gathered from the time you were born will cling to you, sustain you, and attract even more."

"I understand. Thank you," I said. Perhaps I had heard so many platitudes that now I dreamed them.

"There is more," he said.

"More?"

"More important than the love given to you is the bounteous love you will give others."

Then he caressed my hair and hummed a familiar tune as I relaxed. But before I fell asleep, I asked him about the song.

"I don't know the name," he said. "Someone from Arizona sang it."

Sleep deepened, but just as night enveloped me, the image of my father briefly shone like a silver moon before fading into the darkness.

25 The Visitation

Michelle Kaneko messaged me early the following day.

"Luis and I want to know the clue Rod spoke of last night. We're on our way now. Would you care to join us?"

"Go ahead with your plans. I need more time."

"As you wish, Cherie. Nurse Kim will escort you when you are ready."

No escort was needed. I knew what to expect but did not rush to what I dreaded. Viewing Collin would be a fresh heartbreak, but it was necessary. I saw where he died but needed to face the reality that he was gone. And maybe I could find clues to what happened. So, I dressed, took a sip of coffee, and then let the cup grow cold in my hand as I stood, paralyzed by the bitter hailstones of circumstance. Jinae Kim arrived within half an hour, interrupting the storm.

"I'm here. Ready when you are," she called from the entry.

I grabbed her by the elbow, steering toward the nearest spoke street. "Let's get this over with."

My friend was alternately silent and chatty, walking quickly or more slowly as she followed my lead. She was like a favorite all-purpose jacket on Earth, ready for all things and able to become what I needed. That was Nurse Kim during our walk toward the WayPoint Clinic.

We entered the clinic portal, and once in the corridor, she grabbed my wrist and locked eyes with me. "Collin first, or Thaman?" she asked.

"Are the Kanekos here?"

"They've come and gone. So … Collin or Thaman?"

I had been composed during the stroll, but suddenly, her image wavered as tears filled my eyes, and I could not reply.

"Collin then," she said. "This way." With only a nod to Lilith, she pulled me past the welcome desk and into the Triage Room near the nurses' lounge. Collin must be behind the curtain near the back. We waited a moment for the chilled air to warm. Then, when I nodded, she split the cling seam, opening the curtain, and we passed through.

I fiddled with my peridot ring before stepping forward. There was the love of my life, my beautiful husband-to-be. His eyes were closed, and his lips didn't part into a smile. But it was Collin, and I imagined his dimples deepening as they flinched and that he'd wake with a wink and a grin, his hands reaching for mine. In the hum of the recycler and the rustle of the cling sheets, I heard him say, *"It's all right, Sugar Spring. I love you."*

I sat on the stool beside his gurney and took his cold hand. His chest did not rise; his veins did not pulse.

"Would you like to be alone?" Jinae asked. And when I nodded, she left me, promising to be right outside the door.

I tried speaking to him like we did while we were separated, he in Sanctuary Cave and I at home. *"What happened to you? Who did this?"*

There was no answer. But Collin's hand slipped from my fingers, and when I rose to lay it on the gurney beside him, I noticed two terrain suits on wall pegs by the door. One would fit Collin, the other Thaman. *What could they tell me?*

There were only traces of tunnel dirt on the back sides, so I twisted the hangars until the suits faced me. The pocket under Thaman's name tag had exploded. It wasn't just ripped; the pocket face had burst into shreds, and the damage extended into his chest covering, probably digging into his protective undersuit.

Collin's suit had the same damage. *What had happened?* I looked closer and found charred fiber around his cuffs. Something had struck the weakened fabric, slashing it past the wrists and along the left sleeve of his suit. That force had damaged his arm down to the implanted chip.

I returned to Collin's body, examining his arm where the damaged sleeve had been. One of the doctors had masked the burns on his hand and lower arm with artificial regrowth. I pushed his cover aside to see his chest. That injury had a surface covering, too, but it didn't hide the extent of his wound. *What strange new weapon was this?* My head rested on his chest as I grieved. *What have we done to you?*

Then I heard him again. "Don't be sad. You will figure this out and finish what we started. I'm always with you."

He was.

But he wasn't.

I smoothed the covers over my beloved Collin's body. Those hands would never touch me again, and I'd never feel his lips against mine. I reached to caress his hair but found it stiff and unyielding.

So, I stood, whispering, "Thank you for everything, darling."

Collin wasn't on that gurney. Perhaps he was with the angels, as Michelle said. But my father, or was it Ray, had spoken the truth. Collin would always be with me because he was part of me. I felt his heart beating in my chest, his blood mingling with mine. He had imbued me with his resilience, and the steel he put in my spine was permanent. I'd no longer walk around bleeding from the slashes that absent parents, fickle friends, and Edward had delivered. Collin's love had healed those wounds, too.

I was no longer the sad Earth child spawned by my beginning. Earth was my genesis, but Mars had tempered me. This Spring was unbroken—sad but whole at last.

As I lifted his hand, squeezing those fingers for the last time, I placed his hands against his body and pulled the covers to his neck.

"You will live as long as I do," I whispered. "I will finish what we started and get you home."

***

After one last kiss on his forehead, I left the room and found Jinae Kim waiting beyond the door.

"Would you like to sit down? I can find a coffee," she said.

I took a deep breath. "No, I'm OK. Tell me about Thaman."

"He is still unconscious but on the mend. His body is recovering, and we expect his mind will be fine, too. But no one knows how long that will take."

"I saw the rips in his terrain suit. What could have caused that?"

Jinae took my hand in hers. "They are keeping the investigation under wraps, but the database doesn't show a previous suit malfunction that injured the wearer in such a way. They are discovering all they can from science—running down clues from tests and observations, but we should know much more when Thaman wakes."

"*If*...." I replied.

"Yes. If."

"Do you have any guesses?" I asked.

She nodded. "You know what guesses are worth in a case like this. Look for yourself, and then tell me what you think."

She led me to the welcome desk, where she assumed her post, and Lilith stood to greet me.

"I'm sorry for your terrible loss, Dr. Graviston," she said. "I hope you take some comfort in knowing that Thaman is expected to recover."

The impact of bereavement showed in her eyes, and I wondered how recent her loss had been, but I only thanked her, adding, "I'd like to see Thaman, if I may."

"He's in room 407. I'm on my way there. I'll walk with you, but you must know how to get there. I hear you were once detained in that room," she said as we started down the corridor.

"Yes, Dr. Fulbright and I were held there at separate times. Those dark days led to the investigation that brought Neils Westergaard here."

"Yes, Neils hinted at that, but he keeps most of his investigation to himself. I hear Bernadette Duval was a part of the mischief."

I nodded. "She was."

"Everyone is tight-lipped about her. Thaman and Giles told me more than anyone else. They did not have a good opinion of her."

Was Lilith probing for sensitive answers? What was she up to? I studied her face but found nothing to rachet my suspicion ... yet. So, I replied, "She was a complex person, but as part of an ongoing investigation, I'm not free to speak of her, either."

"Of course. I apologize," she said.

Alissa Arvani and Neils Westergaard whispered in a side office, but I could not hear them. Then, we reached room 407, where Wolfgang Fulbright and Elly Petersen hovered over Thaman's bedside.

"No change?" Lilith asked.

"None," Elly replied, shaking her head. Then Lilith patted my shoulder and left for her other duties.

Elly asked, "What do you make of this, Spring?" She pulled the cover from Thaman's chest and found a wound matching the one I saw on Collin. The burn cauterized the wound, but synthetic skin completely replaced the center. "How deep did it go?" I asked.

"Thaman's injury was not as deep as Collin's. The damage pierced through his skin but not into the body cavity. There was serious compression damage to the left lung and less severe damage to the heart. Alissa believes he will recover, but we are keeping him sedated for now."

"Something caused this, and I suspect a scanner was involved. From my visit to the cave, it looks like Thaman had it first, and Collin took it with him into the tunnels, where he was injured."

Elly shrugged, "No one reported a scanner on Collin or Tham. If there was one, where is it now?"

"I don't know. Maybe the accident happened some other way." I turned to Tham. His monitors indicated a deep, restful sleep. "Have you been his attending physician from the beginning?"

She shook her head. "Alissa was the internist; she was on tap to care for his heart and lungs. He became my patient today."

Elly was our specialist in invasive diseases. "Is it cancer?" I asked.

"There is no sign of cancer," Elly replied. "But these wounds and the undersuit we removed have two radiation signatures. One is from an iridium compound, and another is used on Earth in iridium detectors."

"Do we mine iridium on Mars?" I asked.

"Not that I've heard," she said. "No one has reported iridium so far."

"Could there be a deposit in Sanctuary Cave?"

"I can only guess. We don't have iridium detectors on WayPoint. There has been no need before now."

"So, no iridium scanners here, then. But why would either of these compounds strike at the chest? Radiation doesn't make choices."

"Indeed not. We have created complex instruments to target radiation, but in nature, we've never seen it directed to a specific point."

"Then how did both these men get hit in the chest?"

Elly shrugged. "We aren't sure."

"Neils Westergaard must be hot on the scent to find that answer," I chuckled.

"He doesn't make much of it. He's more interested in tracking Thaman's steps in the cave. And since he can't do much on his own, he hangs out here hoping for Thaman to revive."

"Oh, joy," I whispered, hoping to hide the sarcasm.

Neils surprised me by joining us in the room. "And what joy do you find in our injured friend?" he asked.

"None, none at all," I stammered.

"Are you sure Collin said nothing about finding Tham in the cave?" Neils asked.

"No. He left home to answer Tham's call, but he didn't mention his name again."

Lilith returned to the room to change fluids for Tham, and Neils instructed her as Elly escorted me out.

"I want to be the first to know when Thaman wakes up. Will you promise that, Nurse Marchand?" Neils asked. Then, after she promised, he asked, "When is your break this evening, Lilith? Are you free for dinner?"

He pushed the door shut, and we walked away.

I stopped at Jinae's desk to thank her for helping me face an ordeal I had dreaded.

"Oh, sure. Leave me alone at the grindstone," she said, grinning. Jinae preferred teasing to anything serious, but in this case, her eyes softened, and she smiled sweetly, taking my hand. "It's what friends do," Jinae said. And even though she'd prefer a punch on the arm, I bent to hug her, echoing a whispered, "Thank you."

She touched my face briefly and then pushed away, no doubt hoping I would miss the tear on her cheek. "Off with you. These reports won't file themselves."

Elly grabbed my arm. "I'll send her off, Jinae. Don't worry."

But when we reached the portal, Elly followed me through to Ring Street.

"How do you feel, dear?" She asked.

"Empty. But on my feet," I replied.

"What will you do now? Is there any way I can help?"

I shook my head, not knowing which way to turn. But then I thought of something I should know. "Who was the first to reach Collin?" I asked. "Was it someone alone or a party? Who can tell me what they found? I only know what Luis told me, but I don't think he was the first to arrive at the cave."

"No, it's doubtful Luis was the first. And I found it odd that Marvin alerted Collin to trouble before anyone else knew about it. The distress alarm that sent the clinic running came later. Andy grabbed Dr. Fulbright, leaving Alissa and me to set up the emergency station in the triage room. But Rod Alexander and Neils Westergaard were already there when our doctors reached the cave. I assume those two rode together. Does it matter, dear?" she asked.

"Something puzzles me," I said. "I need to sort it out. A quiet moment in Destiny Temple may settle me."

"That's a good idea, Dear. Would you like company?"

I gave her a quick hug. "Not this time. I need to be alone with my thoughts for a while."

She patted my shoulder. "All righty, but I'll call you in the morning. We'll see how you feel by then."

"Til tomorrow," I said, turning toward Destiny.

26 Contemplating Loose Ends

While walking through the Temple door, I remembered meeting Elly on a night when I was particularly rattled. I was new to Mars and had just come from a secret meeting with the reportedly delusional Dr. Fulbright. My wild-haired predecessor had warned me I'd meet a stranger in trouble, and Dexter had warned me against meeting Fulbright.

On that night, I had no idea who Ray was, but since I arrived at WayPoint, he had sorted through my thoughts to harvest my memories for images of friendly faces—people I had once loved or trusted. Later I learned that he used those faces to help me accept his shocking message for Mars.

Collin joined me on a mission to help Ray, but now I had to carry on our mission alone. Well, nearly alone. Fulbright and the Kanekos knew what Ray was, and Milo and Maria had hints. Besides my friends, the dark forces behind Bernadette Duval, Dexter Craig, and Garrison Mathis wanted something, too. *Who were they?*

It wasn't clear if those dark seekers knew Ray existed, but they kept probing for something. Was it knowledge? Status? Power? Whatever it was, Bernadette desperately wanted that prize, and she used the promise of it to keep Dexter Craig dancing on a puppet string at her command.

The dangling carrot of having everything he desired, including prestige, wealth, and the attention of Bernadette, had been too much for Dexter. He had no idea what she was after, but with such power at stake, he followed like a lemming, and her plans led them both to destruction.

But now, staring at that same cosmic vision, a question loomed. *Was I any stronger than Dexter had been?* If the dark forces behind this could grant my greatest desire, would I stand against temptation any better than Dexter had?

As soon as I thought of the question, Ray gave me a mental answer: "Of course you would. I believe in you, just as you once chose to believe in me against all you knew or hoped for."

All I had hoped for had come and gone. And to have it again was the one thing that might tempt me, but no one could promise that. All the wealth, power, and prestige the dark forces could offer wouldn't be enough. *No one could return Collin to me.*

I looked for Ray in the Blue Room, and even though his voice was clear, I could not see him. Then, my search was interrupted by another alert flashing on my wristband.

Michelle Kaneko wanted me in the Memorial Room. It took an effort to leave the comfort of the weaving planets and undulating mists in the Destiny display, but Michelle was insistent.

***

Access and decoration of the Memorial Room were under my control, but the door was locked against me until Michelle allowed me to pass. Then, even before a greeting, she asked Marvin to put the room on secure lock-down before assuming privacy mode.

"What's happening?" I asked.

"I have something for you," she whispered, stepping aside to reveal what I assumed to be two of the sample memento niches that our 3D designers had been working on.

"Is that how they will look?" I asked.

"We won't know that until our craftsmen on Earth get the order, but these are Collin's designs, and I thought it would be fitting for him to have the first one. We can change it later if you like, but we must have his memorial soon, and this should be part of it."

Then she opened a tote and set Ray's cask near the stone niche. "We should hide this here. Ray is shielded, and security is set to the highest level. There are only rare visitors in this room, and since you manage this for us, you will be here when anyone else is. He will be safe with you as his guardian."

I examined the niche, a small stone box with one door. There was room for the barrel shape that held Ray. Collin had chosen his materials well; the whitish niche was the same alabaster color as the cask.

The truncated cones, one atop and one below the barrel, were shorter and broader than I remembered. But then, I had only seen the freed cask once in the dim light of a cluttered cave. If the cones ever had points, they plunged deep into the melon shape from above and below.

I placed the cask into the stone box with one cone resting on the floor and the other up like a tabletop. Collin's tiny rock hammer would rest there like a geologist's trophy.

Two of the markings on the cask held the blue charms I had once worn as a heart pendant—Ray's shields. But when in place, they did not look like add-on ornaments. They melded into the cask like they had grown from it, iridescent blue veins in alabaster skin. I turned the cask so that the shields were not visible from the niche door.

"What kind of lining is this?" I asked.

Michelle nodded. "That was Luis' idea. Ray's shields may hold, but since this location may put him closer to humans, he added another layer—thick Dragon Skin."

"Like Kevlar?" I asked.

"Similar, but much more efficient than Kevlar for shielding radiation. Does it suit you?" she asked.

I paused a moment to connect with Ray. "*Do you feel any intrusion?*"

"None at the moment," he replied.

Then I turned to Michelle. "When will it be mounted?" I asked.

"At any time," she replied. "The brackets for these two niches are mounted now. Does this suit you, then? Luis and I should be able to talk to Ray here if you are with us, and we can control who might be listening."

"Yes, and I can remember Collin while talking to Ray, too. It's a good idea."

"The room will be sealed with access to only you, Luis, and me. We three will be notified if anyone else tries to enter. The niches have fingerprint locks; I'll activate them later today." Michelle paused as she turned to me. "Would you like some time alone here?" she asked.

The thought of Collin's body on the gurney was still too fresh, and I had clues to follow, so I declined. "I'll bring the hammer here this evening and meditate then. Now, I need more information to solve my puzzle."

"As you wish, cherie," she said. "You go first, then. I'll lock up here."

After a hug, I returned home to make a very long-distance call.

***

Messages to Moon's Threshold Station were tedious and laggy; by necessity, we kept things to the point. Several unanswered messages from Jefferson Stafford needed replies, and I had a question: *were there iridium deposits on Mars?*

I warmed soup for supper and prepared to wait, but his reply came in less than half an hour. He expressed his condolences about Collin and replied about iridium, saying there had been no ore samples or mention of an iridium detector in his database. Later, there was a follow-up message saying that a non-specific radiation scanner was sent from Benjamin Hessling to Director Morsey on Phobos a few months back. The Phobos geology team wanted a targeted radiation detector for scanning crevasses and a smaller version to check rock samples.

Hessling. Where had I heard that name? I reread Jeff's messages and found that Hessling was an acquaintance of Ross Hashimi, but merely knowing someone meant nothing. One of the main tasks on Phobos was studying the soil for signs of a previous atmosphere and the early composition of Mars' surface, but as far as I could see, his info didn't matter to my investigation.

I plowed through days of messages from Jeff. Garrison Mathis was still in the hospital, his condition worsening. There was still no word on the cause of his distress, and his trial was still on hold. He was under hospital guard, and all visitors were vetted.

My soup was gone, and I desperately wanted to talk to Collin. He knew the answers I needed, and I missed him. The last tangible connection I had with Collin was to finish his niche. So, I grabbed his hammer from the box near my bed and headed for the Temple Memorial Room.

Michelle was true to her word. I could access the room, but an alert was immediately sent to the Kanekos: *"Dr. Graviston has entered the memorial."* No other alarm sounded, and the room locked behind me automatically. I used a step stool to reach the corner cupboard where Ray's cask rested in brackets. But when I reached for the little door, Marvin's red activity light glowed before me.

"Privacy mode, please, Marvin," I said.

"Complying." The red light faded to a dark plum.

Then I opened the niche, balanced Collin's little hammer on the upper cone table, and snatched it back. The hammer was part of Collin, something he had used much of his life. It held his DNA and enabled his curiosity about geology and caves. He had probably used it to mine the peridot and garnets in my ring and maybe even the labradorite he used to carve my fake duplicates of Ray's charms. *Was it still warm from Collin's hands? Was his spirit there?*

Ray joined my thoughts. "Collin is not in the hammer. Let it go," he said.

"Where is he?" I asked. "Can I still reach him?"

"He is no longer in our realm," Ray replied, "I cannot assess your ability to reach him, but he will reach you through your memories of him."

I nodded. "I said it earlier today. Collin will never die as long as I live."

"That sounds right to me," Ray said. "And he left a message for you."

"He did? How?"

"Before Thaman became a tenant of the cave, Collin and I had time to discuss many things. He helped me understand human love, especially the bond between a man and woman."

"That sounds personal," I said.

A raspy sound followed that I recognized as Ray's attempt to chuckle. "I do not refer to mating. I could figure that out. But he told me about the bond of love. He passed through the Blue Room as he was dying. He worried he had let me down, but his last thoughts were of you."

"What did he say?"

"I can show you. Call Collin's hologram."

Of course. Ray could affect electrical systems and use holographic bodies to communicate visually with those on Mars. He had spoken to me as a virtual gondolier, Eldredge Osgood, and Vince, the Virtual boxing coach. I had no doubt the alien could show me an enhanced version of Collin through his memorial hologram.

"Collin Grant," I commanded.

And there was Collin's memorial image, sitting on a boulder, hat pushed back from his brow, chewing on a blade of grass, and grinning from ear to ear.

"Hey, Sugar Spring," he said. "This is not the end I hoped for us."

"Me either," I said, tears streaming.

"Now, now. Don't get too weepy. It's not the end of our love. It's only the end of me, and I'm sure you'll carry on with what we started."

"What if I don't want to?"

"You want to; you just haven't accepted it yet. But what we gave to each other lives on. You made me happy."

"And you made me stronger," I said.

"You were always strong enough, but we amplified each other. We had real love. And it's like all other critical elements in the universe: neither energy, matter, life, thought, and especially not love can be destroyed. It just changes form."

I turned toward the ceiling. "Ray, Is that you speaking?"

"Maybe a little of me slipped in," he said, "but Collin's feelings for you are as he explained them to me."

"It's me, Sugar," Collin said. "Ray and I had long conversations; he taught me about space, and I taught him about humans. You and I did good for each other. Meanness fades, especially when good erases it, and when we embrace goodness, it spreads through the cosmos. We made each other better, Spring. And the love we shared will make everything better. Nothing is wasted. You're right; I'll live as long as you do, and who knows what comes after that."

I reached to touch him, and the sense of touch generated between my suit sensors and the advanced holographic programming allowed me to feel the warmth of his arms and how his muscles rippled beneath my fingers. After removing the grassy blade, I kissed him again, held him, and said again that I loved him. I held him tight, knowing I couldn't hold on for long.

"I won't be able to see you like this again, will I?" I asked.

"No. Not unless Ray helps. When you view my hologram, you'll see the image of me you created for everyone else—me sitting on an old hard boulder." He patted the granite stone. "Thanks for the rock to lean on." Then he chuckled as he rested against the rock and took his hammer in hand. "But don't forget; I was also your rock to lean on, and you can always find me in your heart."

I nodded, and he waved as the holographic image faded.

"He told you all that?" I asked Ray.

"As I said, it resulted from our conversations and his desperate need to leave a message for you as he passed from this realm. All you heard him say was genuinely felt."

I stared at the closed hologram door, wishing Collin would

reappear. Then, with a deep sigh, I turned away from the wall where he vanished.

"Will you be safe here, Ray?" I asked.

"I think so. And if Marvin doesn't do it first, I'll alert you if there's an intruder. But we can meet in our Blue Room whenever you like."

"Thank you, Ray."

"Collin didn't want to leave you, and certainly not with things unspoken," Ray said.

I nodded. Then, after a silent moment, I replaced the hammer and locked the niche and the room. Ray was safe there, and Collin was safe, too.

I slept peacefully that night.

27 Another Inquisition

Mars was always cold, but the month of Virgo was upon us, the cusp of Martian winter. Although the transparent galley window was thick and full of insulating gas, I imagined frost decorating the view. Who cared? True, I had found a measure of peace, but every corner of the world was chilly for me now, and frost suited my mood.

To make things worse, Neils Westergaard wanted to see me soon. Today, if possible.

More frost. Why not? I agreed to meet him in the conservatory around 13:00.

As I walked toward Taco Marciano for lunch, I noticed that the decoration of Central Park was shifting toward winter. Flocks of birds in V-formation headed south, and the browning leaves that whirled around the park benches now fluttered away in the virtual breezes. Even the distant mountain vistas appeared snowy.

Inside, the café décor was still tropical, and Dr. Fulbright seemed out of place amid palm trees as he beckoned me to sit beside him.

"Did you ever hear of snow on Mars?" I asked, pointing behind me to the virtual display outside.

"I've heard of it," he replied. "But I haven't seen it myself yet."

"Where does it snow?" I asked.

"Near the poles. But I think it's dry ice, nothing pleasant for humans."

"Too bad," I replied. "I could use a break, maybe a ski holiday."

"Then you'd better go virtually," Wolfgang replied.

Maria stopped by our table, excited about a new menu item. "You should try the shrimp tacos," she said. "Lab-grown shrimp is out of the experimental stage. We'll be able to have fresh shrimp every day."

"Have you tried it?" I asked.

"Of course I have. I wouldn't recommend it otherwise. I can give you a sample today, and if you like the taste, mention it in Friday's Council meeting. Today, Milo is hosting a taco party for his crew," she said. Then, from behind her hand, she added, "It's really a taste test for me."

"We're all your guinea pigs now, eh?" Fulbright asked, winking. "Well, if it's free, why not?"

"No charges against your allotments this time." Maria winked as she shifted the pencil in her hair. "I'd better be sure Milo's order is ready. Yours will be right up."

Giles and Beth were next to stop by while on their way to pick up Milo's order.

"How's Thaman?" Giles asked.

"Still unconscious," Wolfgang replied, "but Alissa is gradually taking him off his meds. If his vitals remain stable, he might awaken soon."

"Let us know," Beth said.

Giles, not one for emotion, teased instead. "Yeah, let us know. I want to see how many brain cogs he's lost."

Beth jabbed him with her elbow, adding, "We both want to wish him well."

The couple moved toward the take-out counter, but I held her back. "Beth, I have a question for you. Do you remember if Ginger ever delivered a package here from Benjamin Hessling?"

She shook her head. "I can't recall, but you can ask Milo. He'll have a record."

"Wait. I remember hearing the name Hessling," Giles said. "Tham and I didn't know each other well then, but I remember him walking through a site, yelling the sender's name. I asked him whether he was trying to whistle or clear his throat. He didn't like my joke but stopped long enough to show me the label. It was from an earth-side man named Hessling. I don't recall the recipient, but Thaman might."

Beth pulled his arm toward the counter, adding, "It should be in the transportation logs. We can ask Milo."

Lunch came soon after, and I gave Maria five stars on the recipe.

Wolfgang pointed to his plate. "This is my new favorite. Count me as a regular."

Maria grinned, and Dr. Fulbright walked with me as far as the clinic portal. Then he hurried to check on Thaman, and I turned left toward the conservatory.

***

Inquisition

I was alone when I reached the conservatory, but I didn't mind a moment to remember meetings with my patients, especially Collin. Our first meeting had been in the conservatory, where he immediately impressed me as a fresh-eyed cowboy with a buoyant spirit.

But Bernadette Duval was alive in this room, too. After my flawed first group session on Mars, she marched in on spiked heels to rebuke me, and weeks later, in the same room, she pitched a promise of power to Dexter Craig as I huddled with two of my patients, listening from behind the vines hanging from the observation deck.

I wondered if Neils Westergaard had prepared for meetings as carefully as I had in those early days when I was new and insecure. Probably not. Neils had too much swagger to bother with details.

Five minutes late, Westergaard traipsed through the door, tossed his tablet on the front table, and waved needle-like fingers toward the opposite chair. He studied his screen as I approached and only looked up when I sat.

"Dr. Graviston. Finally, a chance to get a few questions answered."

"That's why I'm here," I replied.

He nodded and started his investigation. "I've never understood how the four of you were in Sanctuary Cave on the night Duval died. Can you explain that?" he asked.

I cocked my head. "Isn't that in the written reports?"

"There's a record, but I still don't understand it. You were held in the clinic while Bernadette Duval was in her quarters in the Icehouse. Then, she left with Dexter Craig, and all three of you ended up in Sanctuary Cave with Collin Grant. How did that happen?"

The movements of that night were tricky to choreograph, and I couldn't mention Ray. So, I used a version of my story that didn't reveal the alien.

"Garrison Mathis held our Prime Minister, Luis Kaneko, under house arrest, claiming Luis was hallucinating. Evidence was uncovered that a coup was in progress, so when Kaneko was liberated, the residents of the Icehouse figured trouble would follow. Collin arranged to get me out of harm's way in Sanctuary Cave."

"Yes, a place designated for refuge in times of trouble. But how did Duval and Craig get there?" he asked. "Were they hunting for you?"

I shrugged. "Bernadette's story was wild. Contrary to evidence, she had convinced herself that Wolfgang Fulbright was still on Mars. She recruited Dexter to help find him."

"Where did she look for him?"

"Records show that she and Dexter went to a deep farm where they thought he had been. When they gave up there, they stopped by Sanctuary Cave. She had become a victim of the same hallucinations she projected onto Luis Kaneko. She was incoherent and apparently without good judgment. She eventually ran unprotected to the Martian surface and died there."

"And didn't you fall prey to those same hallucinations?" he asked.

"Bernadette said so, but her behavior proved she was not mentally healthy. There was no one on Mars with credentials to diagnose hallucinations besides me, and I wasn't seeing things."

"Was there anyone around to prove *you* were not hallucinating?" Neils asked.

"Read the depositions. Everyone who had known me since I came to Mars vouched for me. They would have noticed changes in my behavior but did not."

"But they weren't experts, and Garrison Mathis didn't vouch for you," Neils replied.

"They weren't experts in psychiatric sciences, but they were witnesses to my behavior. Garrison Mathis was an astronomer, so what expertise did he have? The Commander of this base, Luis Kaneko, saw I was fit to function, and all the members of WayPoint agreed that he and I were both mentally fit. Since then, Wolfgang Fulbright returned, and he and I have confidence in each other."

"So, is this a case of the insane diagnosing the insane?" he asked.

"Of course not. How could WayPoint have functioned in the months till you got here if that had been the case? And why would they have released Fulbright to return unless he was proven sane?" My hackles were rising, and I had about had enough. "What is your point, Mr. Westergaard? What are your credentials, anyway? No one has explained how you were appointed to head this investigation. Why is that? Who sent you here?"

"Don't try to turn the tables on me, Dr. Graviston. I've had plenty of experience in the courtroom, and I know all those tricks."

So, he was an attorney. "Explain this trick, then," I said, palms pressing the table. "Who besides me cured five WayPoint victims of hallucinations before you arrived? What citizen of WayPoint would you trust to handle psychiatric evaluation more than me?"

He shrugged. "I hear you had some electronic help curing at least Collin Grant."

"Are you referring to Eldredge Osgood?" I asked. "Did you know him on Earth?"

"Everyone on Earth knew of him. He was a public expert on the human psyche."

"I see. Well, would you take Osgood's opinion as an expert regarding my sanity?"

"I might."

"Then let's ask him." I spoke to the message board. "Marvin, show us virtual Eldredge Osgood."

"Am I permitted, Dr. Spring?" Marvin asked in his usual monotone.

"Seek permission from Luis Kaneko," I said.

In a moment, Marvin played a message in Luis' voice. "Dr. Graviston introduced WayPoint Station to the Eldredge Osgood virtual psychology program, and she and Dr. Fulbright have my permission to use these files to benefit the WayPoint Council or improve the health of WayPoint citizens."

A private message flashed on my armband. It was Luis adding to his permission. "Feel free to use Osgood to assist with your personal well-being, Spring. These are difficult times for you, and if counseling from your mentor is helpful, please take advantage of all the comfort Osgood may offer."

When I finished the message, my Teddy Bear mentor appeared in his tweed coat with elbow patches, holding a pipe in his hand. "Good day, Spring," he said. "How may I be of service?"

My heart warmed at the holographic image of my old friend. His visage recalled the days when the real Osgood stood on my deck as we admired the view of the Nevada wilderness. He had been my mentor throughout my Doctoral research. But far more important than that, Eldredge knew my unsteady background and the precipitous choices I had faced then. Dr. Osgood offered the comfort of a fatherly arm when I most needed it.

Surprised by the sudden arrival of an unexpected witness, Neils cleared his throat before speaking. "Eldredge Osgood?" he asked. "Of Earth's Coulton University?"

"The one and only," Osgood replied. "At least I am the only virtual program based on the sum of his visual bearing and professional knowledge. Original Osgood also updates me with personal memories, particularly those related to my purpose on WayPoint."

"And do you have an opinion of Spring Graviston?" Neils asked.

"Dr. Graviston is an outstanding practitioner of the Psychological

Sciences. I recommended her as a candidate for her position at WayPoint Station."

"And have her skills been diminished by her presence on Mars?" he asked.

"They have not," Osgood replied. "Since her practice here, Dr. Graviston has become the ultimate expert on how living on Mars impacts the human psyche. Even Earth's Osgood refers such questions to Dr. Graviston."

"Satisfied?" I asked.

"Are you playing a trick on me, Dr. Graviston?" Westergaard asked.

"I wonder if the tricking is on the other side of the table, Neils. What are you trying to prove on Mars?"

Neils' eyes blazed as he stood. "Wait just a moment," he said. "I am the investigator here, not you. And *you*, Dr. Graviston, are here to answer."

"I would not want to stymy your inquisition, Neils," I said. "Please continue."

"Don't play with fire, Spring," Neils replied.

I raised my chin. "There is no fire on Mars, Sir."

"Don't taunt me," he said. "You might be surprised at the result if you go too far."

"Are you threatening me?" My anger flared at Neils' attempt to bully me. *Was he dangerous?* That thought brought a new question to mind. I pressed the table's edge. "Mr. Westergaard, have you discovered the cause of Collin Grant's death?"

Neils pursed his lips till they trembled and then spat a reply. "That's not the mystery I'm here to solve. Marvin, close the Osgood program."

Osgood vanished, but Neils couldn't silence me. "Did you kill Collin?" I demanded.

"Of course not. I was the first to report him dead."

"The first to report him dead, or the last to see him alive? What do you know about the one clue we have—the radiation signatures related to iridium?"

"Less than you do, I'd guess. I know very little about the geology of Mars. Your partner Collin was a specialist, though. What did he tell you about iridium on this planet?"

"So, are you turning the tables now?"

"Perhaps, but you are avoiding an answer. Are you hiding something, Dr. Graviston?"

"Collin never spoke of iridium. But he did tell me that after he was suspected of hallucinations, all the samples he studied were examined first by his supervisor, Roderick Alexander. You are very close to Alexander, aren't you, Neils?"

"Rod and I have spoken about the iridium clue, and he has no idea what it could mean. But let me remind you, Mrs. Graviston. My job here is to see if there were any suspicious circumstances related to the deaths of Dexter Craig and Bernadette Duval. Unless the recent mishap in Sanctuary Cave resulted from the deaths those months ago, Thaman Bakshi and Collin Grant are no business of mine." Neils' face was as red as a Martian rock as he gathered his papers and stomped out of the room, muttering, "This behavior will be reported to the Council."

I watched him pass through the conservatory door, steaming from both ears.

Marvin cleared his virtual throat, then asked, "Did I just witness a kerfuffle?"

"I'm afraid so."

"Westergaard's heart rate and temperature are elevated."

"Should you be telling me that?" I asked.

"Reporting to a WayPoint medic falls within my parameters. But I see you are upset, too. He seemed threatening. Would music calm you?" he asked.

Soon, soft strains from a pastoral symphony filled the room as Marvin's busy light went dim.

I watched, mesmerized by the green tendrils dangling from the observation deck. The music gathered me into the magic of rhythm and tone, and maybe it helped me make sense of the situation. Neils

Westergaard was right about one thing. Getting answers about Collin's death wasn't his problem. It was mine, especially if Westergaard had a hand in it. But I needed help, and Thaman was the place to start.

I left the Conservatory and ran into Elly Petersen as she started up the stairs to the Icehouse living quarters. When she saw me, she turned abruptly and threw her arms around me. "How's my girl doing?" she asked, pushing me back to see for herself.

"I'm OK."

"Not that OK, I'd wager. How could you be? We should talk."

"Anytime," I grinned.

I could always trust Elly to watch out for me, but she was not one to leave matters at loose ends. "I miss our breakfasts together," she said. "Let's meet Saturday morning in the park; I'll bring coffee and rolls. You bring your mug."

I laughed, replying. "That sounds perfect. I'll see you then."

She waved on her way home, and I rounded the corner to the clinic portal.

28 Partners for a Solution

After a quick hello to Jinae Kim and Lilith Marchand, they directed me to Dr. Fulbright in room 407.

"Is he in prison again?" I asked.

"No," Jinae said with a snicker. "But he drew your old jail cell. Just lucky, I guess."

"What do you mean?" Lilith asked.

Jinae explained. "Our old administrator, Bernadette Duval, proclaimed Spring was hallucinating and locked her in that room. Of course, there was no truth to it, but Ms. Duval was trying to keep anyone from helping Luis Kaneko back to power."

Lilith raised her eyebrows, asking, "Is that kind of underhandedness common here?"

Jinae shook her head. "Not anymore. Don't worry. Thaman will be fine there. Dr. Fulbright watches him, and so do Rod Alexander and Neils Westergaard. He has guards around the clock."

"Perhaps I should watch him more closely, too," Lilith said.

Jinae walked with me as far as the central nurse's station, where she paused to point to 407 at the far end of the hall. "Lilith misled you," she whispered. "She's in Thaman's room more often than Westergaard is. Why would she suggest otherwise?"

"Who knows? But it's worth considering," I said, shrugging. Then,

I continued to 407. As predicted, Thaman was surrounded by self-appointed guards. Rod stopped scrolling his tablet long enough to nod in my direction. Neils Westergaard huffed a greeting. He must have been unhappy to see me again so soon.

"Greetings, Dr. Spring," Fulbright said as he examined a tube attached to Thaman's arm. "I'd ask you to sit, but I don't believe we have a vacant seat now."

"She can have mine," Neils replied. "I should get back to my reports. Buzz me if there is any change here."

Fulbright muttered, "Aye, aye, Captain," but Neils was clacking down the hall and probably didn't hear the sarcasm in his tone. Wolfgang nodded as he waved me to Westergaard's still-warm chair.

"How's the patient?" I asked.

"About the same. Being unconscious will ease the demands on Thaman's body and help him heal."

"How long will that take?" Rod asked.

Fulbright searched his pockets for a moment, then, without finding whatever he was after, he ruffled the hair over his left ear and replied, "Same answer as yesterday. The recovery time depends on Tham, but he's getting stronger. It's a matter of weeks, I'd say."

"Weeks," Rod huffed. "Then I'll take a break, too. Back soon." Then Dr. Alexander followed Neils past the central nurse's station.

Fulbright rolled his eyes, and as soon as Rod was out of earshot, he asked, "What brings you here, Spring?"

"I'm checking on Tham, for one thing," I replied. "Will it be weeks till he's conscious?"

Wolfgang sat close to me, whispering, "More like days. But I don't like the vultures hovering over him, so I keep them guessing. Tell me, what else is on your mind, Spring?"

I bent my head to his. "I need to find out what happened to Collin. Has Tham said anything? Has he roused at all?"

"He has not. He would be a good source for you, though. I'm sure whatever killed Collin was the same thing that injured Tham, but as you see, others are standing in line for his answers. Unless he wakes up in the middle of the night, you'll be on a long waiting list to hear anything Tham remembers. He trusts you and me, but his sense of judgment is still iffy. He trusts the others waiting for him, too."

I sighed. "Then I'll have to solve it with the puzzle pieces I have. You might hold clues, too, Dr. Fulbright."

"Maybe, but my only problem to solve lately has been how to keep Thaman safe. Do you have ideas?" he asked.

"I have questions. But if we put our heads together, we may find some answers."

He nodded and checked the hallway. When he found no one to overhear us, he closed the door and set the mirrored window to one-way mode. We would see anyone approaching before they saw us. Doctor/Patient interviews were set to private. We were safe until someone else arrived.

"So, what's your puzzle, Spring?" he asked.

I looked at the monitors attached to Thaman. "Can he hear us?" I asked.

Fullbright shrugged. "We aren't sure what he can hear, but from the monitors, I'd say he's out of range of interpreting what we say. Music will help." He piped music into Tham's auditory track, giving us another safety precaution. Then he nodded for me to continue.

"Do you recall telling me that in the first days, Ray experienced interference when communicating with you?"

"I do," he replied.

"Can you give me any details? Was it often? Cyclical? Did it last for long?"

He shook his head. "I don't recall a pattern." He sipped coffee before asking, "What are you trying to discover?"

"Well, I suspect the interference is either an attack on Ray or an attempt to gain information about him. Following the changes in the interference may point to the source."

"Ray attempted to contact me after I picked up that trinket from Hashimi's pocket."

"The day you found him in the desert, right?"

"Yes, but Hashimi died before we reached him."

"I touched that trinket on the day I arrived on Mars. You sent it to me via Milo. After that, I started seeing images from Ray."

"Was there interference then?" he asked.

"Not at first. I believe sometimes I only saw him in my head as if he projected himself to me, and we had no interference then. The first time was when he appeared in a virtual program. He seemed alarmed about something, and then he vanished."

"That makes sense. Static often occurs in electromagnetic communications."

"Did that happen to you?"

Fulbright shook his head. "In those days, I had no idea what I was experiencing, so I can't say if the static occurred in my head or through electromagnetic waves."

"Is there anything you can remember about it?" I asked.

"We now believe Hashimi was one of the earliest victims of hallucinations. So, since I found Ray's trinket when he died, the conclusion is that the images and the static relate to the hallucinations. When else were you aware of static?" he asked.

"Before we found Ray's physical location, he complained about the interference becoming more regular and frequent. He felt it followed a pattern and lasted for short periods before it eased up."

"That sounds like a widespread interference, perhaps a routine sweep, not specific to him."

"I'll ask him."

A moment of personal communication in the Blue Room provided the answer.

"Ray says even before we communicated, he experienced interference with what he calls his processors. From the time he landed here and detected a sentient presence, he was continually processing the data around him, organizing the information from this planet and its beings. He sensed static even before he tried to communicate."

"So, was Ray affected by random sweeps before you and Collin found him in the cave?" Wolfgang asked.

"Yes. And it changed again after we shielded him. There was no static for a while, but then it became stronger and less often with no regularity. It was intense the night Thaman and Collin were injured."

"So, the static was no longer random but more directed?" Fulbright asked.

"Sounds like it. Could it have been iridium scanners at close range?" I asked.

"That would explain the radiation signature," Fulbright said. "There were residual signs of iridium and iridium scanner elements around the torn fabric in the damaged terrain suits."

"Then, they were iridium scanners that either met with a catastrophic failure or …"

"… or they were weaponized," Fulbright concluded.

"But I've never heard iridium mentioned on Mars. Where would such scanners come from?" Fulbright asked. "And I can't recall iridium being used in a weapon."

"They have scanners on Phobos. Perhaps one found its way to Mars," I replied.

"So, the seekers shifted from wide-ranged scanners to smaller, targeted ones, but why would they do that?" Fulbright asked. Then he snapped his fingers. "Of course. They found a clue to narrow their search."

"Yes. Collin and I started targeting Sanctuary Cave when we found out that was likely where Hashimi found his blue charms. It became our best target in our hopes to find Ray."

Fulbright stroked his beard, saying, "And Bernadette and Dexter's deaths drew everyone else's attention to the cave."

"That's when Kaneko shut it down to the public pending an investigation," I said.

"Making it even more appealing to the seekers," Wolfgang added. "But who could have brought close-range scanners to the cave? Who had one to bring?"

"Jeff Stafford from Threshold Station said Hessling sent a targeted radiation scanner to Phobos. That's the only one I can track down."

"Could someone have sent it here?" Fulbright asked.

"Beth said Milo would know."

"Then there's your next clue," Fulbright said. Then he nodded toward the mirrored window. Someone was coming.

I opened the door to leave while Wolfgang reset the mirror to two-way views.

Rod Alexander only grunted as I passed him in the hallway. Rod may have access to Thaman before me, but I'd hear soon after. Wolfgang Fulbright was on my side, and I knew where to go for more answers.

29 An Unexpected Encounter

I rushed to speak to Emilio Torres at Taco Marciano before the Council meeting on Friday morning. The café was in an unusually festive mood for that time of day.

"Am I crashing a party?" I asked.

Milo, Beth Martin, and Giles Cardiff laughed around a table as Maria plopped plates of lavishly decorated Carmel and Cinnamon Cream Tortillas at each setting.

"Make room for Dr. Spring," Beth shouted, beckoning me to the table.

The men dragged up a chair. "Is it someone's birthday?" I asked. "What did I miss?"

"Do you remember the improved ice cream I told you about?" Maria asked, waving her hand over her new creation. "The cream in that makes a nice custard filling, too. So, we have a new breakfast dish, Crema Maria. Sit. Try it."

"Is this party another taste test?" I asked.

"More than that," Beth replied, giggling. "You'll never guess. We found Ginger!"

"Are you kidding me?" I asked, smiling nearly as wide as Beth. "Where was she hiding?"

"We were assigned to deliver supplies to the drop point, and when we got there, Ginger was there with her lander," Giles said.

Beth's eyes were wide as she continued the story. "She said she waited to speak to the delivery person and hoped it would be me."

"How did that happen?" I asked.

Milo, only slightly more subdued than Beth, picked up the story. "The drop was scheduled, and I sent Beth hoping she'd see Ginger," he said.

Beth replied, grinning, "I asked her why she didn't answer my messages and why she didn't stop when she saw us the other time. The dust devils must have covered us the day she flew by. She didn't see us."

Giles leaned forward, "Ginger said Marvin told her Beth was worried, and she figured she'd ease Beth's mind."

"You'll never guess what else. Ginger told me she has a boyfriend on Phobos. He works in the labs and doubles as a medic. Ozy Platt is his name."

"Speaking of packages from Phobos, did Milo find out who sent the package from Hessling that I saw?" Giles asked. "The one Tham was to deliver?"

"I found it," Milo replied. "It was from Hessling originally, and The Phobos Investigation Team forwarded it to Garrison Mathis, Science Secretary. I checked our records, and since Mathis was no longer in WayPoint, we delivered it to the new Science Secretary, Roderick Alexander."

"Do we know what it was?" I asked.

"Yes," Milo replied. "When the package could not be delivered, I was required to inspect it before it could be redelivered. It was a small, unlabeled machine that we delivered to Rod. I don't know what it was for, but it wasn't heavy; it would fit on this dessert plate."

"A scanner, maybe?" I asked.

Milo shrugged. "Some kind of small machine."

"The package we picked up today goes to the same person, Rod Alexander," Beth said.

"Was there no packing slip?" Jinae asked.

"We didn't open it, but the package was marked terrain samples," Giles replied.

"I'm on my way to the Council Meeting. Rod will be there, so I can hand it to him if you like," I said.

"Thanks for the offer, but I'll get it to Maria. She'll be there, too; she can deliver it."

"I'd better scoot; Luis hates tardy council members," I said, pushing my chair back. "Thank Maria for the yummy treat. I'll be back for more."

***

I jogged to reach the Council Hall in time. Luis frowned as he scanned vacant seats, but I slid into the chair Jinae pushed toward me before he turned in my direction.

"Greetings," Luis said. "Our meeting may be a little shorter than usual today. But before I explain, I should mention our loss of Geologist Collin Grant and the injury to Thaman Bakshi. Dr. Spring Graviston is preparing Collin's memorial display, and we will advise you of a remembrance service soon. The accident is under investigation, and details about how this occurred and Thaman's status will likely be in Dr. Graviston's remarks."

Then he turned to me. "Spring, if you prefer, we can let Jinae brief us on those matters. There is no need to put you under further stress after the loss of one so close to you."

"Thank you," I replied. "Since Jinae has the most recent information on Thaman's well-being, I'll let her cover that part of my report."

Jinae, startled by her unexpected call to speak, flipped through her screens to be sure her facts were aligned.

"Will that suit you, Nurse Kim?" Luis asked. And when Jinae bobbed her head, he continued. "Our Communications Secretary, Peter Ulikov, has news that will raise more questions than usual. So, he will go last instead of first today. We will begin with our acting

Prime Two, Neils Westergaard."

The room rustled with whispers and shifting seats. No doubt there were reasons behind this change, but we'd have to wait for Kaneko's explanation.

Even as our acting second in command, it was clear that Neils had not been briefed on the matter at hand. He cleared his throat as he flipped through his screens to begin his address.

"Since Nurse Kim will brief you on Thaman's well-being, I will shorten my remarks about the status of my investigation. First, since Thaman and Collin Grant were assisting with an inspection of Sanctuary Cave as related to the deaths of Bernadette Duval and Dexter Craig, we are doing all we can to find the facts related to that incident and if that tragedy is linked to the incident involving Collin and Thaman. So far, there are few clues, and we hope to learn much more when and if Mr. Bakshi regains consciousness. Dr. Kaneko will have any information as soon as I do, and he will relay that to all WayPoint when that time arrives."

"Thank you for that update, Dr. Westergaard. Next is the Human Resources report, and I believe Dr. Graviston has passed at least part of that to Nurse Jinae Kim."

Maria Torres slid into the room, carrying a small box. Since Jinae was speaking, she settled the box on my table and silently found her seat. The box was about ten centimeters square, and as Giles had said, it was labeled *Terrain Samples*. But as I picked up the small box to read the label, I noticed the silence of the contents. The package had the heft of a small rock, but no sand slid over the bottom, and no pebbles clattered against each other. As silent as the box was, I assumed it had been well-wrapped and tightly bound to keep the contents from moving. But there were other labels on the box. One was partially obscured, but from the label design, it was in the red, pale green, and dark blue logo of the moon's Threshold Station. That one was covered by another label, stamped with only one word.

When Jinae had finished her report, she returned to the seat next to me, and I pushed the box toward her. She read the label, picked up the box, and mirrored my curious look.

"*Replacement?*" she mouthed. I nodded with a tiny lift to my shoulders. "Why would anyone replace soil and rocks?" she whispered. "And why would anyone send moon rocks here?"

I had no answer, but I planned to prod for one when I handed the box to Dr. Alexander.

Reports came and went. Maria shared her news about fresh Martian-grown shrimp and improved creamy desserts, and finally, it was time for Peter Ulikov and his big news.

Garrison Mathis was out of the hospital, but he had been found guilty of a coup against Luis Kaneko WayPoint Station. Garrison would spend months or years under guard until his rehabilitation treatment proved successful. But even if the authorities assessed him as fit to behave among the human population, he would never return to Mars nor lose the badge of dishonor he earned from trying to steal power from our Prime Officer, Luis Kaneko.

Neils Westergaard and Rod Alexander whispered at their table until the questions between them demanded an answer from the council. Rod Alexander asked it. "But what now?"

Luis nodded. "Now, we shall reassess our staff and fill in the holes. Other than that, we go on as usual."

"And what about me?" Neils asked. "Will I continue in the role of Prime Two?"

"For now, you will," Luis replied.

Peter Ulikov had news on that front, too. "Harvey Cross of Earth's Council has approved a replacement. His personal assistant, Elias Meersham, is in transit now."

Luis nodded, "But until he arrives, Neils will continue as our acting Second Officer. To make things run more smoothly, I am authorized to name Dr. Spring Graviston as the official Secretary for Human Resources. Congratulations, Spring," he said, and there was mild applause in the hall.

Then he turned back to Neils, saying, "I recommend you wrap up your investigation as soon as possible. You will return to Earth on the ship that brings our new Prime officer, Elias Meersham."

"Is that it?" Neils asked. "Was Harvey Cross upset with me? Was I too slow with my report?"

"No, I don't think so," Luis replied. "He suggested another task you can do for us. It's something of an investigation—right up your alley."

"What kind of investigation?" Neils asked.

I wondered, too. Would this take Neils closer to Ray?

Luis grinned. "Harvey suggests you might help us pack Garrison's belongings. Now that we know he will not return, we will move you into Garrison's quarters, and you can sort out what should return to Earth and what should remain here for the use of our new Prime Two. Cross thinks you should be well-suited to the task, and I see his point."

"Of course," Neils replied. But deepening brow furrows proved him unsatisfied with his new task. Perhaps he wasn't finished with Sanctuary Cave.

As Luis had predicted, there were many questions, most relating to how this change affected them individually. Jinae and I had our concerns answered, and we had the news to share with the divisions, so I nudged her to leave. But she pointed to the package we hadn't yet delivered, and I carried it to the person named on the label, Rod Alexander.

Rod was surprised at the delivery, but Neils Westergard grabbed it from his hands, his eyes widening as he read the label and showed it to Rod.

"What's that all about?" Jinae asked.

I shrugged. All I had were my suspicions.

Jinae chuckled. "Let's have lunch; maybe food will fire up the gray cells."

We could do nothing else in the Council Hall, so I agreed. "Why not? Tortilla soup?" I asked.

"Sounds right to me."

We dropped by Maria's take-out counter for soup and carried our lunch to a park bench to tank up and share ideas.

"I don't suppose there's any news on Thaman reviving, is there?" I asked.

Jinae shook her head as she slurped. "No. Not since I gave the report today. All steady there."

"Fulbright said he would keep me up to date."

"You can trust him."

"Will you be sure that Dr. Fulbright knows what happened here? Tell him everything, even about the package."

"Certainly," she replied. "Do you think the news about Garrison Mathis will impact anything here? Everyone on the station knew he was guilty. His arrest was just a matter of timing."

"True. I can't imagine more than a few more personnel shifts—like when you took over for Bernadette and Fulbright returned to cover my patients."

"Yes, it did turn the ground over here. But is the role of Prime Two all we must replace?" she asked. "That can't be that much of a change. Neils knows nothing about his job anyway."

"True," I sighed.

"Will it change the mystery you're trying to solve—the one about what happened to Collin?"

"Hm. I just realized that no one is assigned to figure that out. Why is that?"

"The medical staff is part of the investigation. So far, we only have clues from the bodies and how they were discovered. But maybe we haven't been told who is working on it."

"It isn't Neils. He told me as much at my inquisition. That's not his mystery to solve. Who else could it be?"

Jinae shrugged. "The only ones allowed in the cave are Rod Alexander and Neils, but they hang out at the clinic too much to be investigating elsewhere."

She made a good point. Who could be investigating? "Hm. You're right. Rod doesn't seem to be investigating unless Thaman is his next clue. Could that be all they have to go on?"

Jinae shook her head. "Lilith hangs around Thaman, too, but I don't think she's ever been to the cave. An investigator would have to go there, wouldn't he?"

What was I overlooking?

We had finished our soup, and Jinae needed to return to her post.

"Do me a favor if you will," I said. "See if you can find out what Lilith is after. She's a newcomer and might be here for more than a job. See what kind of questions she asks. All my suspects are under the clinic roof. Let me know if there is any change in Neils, Rod, or Lilith. It would be good to watch for a change of personality."

"OK. I will, but Lilith doesn't seem devious, and Neils will be moving out," Jinae replied.

"Those good at being devious are clever not to show it," I replied.

"You're probably right," she said, waving. Then, we returned to our duties.

30 Left Behind

Not much happened during the remainder of Friday. There was no word of a change in Thaman's status. WayPoint buzzed about Garrison Mathis's fate, but I did not want to be part of the rumor mill. So, instead of joining in the speculation, I concentrated on my official report of today's Council meeting for the Human Resources crew.

After that, I was lost. WayPoint was in for another shake-up, and we hadn't resolved things. Ginger, Neils, Rod, Thaman—would these pieces ever connect?

"Having a night in, are we, Dr. Graviston?"

It was Marvin. I'd shut him down, but maybe I'd ask him a few things first.

"Marvin, is anyone investigating Collin's accident at Sanctuary Cave?"

"Besides you?" the disembodied Marvin replied.

"Yes, besides me. Anyone official?"

"Dr. Kaneko has posted a guard in the cave when Rod Alexander can't be there. And I believe Michelle Kaneko is following up on interviews."

"Are you allowed to tell me those things, Marvin?" I asked.

"You are aware of my protocol, Dr. Spring. If I were not allowed to tell you, I would not do so."

His reply made sense, but it would also make sense to say that if he had something to hide. *Wait. What was I thinking?* Marvin hid nothing except facts prohibited by his programming. But I was still curious.

One more query.

"What is the status of Thaman Bakshi?" I asked.

"There is no change," he replied.

OK, one *more* query.

"Marvin, I saw Beth Martin earlier today. She had an encounter with Ginger Welsh. Did you tell Ginger that Beth had been looking for her?"

"I have not spoken to Ginger Welsh, Dr. Graviston. Since she moved to Phobos, she is not in my normal communication chain."

"I see. Maybe Beth was mistaken."

"That could be the case. Beth has been mistaken before. Didn't she once put great confidence in Ginger Welsh? Enough to help her with a deception?"

"Hm. Yes, she did. Do you think Ginger might have misled Beth again?" I asked.

"You ask if such a thing is possible. Of course it is."

"But possible doesn't make it so," I replied.

"Correct."

"Privacy mode, please, Marvin."

"Complying." Marvin's attentive light on my wristband went black, and I held off momentarily before turning out my house lights. The darkness was lonely without Collin, but I was a big girl, so I turned out the lights to sleep.

Sleep didn't happen, though. I flailed under the bedclothes, dissatisfied that Collin had left me behind, and I couldn't conjure him home. Finally, the sheets won the fight, and sleep came without me knowing.

Then I dreamed about Collin. My head rested against his shoulder, and he stroked my hair as he reminded me that his work on WayPoint was done, but I still had duties—a purpose.

"But I want you here." Then I wondered if this dream Collin had any answers for me.

"Can you tell me anything about what happened in the Cave?" I asked.

He chuckled, "If I'm a dream, I won't know anything you don't know. Ask it and see."

"Who injured you? How did it happen?"

He shrugged. "There was a loud noise."

"I know that," I said.

"See what I mean?" he replied. "But before the explosion, I heard a voice. It gave a command, and then the lightning struck."

"But who had a reason to hurt you?" I asked.

"I guess it was an accident. After all, who would have any reason to target me? What problem is a geologist to anyone?"

I didn't know. But I added, "Even if you are a dream, I'm glad you're here. I miss you."

I'll always live where you walk," he replied.

He was right. Like it or not, I had to keep walking."

***

The following day was Saturday, and I had a date to meet Elly. My dear friend had promised to bring coffee and rolls, but I dropped by Maria's to surprise Elly with the new caramel cream treat. I found her on a bench beneath a bare-limbed virtual tree. She had her yellow mug, and I brought its twin. Elly had used that mug to ground me, stabilize me, in my early days on Mars.

When I moved in with Collin, she gave me one from the pair to remind me of the love and friendship between me and my surrogate Martian mother.

I saw what she was doing. Collin was not the only one tied to my heart. He was not the only one in my life. Elly grinned as I approached, and when I revealed the sweet tortilla, she chuckled and tossed the sausage roll back to the plate as she grabbed the creamy treat.

"Always eat dessert first," she said. "Didn't I teach you that?"

I chuckled. "I don't recall that lesson. But you taught me a lot of things."

She laid her fork aside to place a hand over mine. "I'm glad I had a part in your life; you've made me very proud."

"I'm a mess. How could you be proud of me now?"

She grinned as she leaned back to study me from a distance. "You were always capable, but I admit, you were something of a mess when you arrived at the Icehouse. You didn't believe in yourself even though you had every reason to."

"I feel like nothing now. Collin was my backbone. He made me strong. Now I'm standing up, but that makes me easier to knock over. Who will hold me up now?"

She shook her head as she sipped from her yellow mug. Then her eyes met mine. "He helped you stand, and now you are ready to stand alone."

I shrugged. Telling Elly she didn't know what she was talking about would be rude, so I kept quiet.

"I saw that eye-roll," she said. She took my hand again. "Listen to me. You were always interesting, smart, strong, and thoughtful. You only lacked the belief that others saw strength in you. It's hard to believe in yourself when you don't see that in the eyes of others. We in the Icehouse believed in you, and you let go of your Earth-born self-doubt and began to believe in yourself, too."

Could she be right?

"Collin believed in you, but now he's moved on. I believe in you, but I may be gone someday, too."

"Please, no," I said, squeezing her hand.

She smiled. "Not today. But one day. And when that day comes, if those of us who love you did our job right, you will have enough belief in yourself to carry on. Mars always needed you to be strong. But life can make that difficult. You're there, girl. Maybe you're knocked back a little, but down deep, you know I'm right. You have enough confidence to share. Confidence to inspire."

It was hard to admit the truth in what she said, so I thanked her for it. “Mars elevated me beyond the low state I was in before I came here. You are a big part of that.”

She nodded. “Mars is lucky you came here. We thank you for all you have done here, and I believe you have much more to do. I remember the night you called me to your quarters, afraid you had gone insane. You never explained that to me fully. I know you keep secrets, even from me. But I suspect you have a good reason, and Mars will be very grateful that you are here when the time comes. I believe in you, and you must never doubt that, even when I move on.”

I squeezed her hand in mine, and she must have known tears were close.

She grinned. “Not today. I promise.”

Then we finished our coffee and food with happier thoughts and giggled over the times we had enjoyed on Mars. And I left with the most joy I had felt in days. Elly believed in me, and she was right. I believed in myself, too.

“Do you have time for a walk?” I asked.

“Not today; Doctors must sometimes work on Saturdays, too. But you should enjoy your day.”

She was right.

Our bench was near the temple, so I decided to check out Collin’s memorial and chat with Ray.

31 Ray at Home

If anyone was in the temple that Saturday evening, they were in the Rim of Forever. I passed no one on my way to the Memorial Room. But Luis had announced there would be a memorial service soon. So, I closed myself in, sat on the viewing bench, and replayed Collin's holographic farewell. It wasn't enough for me, but it would suffice for coworkers and acquaintances.

His tangibles niche passed muster, too. When I held the hammer, it was almost like holding his hand. Luckily, if anyone needed to touch something from the niche, I would oversee that, and it wasn't likely to happen unless his family came to visit Mars.

The service would not be set until we knew Thaman's status, so I put the hammer back in place, locked the niche, and sat on the viewing bench again. Ray spoke to me before I called to him.

"Good evening, Dr. Graviston. Is all well?" he asked.

As soon as he spoke, I was across the table from Ray in the imaginary Blue Room, where we met face to face. He saw my face through my captured memories or as others saw me, and the long-legged silvery being was Ray's version of how Collin and I expected an alien to look. It wasn't grand art, and neither of us had given much thought to alien appearance, but Ray had planted an iconic image that we both identified as a spaceman.

"Tell me, Ray, what do you do when you are here alone? Is it boring?"

"This spot is much more interesting than the cave. People come and go, and I can tap into their thoughts. I'm learning more about humans, and it's not just what's on their minds. I'm learning how they feel about each other, what drives them, and, maybe most practical of all, I'm learning more about how they communicate with language."

"But you communicated with language on your home planet, didn't you?" I asked.

"Yes, we had a language, and since we have a gaseous atmosphere, we communicate with sound, too, but not exactly as you do. Our speech organs were quite different, and so were the sounds we made."

"You never told me. What is your planet like? Where is it?"

"You can't see my red dwarf star without a telescope, but we could see your hot, yellow sun. We've known about your star and the planets around it for eons."

"Where is your red dwarf? I mean, where in the sky."

"Hm. I'll borrow some images from your Destiny display. There." Now, we imagined a screen on the wall of our meeting room, and he showed me the corner of the sky where his people had been born.

"Is that Aquarius?" I asked.

He paused a moment, researching. "Yes, you call this configuration by that name."

"And one of those stars is your home?"

"No. Several of the stars you see there have planets around them, and my star would be within this star group from this point of view, but it's too small to see from here."

"What's your planet like?"

"Much like yours, at least as planets go. It's rocky and holds water, but our sky had seven nearby planets instead of the moon you view."

"Is there life on all of them?"

"Not all, not anymore. But when I left, sentient beings lived on several of them."

"So, your home world knows of beings from other planets. Are they friendly?"

"They were when I left, but I haven't been home for a long time."

"Why not?"

"Because I accepted the challenge to come here, which took much screening, education, preparation, and time."

"Will you ever go home?"

"That is unlikely. It may even be impossible. But that was part of the challenge I accepted. When I agreed to come here, the plan was that I would become something different. If we are lucky enough to collect my pieces together, I will become a new being that is something between my kind and yours."

"An ambassador, like you told me before," I said.

"That's correct. With my new body, I'll be a bridge between our peoples."

"But we won't be able to speak to your people if our speech organs are so different."

"That's probably true, but speaking to each other is not as important as understanding each other. That is vital. Both cultures should know how we expect to be treated, what our common values are, and what rules we will follow. We must agree on those things."

"It's such a long way to come, especially since you have neighbors near you. Why did you take such pains to visit us?"

"The stars in Aquarius are not as near as they appear. Our planet is much closer to your sun than to some of those. The stars of Aquarius appear to be a cluster, but you can't judge how deep in space the stars are as you look at them from this viewpoint. But yes, there are stars in Aquarius with planets and living beings closer to my home than your sun."

"That's amazing."

"It is. But I see you have other matters on your mind. What troubles you today, Spring?"

He was right; trouble followed me, and maybe Ray saw that. Had he always been concerned and caring? Were the people on his home planet like that, too? I hoped to find that out someday, but I had other pressing questions.

"I need to find out how and why Collin was killed. I need the truth of that," I said.

"You know he died trying to save Thaman and me. Isn't that enough?"

"But how did it happen? Did someone try to hurt him?"

"I was with him when he was injured. No one else was with us," Ray said. "I saw neither a reason nor a motive for danger?"

"But did someone cause an accident? Was someone or something trying to hurt you? Did they plan bad things for WayPoint? Did you hear a voice?"

The tone of his manufactured, imaginary voice became sadder as he repeated, "No one was with us. I was unable to perceive motive."

"Maybe you can help me find out," I said.

"I'll do my best. Do you have information that may help?"

I nodded. "We suspect our radiation scanners caused the static you experienced."

"Yes, you humans seem quite vulnerable to that."

"And you are not?"

"Not as much as you are. You see, traveling across great distances either takes great energy or a very long time. But the energy is less, and the speeds can be greater if we travel at low mass. That's why I travel bodiless, and the pod I traveled in ..."

"The part of you I put in the niche?"

"Yes, that part. The shell you see is very dense but very light. It's impervious to most forces, but the organization of my components is sensitive to electromagnetic forces."

"So, you're more than particles?" I asked.

"I am currently a form of plasma with an organizing structure that allows me to remember and learn. Additional learning components woke when my vessel recognized sentient beings on this planet."

"And what about the other part of you? The part we haven't located yet?"

"It is not where it should have been upon my waking, and there's the problem we must solve."

"But what is it like?"

"I did not see it, but I assume the exterior resembles the container around me. It may be larger because it carries some heavier particles and the information that will allow it to use molecules from this planet to create a body for me."

"A body somewhere between a human body and the one you had on your planet."

"It will be a body that allows me to communicate more easily with those of your kind. But it will be a body reconciling Earth and Mars more than Earth and my home world. Living on Mars will be easier with my new body than for Earthborn creatures."

"I've noted the changes in the static you observed. It changed from random to a tighter range and finally to targeted. It may have been the targeted source that injured Collin."

"Why? Was Collin looking for me?"

"No. He knew where you were. But he may have gotten in the way of danger. Could a radiation scan have caused the traumatic injury?"

He paused a moment, then said. "My particles do not emit radiation, and I am shielded against damage by it. But a machine that detects radiation on Earth might react badly to my home world technology. I don't know enough about either to say directly."

"Have you ever heard of iridium?" I asked.

Again, he paused, searching for his reply. "Iridium, as you call it, is an element common in many space sectors. Is it common on Earth?"

"No. It's rare and is found mostly in deposits left by meteorites."

He nodded. "Then my planet may have created alloys of it that Earth never imagined. Trouble might come of that, especially if the probe seemed aggressive."

"But if it can be trouble, why would Earth search for it? I'm certain that your presence here has been kept secret. It's more likely they were searching for a mineral deposit."

"Perhaps they search for it because it is unusual. Sentient beings are often curious about the unknown, and scientific advances might benefit humankind. Could that be the motive?"

"It's possible. But I think many Earthmen would sooner face danger for wealth or power than to benefit mankind."

"Hm. Then, it's more important than ever that we begin to understand each other. The cultures near my planet have learned that uplifting and protecting sentient beings is far more important than personal wealth or power."

"I understand. But what happens if we haven't learned that lesson yet?"

He sighed in his cold, artificial way. "Then my trip here may not be fruitful." He was quiet for a moment, then added. "Let's have positive thoughts. Perhaps I can explain things well enough to help them understand."

"But if they can't?"

"Let's believe they can. If not, there must be an alternative plan."

Ray would say no more about the consequences, but if their Plan A was to reduce a being to particles and send him across the cosmos to convince Earthlings to give up greed, then their Plan B must be a doozy.

Ray must have picked up on my worry. The last thing he said to me was, "Do not fear, Spring. You and I will meet the challenges."

Based on my two conversations that day, I began to think I needed to train a little harder in self-belief.

The survival of Ray, me, and my kind might depend on it.

32 Friends and Foes

Sunday morning was prime time to visit a sick friend, and with luck, Thaman would rouse, and I'd be among the first to hear his story. But even if that failed, it would be a fruitful visit. Besides my former patient, I'd see two good friends, Jinae Kim and Dr. Fulbright.

My Martian family had held me together since Collin died. Jinae's jokes always cheered me, and Wolfgang was one of the few I could speak to about Ray. So, feeling grateful, I stopped by Maria's café and picked up a couple of tacos for my lunch, and then I added a few of her new desserts to share with the medical staff on duty.

Maria smiled as she waited on customers at the counter. However, the stress of restaurant duties and serving as Food Services Secretary showed in drooping eyelids and the gray tresses falling from her ponytail. She didn't get as much time off as she was due. She and Milo were part of my team, too.

But what could I do for Maria? She was a whiz at cooking and had the equipment and ingredients to make masterpieces from very little. I'd have to think of something besides food to thank her.

She laughed as she packed my order. "Is this for a Sunday outing? What kind of picnic has two tacos and four desserts? Are you on some new diet?"

"No, I'm just heading to the clinic to visit Thaman, and I plan to share your new creamy delight with some friends. I hope Neils and Rod don't hang out there all day. Neils tends to rain on my good times."

Maria chuckled, "He won't bother you today. He and Rod are heading to Sanctuary Cave; Milo checked out the transport for them."

"They must have more clues than I do. It's hard to imagine what else they can find there," I said with a shrug. But then an idea struck. I leaned toward Maria. "How about we take a girl's day off? Maybe a shopping trip? Does that appeal at all?" I asked. "I'd love to do something to thank you."

"No need to thank me for anything," she said." But I can use a break from the stress." She drummed her fingers on the counter before replying, "I've seen everything WayPoint shops have to offer, but how would you feel about a road trip? Milo promised me the use of a rover and a drive around the new sites, but he's always so busy. Could you come with me for a drive? We can talk while we tour. How does that sound?"

"It sounds fun," I replied with a grin. "Let's do it. I usually have free time on Wednesday mornings. Can you get away then?"

She propped a fist on her hip. "I believe I can, and I'll be sure to make it so."

"Great then," I smiled as I collected my packages. "Wednesday, it is." Then, with a wave, I was off to the clinic.

***

Jinae usually had Sunday mornings off, but she was at the Welcome Desk, full of her usual perkiness and wit. "No break today?" I asked.

"Lilith has a headache, and I'm covering to give her a few minutes to rest. What did you bring me?" she asked, pointing to my parcel.

"Some goodies from Marias," I replied. "I'll put them in the Nurse's Lounge, and you can share. Maybe Lilith will want to try a new dessert when she returns to duty."

Nurse Kim nodded. "She won't be long; she's worried about Thaman and tries to shield him from Neils and Rod Alexander."

"But they aren't here now, are they?" I asked. "I heard they were off to the Sanctuary."

"True. I hope Neils and Rod stay gone a while. They aren't helping Tham, and their hovering makes the rest of us antsy."

"Gotcha," I replied. "Well, I'll put these in the lounge. The tacos are mine, but you can share the desserts any way you choose."

"Oh, good. If I hurry, I can eat them all," she replied, grinning.

"I'm off to see Tham," I called as I started down the hallway.

Wolfgang was at his charts and monitors, but Tham seemed to be in the same condition as when I visited before.

"Has anything changed?" I asked.

"Not much," Fulbright replied. "But he has moments close to waking."

"I'm surprised Neils and Rod left him alone, then. They seem quite eager to speak to him."

"They are, but I try to keep them in the dark about when Tham might rouse. I'm afraid they will pound him with questions as he's coming to consciousness."

"Do you need a break? I left some desserts in the nurse's room. I can watch Tham for a few minutes."

"I'd appreciate that. Thank you. But please message me if there is any change."

"Will do, Doctor."

He grunted and was out the door, leaving me with a sleeping Tham and little to do. Checking the monitors didn't take long. Then I leaned over his bed and asked, "Are you in there, Tham?"

No answer. So, I spent a few minutes reading his chart. The wounds were healing. His vitals were near normal, and his meds had not changed lately, except that the coma-inducing drug dosages were being gradually reduced. All looked good.

I paced around the room twice, but when I started humming on the third circuit, Tham shifted position slightly.

"Are you there, Tham?" *Was that a mumble? Did he make a noise?* If he had made a sound, there was nothing more.

I walked to the nurse's desk and back, noting that the other rooms on his half of the hall were vacant—nothing to see there, so back to 407. Tham had not changed. So, I leaned back in my chair and whistled a song Collin liked until I heard Fulbright returning. Then I sat up like a proper doctor.

"No change, eh?" he asked.

"None. Tham's the same. But I thought I saw him shift position once, and maybe he mumbled, but I'm not sure."

"Sounds like he'll rouse soon."

"Oh?" I asked.

"Soon-*ish*," Fulbright replied.

"So why do you think Rod and Neils are watching him so closely?" I asked.

"I guess Fulbright wants to add his comments to his report, but he sure is persistent. It's nice to have a break from him today. He's getting pushier, too. And cranky. I admit I can work up a good crank myself, but Rod and Neils are pushing the limit."

"Is this a change?" I asked. "They put me on edge every time we meet."

"It has been markedly worse since Neils heard his replacement is coming. You think he'd be in Mathis' old room, packing up as he was told, but no, he hangs out here, getting grumpier and grumpier."

"Maybe he doesn't do well with deadlines," I said.

"He has weeks, maybe a couple of months. I hope he doesn't plan to be grouchy till the ship comes to take him home."

"Yeah, that would be rough. Has Neils said anything about what's bugging him?"

"Not to me. But I heard him speaking to Rod. He wasn't pleased with how well Rod did some task and vowed he could do it better."

"Was it something in the cave?" I asked. "I heard they were going to Sanctuary today."

"Maybe," Fulbright said, shrugging. "I try not to listen to them unless they mention Tham."

"What about Lilith?" I asked. "She seems a little too interested.

What do you think?"

Wolfgang shrugged. "She's OK. She struck up a quick friendship with Giles and Thaman and asked many questions about what happened outside the cave, but as far as I know, Lilith never wanted to go inside. She seems genuinely interested in Tham."

I nodded. "I hope you're right."

"Don't worry. I keep this room under watch; I'll know when Tham rouses. He won't be awake long without me by his side. You and I well know there's too much at risk to make a mistake."

A third voice surprised us. "What risk is that?"

We both turned toward a curious Rod Alexander.

Fulbright had an answer ready. "Thaman's welfare is part of the ongoing risk to WayPoint. We must prove we can keep our citizens healthy. The project is at stake."

"Right," Rod replied as his brow smoothed.

"What happened to Neils?" Wolfgang asked. "I thought you two were off investigating together."

"Yes, we got an early start but had no luck, and Neils is upset. He's settling into Garrison's old quarters. Maybe he'll take a nap and calm down."

"What did you hope to find?" I asked.

"Neils wanted me to escort him through the raw tunnels, so we both suited up for that. It was the same as when we combed through the protected part of the cave. We found nothing because there is nothing to find."

"Shouldn't you rest, too, then?" I asked. "You must be tired after stumbling over rubble in those terrain suits."

"Na. He ordered me to stay here. He's our Number Two for a while longer, so I have to listen."

I looked at Fulbright, wondering if I should stay. He shook his head. "Don't worry, Dr. Spring. As you see, I have helpers here. There will be no problem keeping watch on Tham. Enjoy the rest of your Sunday."

That was a dismissal if I ever heard one, and he was probably right.

There was nothing I could do until Tham woke up.

"OK then. I'll grab my tacos and go. But when Tham rouses, tell him I promise to bring more. Let him know his friends are eager to know how he's doing."

"You'll be the first, Dr. Spring." He nodded as an eyebrow arched upward under his Einstein hair, and from Dr. Fulbright, a raised eyebrow was as good as a wink and a nod. It was a promise.

33 Dinner With the Doctors

As another step in my mission to thank my friends, I invited the Icehouse physicians to a Monday night dinner at Bistro sur Mars. Elly and Andy Petersen had been my surrogate Martian parents since I arrived under the Icehouse roof. And while Bashir and Alissa Arvani often kept to themselves, they were both mentors, and Alissa came along for girls' nights out when her duties allowed it.

Bashir pulled out a chair for Alissa, but she paused to hug me before sitting. “Thank you for this opportunity to be with you. Bashir and I did not want to impose on the time you need to heal, but we take this as a welcome sign that you are recovering.”

“I am indeed, thanks to all my friends; I don’t know how I could have survived this without you.”

“Grief takes time,” Bashir added. “Be patient. Your happiness shall return.”

“That’s sound advice, Bashir. Now, let’s dig into the menu. I hear this restaurant uses our improved Martian cream to add to new dishes, including some Italian favorites.”

We poured over the tabletop menu for a moment and clicked to make our orders. Chicken Marsala and Shrimp Alfredo were tempting, but there were enough choices to please everyone’s taste and dietary requirements. When our orders arrived, we discussed our dinners and caught up on how things had changed since I left the Icehouse.

"How is the memorial for Collin coming, my dear?" Andy asked. "Are you pleased?"

I smiled while batting back the pain. "I *am* pleased. Collin's hologram appears to be the friendly, happy man he was. Seeing him will remind all his friends of Collin's good nature."

Elly squeezed my arm. "You can't ask for much more than that, dear."

"No. That's the best it can be. But all of you have experienced changes, too. How are things in the Icehouse?"

Andy cocked his head, sighing. "I must admit I'm glad Neils Westergaard will be leaving his office in the clinic. It suited his purposes, but his investigation has interrupted our work."

"True," Alissa agreed. "Westergaard can't keep out of Thaman's hospital room. He gets in my way and must be driving Wolfgang mad."

"I was there yesterday," I said, "Dr. Fulbright is keeping a good watch on Tham."

Bashir agreed. "At least today, Neils is out of the office. I helped him clean out his desk, and he was told to pack up Garrison's quarters. I guess he's busy there."

"It is good he's occupied," Alissa said. "He has become more unpleasant lately."

Bashir nodded, "He seemed more irritable today than when I saw him yesterday in the clinic."

"I wonder if his trip to Sanctuary Cave put him in a bad mood," I said. "Rod said nothing turned up in their search for information."

"Who can say?" Elly shrugged as she replied. "He's never been an easy one to understand."

"Bashir, I apologize for a sensitive question," I said. "While Neils is our acting Second Prime, does he have access to ...." I paused to lower my voice to a whisper. *"to AdMon?"*

Andy cleared his throat, and Bashir sat straight, caught his breath, and leaned in. "Outside this table, few know of the program you mention."

"But you still have control of it, right?" I asked.

He nodded. "There were no instructions to give access to Neils, and I never did. He may be acting as an officer here, but until Kaneko tells me otherwise, Westergaard does not need the secrets of that program."

Andy nodded. "Neils had offices in our clinic, but I manage our staff, and I saw no reason to give him the ability to find out where a citizen is or was at any time or who they might have been with. Only Bashir and Luis have that power now, and Bashir can coordinate with me if he sees reason to pass that information to medical personnel."

"Yes," I agreed. "Even when I had access to AdMon, I rarely had to use it other than under Dexter's direction. Marvin is sufficient. I don't miss AdMon at all."

Bashir spoke up. "Neils probably knows nothing about it."

With that topic closed, our conversation centered on funny incidents with patients, accidental crises we faced together, and the bureaucracy that continued to pester clinics, even on Mars.

"Are the hallucinating patients completely cured now?" Elly asked. "Even Giles and Thaman?"

"Giles is nearly 100%," I said.

Alissa shook her head. "I wasn't convinced it was time to let Thaman go; his judgment skills needed more work. And I worry that his weakness might have led to the condition he's in now. Wolfgang agrees, and he will study Tham thoroughly before allowing him to enter the caves again."

"I agree. But we're lucky Tham relies on Wolfgang. He'll follow his doctor's instructions."

She nodded. "He respects Dr. Fulbright but is also very close to Neils and Lilith. Hopefully, his better instincts will win out, and he will follow Fulbright's guide."

When our party disbanded, the other four returned to their Icehouse quarters, and I went to my rooms, where Collin haunted every corner. That was fine with me; I was comfortable living with his memory.

But in the wee hours of that night, my wristband blinked with a message from Wolfgang.

"Thaman is waking. Come as quickly as you can."

34 The Blues

Who else knew Thaman was awake? Wolfgang had not said, and in my hurry to get to the clinic, I had not asked. I threw pants and a shirt over my body suit, stepped into shoes, and was out the door. The clinic was a short walk away, but this time, I ran.

WayPointers roamed through the spoke streets around the clock. Joggers were common, but I sprinted. Some night owl types waved, and I caught puzzled glances as I raced by with a determined expression, focused only on my destination.

Some probably paused to watch me for a moment. Others shouted, "Is something wrong?" I waved over my head and kept running.

Ring Street was less populated, and I pushed ahead harder. My heavy panting and elevated heart rate drew Marvin's attention. His voice droned from my wristband, "Dr. Graviston, do you require assistance?"

"No," I huffed. "Needed at the clinic."

"I have no medical alerts from that sector." It wasn't a question, and I had no spare breath to reply.

Finally, I pushed through the Clinic Portal. The Welcome Desk was deserted, so I turned down the corridor toward the empty Nurse's Station. I dashed into room 407, nearly crashing into Dr. Fulbright. He steadied me as I braced against my thighs, catching my breath.

"Marvin told me you were on the way," Fulbright said, "but he didn't tell me you were taking the express."

I nodded, panting. "Thaman," I gasped.

"Breathe. We have time," he replied.

My heart rate slowed, and I looked toward the bed where Thaman was still hooked to tubes and monitors.

Thaman Bakshi scanned me through drooping eyelids. "Dr. Spring." It took two labored breaths before he spoke again. "Where's … Collin?"

Oh, no, not that question.

I leaned over his bed while Fulbright replied. "Collin was injured the same night you were."

Tham rolled back on his pillow, then turned to Nurse Marchand beside his injection system, muttering, "He's sleeping, then."

"He's being looked after." Nurse Marchand said as she added meds under Wolfgang's supervision.

I walked to Dr. Fulbright and whispered, "Tham won't sleep again, will he? Will I be able to talk to him?"

Thaman's chin fell to his neck.

"He's sleeping now," Lilith said. Then, once she saw her patient resting easily and Wolfgang approved of his vitals, she added, "He talked a little before you arrived." Then she looked toward Dr. Fulbright to tell more. Wolfgang stood to give me his chair as he explained.

"When Thaman roused, Lilith came to assist me. Rod followed her to the door, and once we saw Tham was stable, we allowed Alexander in."

Lilith shrugged. "Rod was with me in the Nurse's Lounge having coffee. When I answered Dr. Fulbright's call, so did he."

"What did Tham say? Do we know how he was injured?" I asked.

Wolfgang shook his head. "He didn't remember the accident, and he had no idea what he had been doing or how he was injured. Tham must have blacked out from the shock. But he saw Collin's face through his helmet. Collin renewed Tham's oxygen and did what he could to make him comfortable."

I nodded, "We guessed as much. Was there anything else?"

Lilith added, "Before Tham passed out again, he remembered Collin picking up clutter and debris around him. He felt some pain, which wasn't quite so sharp after Tham took the debris away. But there was one more thing." She nodded to Wolfgang. "It's up to you to tell that."

Wolfgang studied his shoes, shaking his head, and then looked up to continue.

"Tham said he was curled up like a baby, but he remembered Collin's face and that his pain eased when Collin tidied up around him, pushed him onto his back, and straightened his body. Then, as Collin arranged Tham's arms, he pried open his fists."

Tham shifted in his hospital bed and opened his eyes again, and Fulbright stopped his story to check his patient's status.

"Let me ... tell it," Tham moaned. "It was ... in my hand," Tham said. "Your ... Dr. Spring's charm." He locked eyes with me as he continued. "From yo. ... your necklace ... blue ... the heart. From ... your fa ... father. Half of it ... in my palm." Then, after a few heavy breaths, Tham added, "Collin ... took it."

Drained from telling his story, Tham closed his eyes again. As soon as she saw he was stable, Lilith said, "That's all he told us. Is that necklace important? Would you like to have it back?" she asked.

Footsteps sounded down the hall as I asked the million-dollar question. "Who else knows this?"

Lilith replied, "Rod was here. He heard Thaman's story."

"But what became of him? Where is he now?" I asked.

"He came to see me," A male voice replied. Neils Westergaard had entered the room.

"Wasn't a message sufficient?" Fulbright asked.

"I requested a report in person and sent him to the cave to search for that blue charm."

"But weren't you just there?" I asked.

Neils nodded. "We searched yesterday but didn't know what to look for, and I'm told the charm is small. It wasn't on either of the injured men, but if it was in the cave when the men were hurt, we should find it."

"No one besides Tham mentioned it. There's a chance he dreamed it."

"It's possible, but I'll stay with Tham in case he rouses again," Neils said. By his bearing and tone, he was eager for information but not as cranky as had been reported.

"Who else knows Thaman is awake?" I asked.

"Not even our medical team," Fulbright replied. "There hasn't been time, but they should know. I'll tell them right after I run these tests."

Lilith nodded, "You don't need me for the tests; I can tell the staff."

I nodded, "I'll tell Luis Kaneko, too. He should know the good news that Tham has revived."

"Will he recover now?" Lilith asked. "Will he remember more?"

"He's on the road to recovery," Wolfgang replied, "And we will know in time if there is permanent damage."

"Just tell me what to do," Lilith replied.

"Thank you, Dr. Fulbright … Lilith. I'll contact Luis now and stop by to explain the situation as soon as he is free. Please take care of our patient," I said, smiling.

When I was clear of the Ring Street Portal, I messaged Luis, and he responded immediately.

"I've been waiting to hear from you. Marvin told me what happened. Michelle and I are here. Come as soon as you can. We're wrapping up a lunch meeting."

I promised I'd be there in an hour, but I stopped by home long enough to change clothes and comb my hair. I shook my head as soon as I walked in. Sure, I'd rushed to throw on clothes and get to the clinic, but had I really left it that messy?

What was that noise?

I twirled around to find my brush on the floor. My hurrying must have jarred it from a precarious position. No matter. There was no time to worry about that. I left the brush on the floor and rushed to the Kanekos' quarters.

There, we connected a few of our puzzle pieces to make a more complete story of what happened the night Collin died.

Michelle recapped for us. "So, Thaman was alone when he was injured. Collin found him and tended to him in the storage room, as we suspected."

Luis nodded. "And Grant cleared some rubble away, which may have included the machine that injured Tham."

"Right," I agreed. "And from what Emilio Torres and Beth Martin told us, it may have been the scanner Dr. Hessling of Mars sent to Garrison Mathis, which eventually was delivered to Rod Alexander. According to Ray, such a scanner might have interacted badly with the alien structure that contains his energy."

Michelle continued, "And when Collin found the blue charm in Thaman's hand, he figured it had been ripped from Ray's cask, leaving Ray unshielded."

"And Collin went to Ray, replaced the shield, and carried Ray and his cask to a new location," I said. "But I guess somehow, perhaps while repositioning Ray's cask, the scanner activated, injuring Collin."

Michelle picked up the scenario. "So, Collin left Ray and struggled toward the Tham in the storeroom, but he could not save himself. That fits."

"And as long as the blue charms shield Ray's cask, he is safe," I said.

"As long as that scanner stays far away from it," Luis added. "But you say Neils sent Rod to find the blue charm?"

"He sent him to the cave, so he's looking in the wrong spot," Michelle said. "I guess that proves Neils and Rod are working together to find … what? Are they looking for Ray?"

"They've given no hint of looking for a being, but according to Bernadette's promises to Dexter, they are looking for something to give them power," I said.

"Prestige is a type of power, and a measure of celebrity would come along with proving alien life exists," Luis added.

Michelle nodded. "Alien technology might bring them fame and wealth, too."

"But who are they working with?" I asked. "Rod worked with Garrison; they both worked with Bernadette, and Bernadette directed Dexter. But why Neils? And who else are they working with?"

"Could it be Dr. Hessling from Threshold Station?" Luis asked. "He sent the scanner that Phobos requested."

"So, was it Rod who partnered with Neils? Or is Neils only a puppet in this, like Dexter was Bernadette's puppet?" Michelle asked.

"What about Lilith?" I asked. "She is close to Neils and Thaman, too."

"I should question Rod," Luis said. "He's under my command and is a cog in this machine. I'll see what I can find out from him tomorrow."

"Sounds like a good plan," I said. "Neils is hanging around Tham, waiting to hear more, and while he wasn't as grouchy when I saw him today, he's in Wolfgang's way."

"Then I'll ask him to dig for info in Garrison's quarters. That should separate Neils from the clinic," Luis said.

"Good idea," I said. And soon after that, I left for my messy room.

35 The Intruder

It was late when I got home, and sadly, the mess was as I left it. No magic fairies had come to pick up the clothes I had strewn, and Marvin had no hands to do it. But I was thirsty after all that rushing, so I stopped by the galley first.

Herbal tea. That would do. Thank goodness the snack cupboard wasn't bare; there was a pack of crackers with fake cheese spread to go with the tea. So, I put the tea in the warmer and set the timer. There was time to pick up my clothes while I waited.

House shoes were buried under my pants and shirt. Even after all these months on Mars, I had never gotten the hang of throwing things in the low Martian gravity; my pants, shirts, and shoes had arched over the sofa instead of landing on it. Collin explained it well: lower gravity requires less time to fall, so things travel farther.

Oh, well. I folded the pants and shirts to fit the drawer and placed the house shoes on the closet floor. Then I took a moment to kick off my weighted shoes and drop them beside the bed, noting that the sound of the drop always took a split second too long, especially when waiting for the second shoe to fall.

WayPointers were rarely free of the weight we wore to help keep our muscles from losing mass in low gravity, and only the most fashion-conscious of us slept in anything other than a body suit. The elastic stretch helped keep other muscles in tone, and the nanite coating was part of the antenna relay that kept us in touch with Marvin, the health monitoring system, and *Ad-Mon*, too. However, that secret program was only accessed when protocol allowed. *Thank goodness for privacy requirements.*

I caught a glimpse of my hair as I walked past a mirror. *Argh*. But I grinned as I remembered Collin asking how anyone could get bedhead before bed.

Tea and cheese biscuits hit the spot, but then I needed to brush my teeth, so a trip to the privy was in order.

The water-efficient hydro-shower was for human indulgence, but we used the air shower most of the time. Measured, fortified water was allowed for cleaning teeth, but as I brushed, I caught sight of that hair again. What a mess of curls. I picked up the hairbrush from the counter and gave my coppery mop a few passes. It still amazed me how bouncy curls were on Mars.

Lights out. Off to bed.

Wait.

Something was wrong.

The brush had been on the floor when I left.

Or had it? Tidying was a mindless action, incidental and routine. Perhaps I had picked up the brush without noticing when I put my clothes away. *That explained it.*

I closed my eyes but couldn't fall asleep without an answer. Did I pick up that brush, or had someone been in my quarters?

Ridiculous. *Go to sleep*.

That wasn't happening. Staring into the darkness didn't help. I couldn't see, so I listened.

The moisture recycler was at work. The galley's chilling engine hummed. Then, a *thump*. Just one.

Was that *thump* from the quarters next to mine? *It could be that*.

I listened for a cycle, the drop of a second shoe, a drawer opening and closing. But there was no pattern—just that one *thump*.

It might have been an open drawer closing. But was it?

Enough.

"Lights on," I said.

Nothing happened. How could that be? Our induction circuits had never failed me.

"Lights on," I said louder.

Still dark.

"Marvin, is something wrong with the power?"

There was no answer.

I checked my wristband. Marvin's light was black. The room was black.

I swung my legs to the side of the bed and felt for my weighted shoes. With both cradled in the crook of my left elbow, I used my right hand to feel my way toward the door.

There was a *tap*. Or maybe a *shuffle.* I froze.

Then, a penlight appeared in the galley passage, sweeping a path toward the door. I ducked behind the sofa, holding my breath as soft steps brushed across the carpeted room toward the door. Someone wanted to escape, and that suited me.

I jumped as the door creaked open, and there was a *bang* and a muffled *ouch.* Someone had made abrupt contact with the door frame. A man-shaped silhouette, back-lit by the ambient glow of Central Park, rubbed his head. Then, as he started through the door, I stood, screaming, and used all my strength to lob one of my heavy shoes in his direction. *Bullseye!*

Now I lobbed my other shoe, straight and hard. The intruder yelled, and I ran for the door while he rubbed his eye. But he caught me by the ankle and dragged me back in, slamming the door behind us.

"Leave me alone. Let me go," I screamed.

But he pinned me to the floor, using his weight against me.

"Shut up before it's too late," he growled.

I knew the voice. "Rod? What are you doing here?" I yelled.

Gloved hands squeezed my throat, but one of my knees was free enough to land a well-placed kick, and I remembered Collin again.

"Don't punch *at*. Punch *through*."

I tried. But he caught my ankle again. It was all I could do to twist free as he writhed in pain while holding tight to my foot. But I slipped from his grip and made it through the door.

Without my weighted shoes, I could leap farther on Mars than on Earth. Lower Martian weight launched me higher, and my trajectory took me farther across Central Park. On my second leap, I was captured again, but this time, it was one of Kaneko's guards, Bruce Cobalt.

"You're all right. I've got you," he said. And he directed his men to find my assailant, but Rod had fled the scene.

"How did you find me? Marvin wasn't working. My lights weren't working."

Bruce wrapped his coat around me. "Your medic alert sounded in the Icehouse, and Kaneko asked me to bring you to him."

Neils Westergaard caught up with us before we left. "What happened?" he asked.

"As if you don't know," I spat.

He turned to Cobalt, "Seriously ... what has happened here?"

"Rod Alexander broke into Dr. Graviston's quarters and attacked her," he replied.

By this time, Michelle and Luis had gathered us into their quarters. And soon Rod Alexander was there too, complete with a black eye left by the heel of my weighted boot.

"I can't believe this, Rod. What were you doing?" Neils asked.

The guards passed a cold pack to Rod, and he held it to one eye while the other rolled at Neils. "You know very well what I was doing."

"I sent you to Sanctuary Cave to look for evidence."

"Well, it wasn't in the cave, and since these charms belonged to Spring, I looked in her quarters. Here. I found them." He pulled my blue stone charms from his pocket.

"Why did you want my charms? Collin made them for me," I said. "Why were you plundering through my things?"

"They are clues into how Thaman was injured. My job was to find them, and I did," he replied.

"I'll take them as evidence," Luis said. "But I think you'll find they have nothing to do with either of the incidents at Sanctuary Cave."

"Of course not," Michelle added. "While Collin was separated from Spring, he carved those for her out of stones he found. She showed them to me."

"Then the stones are worthless," Neils said.

I grabbed them back. "Not to me. They are priceless to me."

Michelle gently took the charms again. "Let us hold them for you, dear. Just until this is cleared up."

I nodded and let her take the charms.

"What will happen to Rod?" Neils asked.

"He will be held in my private containment cell in the Council Hall and under my guards until we have questioned him."

Neils bristled. "But what if it is as he said? He thought he followed my orders."

"If he acted under his own will, then Rod will pay the penalty for crimes proven," Luis replied. "And if he acted under your orders, you will also be liable."

"Say nothing," Neils spat at Rod. "Our solicitors will straighten this out tomorrow."

Rod glared at Bruce Cobalt. "There was no power, and Marvin was disabled. How did you know where to find me? Why do you think I was the attacker? Have you violated authority by tracking me?"

"You'd be wise to stop talking, Rod," Neils hissed.

Kaneko stopped Bruce before he could reply. "As Prime Officer, I have my ways."

"True," Michelle added. "You may stop electricity and even Marvin, but you cannot stop my husband. He has ways to find the truth."

Under his breath, Neils whispered, "Bashir."

"Yes, Bashir received the alert of Spring's distress. That was part of it," Luis said. "And that's as much of it as you need to know."

"Will you stay with us tonight, cherie?" Michelle asked.

"Not if *he's* locked up," I replied, pointing to Rod.

So once Bruce Cobalt had secured Rod in Luis' holding cell, Kaneko sent a team to watch Thaman. Dr. Fulbright sent a sleeping draught for me. After my quarters were swept for danger and the electrical system repaired, finally, the lights went out, and I could sleep.

***

Wednesday

I woke up groggy the following day, but again, Michelle was at my door before I made coffee.

"Are you all right? Roderick Alexander escaped."

"How is that possible?" I asked.

"No one saw anything. There was no intruder alert. But the cell was open this morning, and Alexander was gone."

"Thaman ... is he OK?"

"Yes, Luis checked on him. Cobalt's second in command, Adams, and Dr. Fulbright are with Thaman. All is well at the clinic."

Another alert sounded. This time, it was Marvin.

"Dr. Graviston, you are needed at Collin Grant's memorial. Someone has taken his hammer."

With her longer stride, Michelle beat me to the Memorial Room, but I was on her coattails as we pushed inside.

She twirled as she examined the room, but I rushed to Collin's niche. When I opened the cupboard, blood rushed away from my head. Michelle caught me before I could hit the floor. "Is it so bad, cherie?" she asked. "I'm sure we can find another hammer."

I turned to her, eyes wide in panic. "It's all gone," I gasped.

There was no hammer, and there was no cask.

Ray was missing.

Part IV: Alien Hunt

36 The Hunt Begins

I stared into the dark niche as if searching the cube's black corners would make the cask reappear. It didn't work, and the truth flattened me like a steamroller.

Ray was gone.

Despite all the care we had taken and with Kaneko's support—even after losing Collin—Ray was gone.

I collapsed against the wall, gasping while guilt clawed me. *Collin died for nothing. I had not kept my promise.*

Stop it. *Focus!* This crisis wasn't about Collin or me. *Ray was in danger.* Nothing else mattered.

Michelle, stiff-jawed and worried, crouched beside me with a firm grip on my arm.

Marvin sounded through my wristband. "Dr. Graviston, do you need medical assistance?"

Michelle waited for my panting to steady, watching my eyes as she turned my face left and right. Then she spoke to the cloud, "Send a medic. Now."

By the time Alissa Arvani arrived, Michelle had helped me to a chair. My chest still heaved, but I squeaked a few words: "Where … is he?"

Alissa's injection calmed me, and when my breathing slowed, she asked, "What has happened here?"

"We've had a robbery," Michelle replied. "And a jailbreak. They took Collin's memorial contents."

Alissa nodded. "I see the robbery. Who would do such a thing?"

Michelle craned to peek through the open door. And after Alissa took the hint and closed it, Michelle whispered, "Will Bashir know?" She asked it as a question, but it was more of a request for Alissa to ask her husband, the clinic's curator of AdMon.

Alissa relayed Bashir's answer. "No one was here last night," she said. "No one else until you two arrived."

"Who knew Rod was a magician?" Michelle asked. "First, he escaped our jail, and now he is invisible."

"But how?" Alissa asked.

"Luis is investigating; he may know by now," Michelle replied. "I'll go to him. But will you get Spring to the Clinic? She may need a health review."

"Spring Graviston is functioning at normal parameters," Marvin droned.

"Marvin has never been wrong," Alissa said, shrugging.

"Don't take me away," I said. "I must find what's missing."

"Only if you promise to come in for a checkup later," Alissa said, and when I promised, she added, "Stay with Michelle until she can bring you to the clinic. Make it soon."

Michelle held my elbow as I stood.

"Let's find Luis," I said.

Then, she grabbed my other elbow and pushed me toward the Council Hall.

37 How?

Michelle helped me out of the temple, but by the time we reached the park, I breathed easy and could walk unsupported. Questions bubbled out of me. "How could Rod Alexander have escaped from the Kaneko prison?"

Michelle shrugged. "The five key council members can open the main door, but only Luis can override our detention cell lock. It takes Ministerial protocols. He and his guards are puzzled. No one believed an escape was possible."

"So, only Luis could have opened the cell door," I said. "But he didn't … right?"

"Of course not," Michelle replied.

"Was the lock broken?"

Another no.

"Was anyone drugged?"

Michelle rolled her eyes. "Luis is twenty steps away in the Council Hall. Let's ask him." But our Prime Minister was as puzzled as I, and the two investigators he grilled looked lost as they pieced together clues from the past night.

"Did any guard leave his post?" Luis asked.

"No, Sir," Cobalt replied.

"But some of them left this room? Is that right?"

"Yes, Sir. Most of us did eventually."

"Why did you leave?"

"To enjoy the dinner you sent for us, Sir. And we thank you for that. Most of us had never had a five-course dinner from Bistro sur Mars, and we were quite eager … and grateful. The Shrimp Scampi was delicious."

Luis drummed his table and then turned to Michelle. "My dear, did you order dinner for my guards last night?"

"No, mon cher. I should have thought of it, but I did not," she replied.

"And while you enjoyed this dinner, was a guard left to watch the detention cell?"

I thought Richards might cry as he shook his head *no*. "Who can break your lock, Sir? Isn't it foolproof?" he asked.

Luis sighed. "Apparently not. But all doors were locked, correct?"

"Yes, Sir," Cobalt replied. "The cell was locked before we moved to the dining room, and we rechecked it after we ate. The same is true for the exterior doors. Nothing changed."

"And yet, Rod Alexander walked through both doors with no one as a witness. Is that right?"

Cobalt nodded sheepishly.

"Was the main door opened after I left?"

"Well, it opened twice, Sir. When the dinner arrived, we allowed the delivery person in. She relayed your instructions to eat in the dining room, as French onion soup can be messy," Cobalt replied. But then he added, "I guess if you didn't order the dinner, you wouldn't have cared about the soup."

Luis ignored that, asking, "Did you lock the door behind the delivery tech?"

"Both in and out, Sir," Cobalt replied. "The delivery trolley is still in the dining room."

"Then please interview every man who was here. Find out what they know."

When Cobalt left, Michelle tapped her husband on the shoulder.

"Mon cher, could *you* have opened the cell door?"

"Of course," he replied. "But I was home with you, not here."

"Must you be here to do that?" I asked.

He paused in the middle of a headshake. Then he turned an angry purple, ushered Michelle and me to their quarters, and initiated the AdMon sequence. The log showed that no one had been in the hall around the time of the escape besides the food services technician, the guard who escorted her, and, slightly later, Rod Alexander.

Despite that, Rod had walked out. AdMon had a record of him in the Council Hall at 20:15, but within an hour he was missing and didn't return.

"Did Rod receive any messages?" I asked.

"They would have come through my men," Luis replied.

"Where is he now?" Michelle asked.

After a few more queries for AdMon, Luis looked up, mystified. "Rod Alexander is not in WayPoint Station." He shook his head, but his expression changed as he looked toward me. "Could Ray have done this?"

"Where would Ray want to go?" Michelle asked.

"For that matter, where would Rod Alexander go?" I asked. "Where could he run to?"

Luis had a follow-up, "What about the blue charms? They block Ray; could they block Rod Alexander?"

"Not unless he knew how to use them, and Ray would never tell him."

"Who else knew?" Michelle asked.

"Fulbright, Collin, and me. No one else."

"Let me try one more thing," Luis said. After a few queries, he had more information. "Rod shows up in the records briefly after he escaped. He was in the transportation bay and took a transport prepared for Maria Torres."

"Oh. Maria must have booked that for our road trip," I said.

"So, Rod took a conveniently placed rover meant for Maria and you. Hmm." Luis began looking at me more suspiciously, and my instinct was to find an escape route.

"My love, you cannot think Spring helped Rod escape," Michelle said. "He stole from her only yesterday. We must keep digging for more reasonable answers."

Luis' face remained stern, but after a moment of processing, his jaw relaxed. Then he nodded, saying, "Leave me here to study AdMon for more clues."

"Very well. I promised Alissa I'd take Spring to the Clinic for examination. We shall do that now."

Should I worry that Luis believed I needed to have my head examined? No matter. Leaving him with his riddle worked for me. As soon as we reached the front door, I whispered to Michelle. "I have a lead to follow, too."

"You have ideas?" Michelle asked. "What shall we follow?"

"The money," I replied. "Or, in this case, the dinner bill. Let's see who bought dinner for the guards."

***

The Bistro shift manager was busy with lunch details, but she remembered the dinner order for the guards. How could she forget six five-course dinners delivered around 20:00? The meals were ordered by Luis Kaneko and delivered on time by one of their meal service technicians. We thanked Sissy for the information, and once outside, I tugged Michelle's sleeve and pointed to a bench in Central Park.

We thanked the Bistro staff for the information, and once outside, I tugged Michelle's sleeve and pointed to a bench in Central Park.

"Who could fake Luis' message?" I whispered.

"Well … I suppose I could," Michelle replied. "But I did not do that. We've reached another dead end."

"Well, there is one thing that might be helpful. Since the order came by message, Marvin might know who sent it."

So, we asked Marvin, and not only did he not know, but he had no knowledge of such a message being sent.

"Could the staff be hiding information about who ordered it?" Michelle asked.

I shook my head. "If that were so, Marvin would know about it."

Michelle added another idea. "Marvin would have a record *unless* the message was fabricated. Maybe someone on the Bistro staff arranged it."

"Do you think someone in the Bistro is working with Rod?" I asked.

"It's possible."

"Would Rod share his power-grabbing plan with a café busboy or even a manager? It wouldn't be much of a conspiracy then, would it? Besides, how would Rod get a message to the Bistro while he was locked up?"

"You're right," Michelle said, drumming her fingers on her knee. "It must be a partner in the scheme, but who?"

"Our known suspects are Neils and Lilith, so we should start there. We can't waste time; we must find Ray," I said.

"Careful thought is not a waste of time," she replied. So, we allowed a few minutes to mull over the facts. Rod had been imprisoned under the watch of six guards. Dinner had been delivered to them with instructions to eat in the dining room. The message had been sent, apparently, by Luis via Marvin.

"Did someone interfere with Marvin's message system?" Michelle asked. "Who could do that?"

"We believe Rod left the station in a vehicle ordered for Maria and you. Maybe that's a clue."

"Yes, Maria and I had planned a day trip for today. So, maybe Rod saw a rover cleared for exit and took advantage of the opportunity," I said.

"But where can he run to?" Michelle asked. "Maybe Sanctuary Cave, but that will be the first place Luis looks. How can that help him?"

"It wouldn't help him for long," I replied. "But where else could he get food, water, and oxygen? The rover provides those, but not long term."

Then Michelle got an answer from Luis. "My husband followed up on the transport," she said. "It is as you say. Milo left the rover out for you and Maria this morning, but guess who else visited it—Lilith."

"Lilith? Why?" I asked.

"Do you think Maria invited her to join your trip?"

I shook my head *no*. "It was to be an outing for two. So, when did AdMon show Lilith was in the transportation bay?"

"At nearly 21:00."

"Soon after Rod escaped—that's got to be more than a coincidence," I replied.

"Do you think Rod wanted Lilith to flee with him?"

"Two on the run to nowhere would be a messy complication. It's hard to fit that into the puzzle with what we know now."

"Should we talk to Lilith, then?" Michelle asked. "We were going there to have you checked, anyway."

I shrugged. "If she and Rod were allies, she might not tell us much, but we should see what she has to say."

38: Lilith and Thaman

It was afternoon by the time we reached the clinic. Michelle and I agreed to use my health evaluation as the reason for the visit. We'd approach Lilith's participation in the escape as delicately as possible.

Jinae Kim rushed around her Welcome Desk to greet us in the hallway. "Are you all right? Alissa told me you were injured."

News had spread quickly about my intruder and Rod's escape, but Jinae also knew that something was wrong in Collin's memorial and that I had collapsed there.

"I'm fine. Just worried," I said.

"Of course you are. Who would rob you? And who would interfere with Collin's memorial? Who on WayPoint is that cruel?" she asked.

Michelle patted Jinae's hand, which rested over mine. "Spring is fine, but we are here to be sure. Is Alissa nearby? We promised to bring Spring in for a check-up."

Jinae nodded. "Alissa was called to an emergency, but Elly is expecting you. I'll help you find her." But once Michelle was out the door, Jinae pulled at my elbow to stop me, whispering, "Do you have any idea who did this?"

Those brown eyes held a glimmer of tears, and from my first day on WayPoint, Jinae had been a trusted friend. I bent my head close to hers. "Rod Alexander was in my room, and he might have stolen

Collin's artifacts, too. But keep that to yourself. Luis is still investigating, and new evidence could change the picture."

"How can I help?" she asked.

"Keep your eyes and ears open and your lips sealed. We still need answers."

"You can count on me," she said, gripping my elbow again. "Now, let's find Elly. She's been in Thaman's room most of the morning, but I believe she's in her office now."

"Oh, please tell me Neils isn't in Thaman's room. He's the last person I want to talk to today," I said.

She shrugged. "We were surprised that neither he nor Rod are hanging around today." Then she lowered her voice, adding, "But now I know why Rod hasn't been here. Maybe Neils is investigating, too." Then she pretended to zip her lips and waved as she left me at the door of Elly's examination room.

"Ah, Spring," Elly said, "I've been looking for you."

"I hope those pinchers aren't for me," I said, pointing to her instrument tray.

"No, nothing like that, but you may need a few tests." She asked a few preliminary questions about what happened during the robberies of my quarters and then in the Memorial Room.

To relieve her concern, I gave her Marvin's report. "The cloud says I'm functioning normally."

"Normal for what?" she asked. Then, with a light elbow jab to my rib, she added, "When have I ever trusted AI? I'll see for myself."

I gave her the side-eye as she checked my vision, heart rate, blood flow, heart, and lungs, and finally, she agreed. "You're as normal as you ever are. Now tell me what happened in your quarters. Were you injured?" she asked.

"No. But I gave Rod Alexander a black eye."

She chuckled but quickly shifted to ask about the incident at the Temple. "Why did you faint when you saw Collin's artifacts had been taken? Was anything valuable?"

Elly knew me well enough to tell if I lied, but I paused to decide how close to the truth I should go. The hammer wasn't valuable, and I had no idea how to put a value on Ray, so I replied, "I'm not sure of the monetary worth of anything in the niche, but having any part of Collin ripped from me again is painful."

She nodded. "Did Collin's tools mean that much to you?"

"They were symbols of our plans, hopes, and dreams—problems we solved, ambitions we shared, obstacles we overcame together—those are the excruciating losses."

"And were those things in that niche?" she asked.

Again, I answered too slowly to fool someone as close as a mother. So, she whispered, "Were there things in that niche no one should know about?"

I pursed my lips to hide emotion, but who else could I break down with, if not a mother? When Elly saw my tears, I nodded *yes*.

She whispered again. "Is this trouble dangerous for you?" she asked.

The dam of emotion broke, and I sobbed as I replied, "It's dangerous for everyone. Me, Mars, and even Earth—maybe beyond that."

She sucked in her breath, squeezing my hand. "Is someone helping you?"

I nodded.

She stood. "Everyone in the Icehouse is your family. Call on us; we'll be there for you. In the meantime, we will keep our eyes open. Most of us know that Rod was your intruder. Are there any other bad guys?"

I shook my head. "Maybe Neils. Maybe Lilith. And there must be others, but we aren't sure who else is involved. We're investigating."

She cocked her head to one side, then said. "You know as much as I do about Neils and more than I do about Rod. As for Lilith, she is close to your two male suspects, and she is devoted to nursing Thaman. That's as much as I know."

"Have any of them done anything suspicious lately?" I asked.

She shook her head. "We haven't seen much of those men in the last day, which is odd in itself. As for Lilith, she stays by Thaman's side as much as possible. Last night, I covered for her when she took a supper break around 20:00."

"Thank you," I said. "Please let me know if you learn anything else."

She patted my hand and then smiled as she stood. After straightening her physician's smock, she dropped the mouth of her stethoscope into her chest pocket and handed me a tissue. "I proclaim you well and fit for work, whatever that may be. I'll send a report to Luis. But first, let's visit Thaman."

In 407, Lilith checked Thaman's monitors as Wolfgang Fulbright observed.

"I hear you've had quite a morning," Wolfgang said, offering me his chair. Then he turned to Elly. "How is she?"

"Fit as a fiddle," Elly replied.

I smiled and turned toward the sleeping patient. "Now tell me about Thaman."

Fulbright shrugged, hands spread. "He hasn't been awake enough for me to evaluate his judgment problems, but his body is responding. He's usually quiet when awake, but his wounds are healing nicely. I'd say improving on schedule. Do you agree, ladies?"

Elly spoke first. "That sums it up."

Lilith spoke more reluctantly. "I think Thaman's trouble about making judgment calls will take longer to heal than his body. Of course, I'm not the specialist on such matters, but he has been a friend, and I worry about him returning to work in the field."

Wolfgang nodded. "I don't disagree with what you say, but we must evaluate him fully when he's conscious for more than a few minutes."

"I hope I will be here for that," Lilith said. "Except for Thaman's care, I begin to believe my work here is done."

"Are you leaving?" Fulbright asked.

What was she up to? Was it a coincidence that she planned to leave just when Ray had been taken?

"You've done good work for us, Lilith," Elly said. "I'm surprised you want to leave us so soon."

"Neils' replacement is on the way, so his ship will return to Earth soon after he arrives. Perhaps I should return with that ship."

I cleared my throat. "May I ask what work is done now?"

Again, she paused, staring at Thaman's monitors, but finally lifted her head to speak. "It is time to tell you my secret, I suppose. A job was not the only reason that brought me here; I came to find out what happened to my sister."

"You had a sister here?" Elly asked.

Lilith nodded. "She wasn't well-liked here or on Earth. But she died, and I came to collect the loose ends of her life."

"What loose ends?" Fulbright asked. "Why did you never speak of a sister while we traveled here?"

"I didn't tell anyone, but my family is curious about the circumstances of her death, and if she did harm here, my family sent me to make amends. Now, I believe I have learned as much as possible, and it's time to return to tell my family how she ended."

"Who was your sister?" Elly asked. "And how could your family send you to Mars?"

"You knew her well. My sister was Bernadette Duval, and our family has old and storied connections in France."

I flushed hot; I must have been as red as a beet. My armband flashed. Marvin droned, "Dr. Graviston, do you need assistance?"

Elly rescued me. "We are with Dr. Graviston, Marvin. Stop the alert."

"Complying."

Dr. Fulbright rushed to my side. "Spring, do you want to lie down?" he asked as he checked my pulse.

"Water, please."

Fulbright sat me in his chair, hovering till my pulse calmed. All the while, I was processing Lilith's information. Bernadette Duval was close to Garrison Mathis, Neils Westergaard, and Roderick Alexander. Was her well-timed supper break an excuse to help Rod escape?

"Spring. Should we call someone?" Elly asked.

I didn't know, and Lilith seemed puzzled.

"You had issues with Bernadette, Dr. Spring, but isn't that all over now? Why has this news upset you so?" She scanned the faces around her and finally asked, "If she's having a medical issue, and both of you are doctors, why would you call anyone else? What's this all about?"

Elly prodded me. "Spring, if you have a question, now might be the time to ask it."

I gulped. Was Elly right? It didn't matter. I couldn't hold back anyway, so I spoke. "Lilith, you were in the Transportation Sector last night. Were you there to help Rod Alexander escape WayPoint Station?"

She shook her head. "I didn't see Rod all day. What's happened? Why would he try to escape WayPoint?"

Elly sighed, patting my shoulder.

"Tell her," I said.

Elly turned to Lilith. "Last night, Rod Alexander was a busy man. He broke into Spring's living quarters and robbed her. Then, when Luis Kaneko's men caught him and detained him in a cell, Rod escaped. He left WayPoint station in a transport, and you were seen visiting that area. Did you …"

Lilith interrupted. "I knew nothing about any of this. Why wasn't it in today's news? Why haven't I been questioned? Why would Rod do all those things?"

Now Lilith needed a chair. You could practically see her eyes spinning as she processed the new information.

"Tell us what you know. Why did you visit the Transportation Dock last night?" Fulbright asked.

Lilith breathed deeply to gain control. "I was here with Thaman," she said. "You both saw that and know I took a supper break, a quick burrito at Taco Marciano. As I was leaving, Maria handed me a hamper. She said she planned a day trip with you, Dr. Graviston. She gave me a code and asked me to place the hamper in a rover the two of you would use. The transportation bay isn't far, so I did as she asked."

"And you didn't see Rod Alexander?"

"No, I did not. How many times must I say it?" she asked.

"Was anyone else in the bay?" Elly asked.

"I can't say for sure. There was nothing out of the ordinary. I didn't see anyone specific, but it wasn't isolated either."

"I believe she is telling us the truth, Spring," Dr. Fulbright said. "And her story is easily verified by Maria."

He was right about that. And maybe Rod saw the code as Lilith entered it. But I still had questions. How did Rod know there would be a rover available? Just lucky? Or had Lilith always planned to get food to him somehow? She wasn't off my hook.

"Yes, please call Maria; ask her," Lilith replied. "Am I in trouble?"

"Not much trouble, I'm sure," Elly replied. "But we should tell Luis about this. He may want to question you."

She nodded. "That's fine. I'll tell him all I know. I guess you'll tell him about Bernadette, too?"

"It will be easier to clear you if he has no more surprises," Fulbright replied.

Lilith turned to me. "Dr. Graviston, I hope you can forgive Bernadette someday. Thaman and Giles explained how she treated you, but she had the misfortune of being born to older parents with many duties. She was my much younger sister, a situation that caused her grief, too."

"I don't believe that could be much of a misfortune," Elly said, patting her hand.

Lilith wiped away tears. "Our family had prestige in France, and I was a young woman, loved by the family, respected by our friends, and sought by wealthy and charming men. Bernadette grew up in my shadow. Though of no interest to me, persistent suitors seemed a wonderful whirl of romance to Bernadette. Jealousy became too great a part of her life. That's one reason I traveled to heal diseases; without me, there was no shadow. Sadly, that didn't help much. Her behavior led to one poor choice after another as she grew."

I understood how circumstances could affect self-esteem and how one bad experience can lead to others. And if Bernadette had more goodness in her than I had seen, I was sorry for that. But could Lilith be as much of a manipulator as her sister?

"Call Monsieur Kaneko," she said. "I suppose he'll be glad I plan to leave WayPoint Station."

I had bigger problems than jealousy to solve. I'd let Luis find the truth, but I wondered who would be happier for Lilith's departure from WayPoint Station—Luis or Lilith herself?

"Bernadette's sister," Elly said. "I wonder …."

Elly abruptly left the room, and I didn't stay either. After my farewells and best wishes, I went to find Luis Kaneko. He'd want to hear about Lilith's revelation.

39 The Chase

I headed straight for Luis Kaneko with my news about Lilith. But he was busy, too. So, I joined a meeting in the Prime Minister's office with the Kanekos and Bruce Cobalt, the lead investigator.

Teams of guards had scoured WayPoint, and Luis, with Bashir's assistance, had searched electronically. Rod Alexander's last known position was in the Transport Bay around 21:00; he was no longer in WayPoint Station.

"He isn't in Sanctuary Cave either," Cobalt said. "My team checked the remote farms and research sites, and no one saw him after 21:00."

"So, did he drive out of WayPoint and vanish?" Michelle asked. "How can that be?"

"He's possibly in transit somewhere, but there is another wrinkle," Luis said. "Neils Westergaard has vanished, too. They may have escaped together."

"Can AdMon tell if Neils was in the Transport Bay around the time Rod left?"

"I checked," Luis replied. "AdMon must be glitching. Neils Westergaard wasn't there, but Rosh Hashimi was in the Bay near that time, and that's impossible."

"It certainly is," Michelle said. "We can't find Neils anywhere, and Rosh Hashimi's body was ejected into space from Phobos years ago."

"So, were Neils and Rod partners? Could Neils release Rod from the cell?" I asked. "And even if he could, where could they run?"

Luis rubbed his brow. "There aren't many possibilities."

"How can they evade our scanner links?" Cobalt asked.

Luis looked at me with a question he dared not ask in front of Cobalt. I shook my head no. Ray's tricks couldn't do that. No one else on WayPoint could duplicate the shielding magic without Ray's blue charms and the knowledge to use them.

Luis turned to Cobalt. "They can only hide from us through distance or very efficient shielding, which doesn't exist here, as far as I know."

"Deep caves, then? Or hiding behind sandstorms? Could they have traveled far enough to be out of range?" Cobalt asked.

"It's possible. Our local communication system is effective throughout WayPoint, but beyond that, we rely on Marvin's link with Phobos. Rod has a head start on us, but neither his rover nor his terrain suit will keep him safe for long, and a hamper won't feed him forever."

"Could he hide in a ship preparing to return to Earth or the Moon's Threshold Station?" I asked.

"Life support isn't activated on those ships until near launch time. The terrain suit would save him for a time, but not until the next flight."

"Then Phobos is his target," I said.

"Or a hiding place we aren't aware of," Michelle added. "Perhaps Rod has helpers, a group ready with a fully supplied safe spot."

Luis considered the idea but soon replied, "All our work sites are inside our crater walls or along the outflow trail. To go outside this crater, we launch to the satellite or rarely to the research team on Phobos."

"Can we rule out the old, abandoned sites, the ones they used in early exploration?" Michelle asked.

"Too few supplies," I said.

"Outdated technology," Luis added. "And the logistics of travel would make them a long shot. The most logical destination is the Phobos Food Transfer spot. Rod would only need short-term supplies till another lander arrives to collect supplies."

"And we know the rendezvous site. Milo or his crew deliver there regularly," Michelle said.

"Then, in all probability, that's where we'll find him, waiting for a ride out of town," Kaneko replied. "Gentlemen, gather your terrain gear. I'll order the transport. Emilio Torres will be your driver. He'll choose a vehicle that can carry three guards and two passengers. Hopefully, he'll return with another, Rod Alexander. Hurry. Rod has had plenty of time to get where he's going, and we can only hope he didn't catch a shuttle since his departure."

Cobalt nodded and was nearly out the door when Luis stopped him.

"You and the guards are to capture our runaway, but if there's cargo in that rover, let Dr. Graviston deal with it. The stolen items are sentimental to her, and she knows how they should be handled."

"Yes, Sir," Cobalt said and was on his way.

When the door closed again, I shared my new clue with Luis. "Lilith Marchand has a good excuse for being in the Transport Pod last night."

When I explained, he promised to question her more fully. "But now, back to the problem at hand," he said. "Spring, these men are more than capable of handling a fugitive, but they don't know the importance of the stolen items. If we find what is lost, you know how to manage it better than anyone else. My men will capture the prisoner; you handle the contraband. Is there anyone else you'd like along—someone to help with the … er … special cargo?"

I shook my head. "We shouldn't add to the list of those who know about Ray. I can handle the cargo alone. So, do you believe in Ray now—that he isn't dangerous?"

Luis grimaced, "Not as much as you do, but all the hubbub around Ray makes it easier to believe he's valuable and not on the side of the bad actors we have in WayPoint."

Michelle volunteered to go with me, but Luis rejected the idea. He patted his wife's hand. "If Marchand goes French on me, I'll need you to translate."

"Someone should go with her," Michelle insisted. "Milo will be busy; Spring needs someone she can trust. Can you think of anyone else, Spring?"

"Fulbright should stay with Thaman, but Giles Cardiff is a good choice. He knows where the Phobos drop zone is, and he's a driver. He can get us there and back if we run into trouble."

"But he was only recently released for work," Michelle said. "Are you safe with him?"

"Milo gives him good reviews, and Giles trusts me. When I worked on his hallucination treatment, I learned what makes him tick. He will follow my lead."

"Can you contact Ray now, Spring?" Michelle asked. "Does he meet you in the Blue Room?"

"No. And that proves he's further away than Sanctuary Cave. I could contact him in the cave, even without his communication charms. Even though Giles doesn't know what Ray is, his hallucinations prove Ray can reach him if we get close enough."

Luis nodded. "I trust my men, and I can swear them to secrecy if needed, but it will be best if you can keep Ray's secret from them, too."

"Keep the facts of Ray's origin secret. I get it," I replied.

"Then off with you," Luis said. But as he waved me out the door, he added, "Hopefully, we can find Rod before he leaves the surface. When the rover is prepared and Giles arrives, Milo will call you to the dock."

***

The sun touched the horizon, and I was tired, but the motivation to catch up with Rod and find Ray outweighed my fatigue.

Giles showed no lack of energy. He grinned ear to ear when he saw me coming toward his rover. "Get the lead out, Dr. Spring. I hear we're going on a car chase. How cool is that?" he asked, scrunching his shoulders toward his ears. He buckled his helmet and popped through the rover hatch.

Our versatile midsized rover had four seating sections to handle the six of us and room in the cargo area for Rod Alexander when we caught him. This unit was equipped for longer-term survival with food, water, an oxygen generator, and a self-contained atmosphere transition tube.

Even though the interior atmosphere was human-friendly, we traveled in full terrain gear in case of unexpected events. I strapped in and joined the helmet comm chatter as we exited the bay. "The chase might not be as cool as you think, Giles. But a lot is riding on this mission," I said.

"Will we be able to overtake Alexander?" Cobalt asked.

Milo shook his head. "Rod has a head start, but we hope to catch him at the Phobos Food Drop before he flags a ride to the moon. We have one edge, though. This rover is a caterpillar with full traction, which makes us more sure-footed. The hover driver he has is no Tin Lizzy, but he'll still have to maneuver around the big boulders. He won't be far ahead of us."

"Why would anyone on Phobos help Dr. Alexander escape?" Giles asked. "Didn't he rob you, Dr. Spring?"

Milo replied. "Our geology department exchanges samples with Phobos, so they coordinate through messages via Marvin, not our WayPoint Channel. Rod may have bypassed us to request the lander."

"Wouldn't you know about that, Mr. Torres? Don't you handle the drops?"

"Not necessarily," Milo replied. "Marvin's program is satellite-based. Phobos messages only come to me through Marvin when transport is required at the drop rendezvous, most often for food. Phobos runs their show, and we run ours. Marvin works for both. We mostly communicate when one of us needs something."

"So, the Phobos Station may not know Rod invaded Dr. Graviston's quarters," Giles said.

"It's possible," Milo replied. "If anyone relayed that through Marvin, it didn't involve me."

Cobalt added, "He stole something from Collin Grant's memorial, too. My sources didn't say if Phobos is helping Rod, but the drop zone is an excellent place to look for him. Those were Kaneko's orders, so that's what we do."

Milo followed his glowing map as we drove, concentrating on deep ruts and rocks visible in the rover's lamps. During the long, silent moments, Giles tapped his knees nervously.

"Too bad we can't have music to make the trip pass faster," he said.

Cobalt had a different idea. "I'd like to use the time to discuss strategy and terrain gear protocol with my men." When his request was granted, I asked for a private channel for Giles and me. But Dr. Fulbright sent a message before Milo separated us into conversation groups. Thaman had roused long enough to say that while Neils Westergaard and Rod Alexander were in his room, he overheard them say something about a *Phobos Bus Stop*. Those few words could be a new clue.

Milo shared the gist of the message with all the passengers. "It appears we are heading in the right direction. Neils and Rod were overheard chatting about Phobos before the robbery. Hopefully, we can catch two birds with one stone at the food drop."

Cobalt and his men continued their briefing, and I used the time to go over Giles' progress with the hallucinations. It calmed Giles' nervous tapping and kept my mind off what we'd find at the end of the road.

Milo waved a gloved hand over the bench back. "You're on your own," he said.

So, I broke the ice with Giles. "How are things going with Beth Martin?" I asked.

Giles' green eyes lit up behind his helmet screen. "Subtle much, Dr. Spring? I figured you'd be after my hallucinations, and, lucky for me, Beth Martin is not a figment of my imagination."

I spread my palms a little. "It's a conversation starter."

"Yeah," Giles chuckled, "You did a good thing for me when you helped Fulbright cure me. I like my new job, and Beth is a good kid. I'm glad we met."

"You two seem to click. Maybe you're good for each other."

"Yeah, I guess so," he replied. "Beth can put up with my jokes, and I'm more settled around her. We might turn into something serious," he said.

"What? Is the Big Joker turning serious? How can that be?" I asked.

"Do you think I'm in over my head, Dr. Spring? I've changed some … not enough to be a different person than before, but I'm definitely steadier. And besides, Beth and I have fun together. It's always a good day when I can drive with her. We've seen more of this crater than most, and we like exploring."

"That sounds promising, Giles," I replied.

"You know," he said, "Beth and I thought Phobos might be wicked, especially since her friend, Ginger, broke contact. Beth said Phobos had swallowed Ginger up into some kind of secret, but as it turned out, her friend is fine and even has a boyfriend."

"That was a relief to Beth."

"It sure was, but … wait … you don't think Ginger is in on this robbery, do you?" he asked.

There was a new idea.

"I hadn't considered Ginger," I said. "Garrison Mathis helped her get the job on Phobos, though, and he's in jail for his part in the coup, so who knows? After she moved to Phobos, did you see Ginger more than the time you told me about?"

"Beth and I thought we saw her shuttle another time, but she only talked to us once. And that was to tell us she was fine."

I wanted to return to the topic of his hallucinations, but I needed to step carefully. After all, Ray caused those, and I didn't know where the conversation might lead. But I had to ask.

"No more hallucinations, right?"

"Not a one."

"Has anyone tried to bully you lately?" I asked.

He shook his head. "No, and they better not try. After seeing what bullying did to me, it's a hot-button issue. When a bully crosses paths with me, I go ballistic."

"Have you become violent, Giles?"

"Heck no. I rein it in, but I no longer buy what bullies sell. And you know what else? I feel better in every area of my life. That bullying monkey on my back was just surplus weight, and it feels good to shed it. Now, no one can define me to myself or anyone else. That's *my* job."

"Good for you," I replied.

During the silent parts of our trip, I thought about what we'd find at the drop zone. Hopefully, Rod would be there, and the guards would grab him swiftly. But how would Ray behave? Would he reach out mentally to those men or attack the guards? And most of all, would Ray be safe? And if he was, how would I explain a being like Ray?

As we neared the target, I was surprised by a staticky visit from Ray in the Blue Room.

"What happ … Spring?" he asked. "Spring … are … there?"

In our mental room, only Ray could *hear* my reply. "I'm searching for you now. Can you tell me anything about how you left or where you are?"

The communication smoothed for a bit, but the problem worsened as we drove toward the northwest crater wall. Ray's last clear message was to be careful of danger. But then the messages stopped. Ray was silent.

"Dr. Spring? Are you nervous?" Giles asked. "You're gasping."

I forced a few deep, slow breaths before I replied. "When we reach our destination, let Cobalt's men do their thing first. Stay with me, and if I give you directions, don't argue. Just do as I ask."

"What's happening? What do you know?" he asked. But I didn't get a chance to answer. Milo broke in and set us all on the same channel.

"We're approaching the drop spot. Keep your eyes open for a small rover or a person moving on the terrain. Speak here about anything you see so we will be on the same page."

Cobalt spoke up. "Good advice. I'll take charge now. My men will follow me, and the others should remain in the cab. Are all suits ready for the terrain?" he asked.

"We decontaminated when we pulled away from WayPoint. We're set," Milo replied.

"Good. Be ready, men," Cobalt said.

We all peered into the night, looking for any reflection from our rover lamps, any movement.

"Wow. Look how high the crater wall is here," Richards said.

"It's not just one wall," Milo replied. "Our crater backs up to another one, and their walls push together here."

Bruce Cobalt interrupted. "There he is. Look to the right."

There was movement, all right. It was a suited man running ... but where?

"Where's he going?" Giles asked.

"Maria's rover is behind that boulder," Milo said. "He must be trying to escape."

"Wouldn't driving the rover make more sense?" Cobalt asked.

"That's panic," I replied. "He's made a bad choice."

"Exiting," Cobalt said. "Be sure your safeties are engaged." They were. None of us had removed gear while we drove.

Within a few minutes, Cobalt and his men corralled the man and stuffed him into the little Rover. "We have Rod Alexander, but he's not talking," Cobalt reported. "My men are searching for anyone else."

"Bring Rod to my van as soon as possible," Milo replied. "We can contain him in the cargo hold. Tell us when Dr. Graviston is cleared to examine the vehicle."

"Very well," Cobalt replied. "All I see here is partially eaten food. He either had a meal while waiting or was camping in the rover. He must have had his helmet and gloves off while he ate, so even though he's equipped, he's spreading Earth contamination. We can flush out the cab to come to you, but Runaway Rod probably dropped a few germs on the terrain."

"Hopefully, there aren't enough to be disastrous," Milo said. "But it's a grave violation of WayPoint protocol."

Cobalt sealed the little rover, and the cab interior glowed brightly as detoxifying light killed germs in the air and on the suit surfaces. Rod's face was grim in the green aura, and his eyes were wide in panic.

Once Rod was safe in the crawler, I was allowed to examine the rover. There was no trace of Neils or anything he might have carried. And Rod had nothing except his suit and a half-empty picnic hamper.

"Could Neils be hiding? Carrying contraband?" I asked Milo.

"There's no sign of any disturbance here," Cobalt replied. "There is a safety cabin on the other side of the clearing, but it appears to be untampered. Alexander says he escaped alone when the cell door of Luis' jail flew open, and he took the rover because he found it stocked and ready to go."

"But what about the things in Collin's niche?" I asked.

"He claims to know nothing about that, and he has nothing on him or in the rover."

How could that be? What had become of Collin's hammer and Ray's cask?

"We have two rovers now," Milo said. "Giles is our only authorized driver, so he'll pilot the small one."

"I'll relay a message to Kaneko for orders," Cobalt said. And soon after that, he told us Kaneko wanted his men to return to WayPoint with the prisoner. "The boss has different orders for you, Dr. Spring. He wants you and Giles to watch for a shuttle, at least until he gets a reply from Phobos about their drop schedule. It shouldn't take much longer."

"Oh, good. I got the sporty model," Giles said.

I messaged Milo. "While we wait here, we'll shine the rover lamps in a few directions to see if we can find anything else, maybe a clue."

Milo approved the idea, and Kaneko gave it the OK. So, with his rover detoxed and ready, Milo headed home. Giles drove the small rover, but I had comm controls, so we flushed the Mars air from the cab and then flashed the lamps around the drop spot. We found no trace of Ray or recent disturbance outside the scuffle of boots when Cobalt's men caught Rod.

"Could he have buried something?" I asked.

"I see no sign of that," Giles replied. "Should we look in the safety cabin? If you want to, we can come back during daylight and take another stab at it."

I sighed. *Was Ray in there?* I couldn't ask that question out loud, so I said, "Even with time constraints, we can't leave that cabin unchecked. But let me go in first," I said.

"I guess you're the boss now." Then he grinned, adding, "Except when I'm driving. OK then, let's check it out."

The door was marked Transition. When I stepped into a very short atmospheric cleaning chamber, the vacuums hummed, and a blinding light flashed to kill the Earth germs on my suit exterior. When the second door glowed *Safe Room*, I stepped into a tiny emergency safe zone or a waiting room like you might find at a bus stop.

My helmet was unnecessary now, but I did not remove it. There was nowhere to search. The shelves held two boxes of rations, a water recycler, an oxygen generator, and two hard benches. It wasn't a camp, and since the ration crates were sealed, there was nowhere to hide anything. Ray was not here.

Within minutes, Kaneko relayed Marvin's report from Phobos. No shuttle lander had been dispatched. We were to head home.

But was Phobos telling the truth? Why couldn't I find Ray? Had Rod had time to ship him to Phobos? Had we missed the shuttle?

That couldn't be. Ray had spoken to me near this spot. If a shuttle had arrived between then and now, someone would have seen it. Everyone had been searching the landscape. So, Ray had not gone to Phobos. The shuttle had not come.

I didn't know where Ray was, but I had an itsy-bitsy clue, and I meant to track it down.

40 Confrontation at the Bus Stop

As we pulled away from the Phobos Food Drop site, Marvin delivered a message from Wolfgang Fulbright. News had spread through WayPoint that Rod Alexander had been captured and was returning to the station. But Luis' jail was ready for him this time.

"Have they found Neils Westergaard?" I asked.

"No, not yet. But there's news from the clinic. You can take Lilith off your culprit list. When she admitted to being Duval's sister, Elly remembered a box left in your quarters after Bernadette died. Lilith and Elly found Duval's diary inside. It explains a lot about the coup. You can read it for yourself, but I believe Lilith is on the up and up, but her sister was knee-deep in the take-over."

"Good to know. I'll be interested in seeing that," I replied.

"Did the clue about the Phobos Bus Stop help?" he asked.

"No. We caught Rod at the bus stop—the Food Drop—but there was no sign of Neils or our friend."

Then, I had another thought. Bernadette once said she could unlock any door on WayPoint. So, I asked to be linked to Luis via my wristband, and after turning off Giles' helmet, I asked Luis who had the power to unlock any door on WayPoint besides himself.

"Well, not many know I can do that," he replied. "But it's a power given to me for emergency use, and the backup is the Second Minister, so Garrison Mathis could do that, too."

"Could Neils have discovered how to use Garrison's access? Could he have used AdMon?" I asked.

Luis paused a moment before replying. "I gave him access to Garrison's quarters. But it would have been quite a job to find a way to access the program. If he discovered that, he'd be far more of a hacker than I thought. Still, it's possible."

"That would explain a lot. For example, Could Neils unlock my house, the jail cell, and even the Memorial Room and Collin's Niche?"

Luis sighed. "I'll check that out and see what Rod knows. I'll keep combing Bernadette's diary, too. We're on the verge of answers, my friend. Will you be back soon?"

"I'm not sure. There's one more clue to track here. We should be back home in a few hours."

When Luis signed off, I set comms between Giles and me, and my traveling companion had questions about the side of the conversation he had heard with Fulbright.

"What's the Bus Stop? Was that a code name for the food drop? Why were you and Dr. Fulbright speaking in code?"

I chuckled. "Don't worry."

"OK, then. What are you so interested in seeing?"

"Oh, for heaven's sake, did you memorize the entire conversation?"

"Only the bits that didn't make sense," Giles replied.

"Well, forget that conversation and help me figure something out. I heard some weird static in my comm link as we drove here, and it might be a clue. Can you help me find that spot again?"

"Sure. It's dark, and I don't know where it is, but I'll give it a go."

"Follow this road south until we reach the spot where we made the sharp turn. After that turn, go slow until I hear the static."

"OK, Boss. I'll try." Then he giggled. "I feel like a detective with a race car. Let's peel out."

"If you need speed, you'd better engage the hover drive," I said, bracing for his acceleration. "But disengage the drive after the turn.

I'll need quiet to listen for the static on my channel. Concentrate on getting us home safely, Daredevil."

"Got it," he replied, then he focused on dodging the boulders as he floated over the ruts on the reverse trail.

I hadn't lied. My helmet comm was tuned to Giles, but it wasn't satellite signals that had given me static; it was a personal head-to-head message from Ray. If we passed close enough, I might hear him again.

Giles studied the terrain illuminated by his rover beam, and as we plodded southward to the main trail to WayPoint, I mentally called to Ray but had no luck. Maybe he had moved, or worse, was *gone.*

The rover shifted toward the east, and in that curve, the hover jets lifted over the terrain, and we bumped over a few rocks.

"Easy," I said.

Giles nodded. "Have you heard anything yet?" he asked.

Shaking my head, I added, "Go slowly. It wasn't much of a signal before. Who knows what it is now?"

Giles disengaged the hover and inched along the rough road while I tried to ignore road sounds and my own breathing, hoping to catch any signal from Ray. Every cracking pebble teased me with the hope of popping static or some part of lost words sent straight from Ray's version of the cloud. We couldn't be far from the point where I heard him before.

I focused on Ray, thought of our mental meeting place, and finally, the room with our Blue Chairs appeared in my head. But before I could send a thought, the room vanished.

"Was that a wince?" Giles asked, and he twisted his head toward me again. "At first glance, I thought you smiled, but it was more a wince."

"Wishful thinking, I guess." And I fought off despair, worrying I might never reach Ray again. I couldn't let Ray nor Collin down. So, as we drove, I continuously reached out with his name.

Finally, there was a sharp crackle, followed by words in the static. "I … here. Something … block ..."

"Where are you?" I asked, trying to link mentally with his

telepathic voice.

"Do not know."

"Are you alone?" I asked.

"Don't know." Then he added, "Danger."

"How can I get to you?"

Giles crept toward WayPoint but looked toward me to ask, "Hear anything?"

I shook my head. Then there were broken words, "… as … cask."

"Stop," I shouted in Gile's helmet. "I hear something." Giles pulled to a stop.

I strained to hear more. "…urry … has m … cask."

Why was he breaking up? There was no electronic simulation involved; our communication was head-to-head.

Giles looked for further directions, and when I was quiet for a few minutes, he started back down the road. After a few more undecipherable crackles, all went silent.

"Dr. Spring, are you crying?" Giles asked. "I've got a few jokes if you need a laugh."

I shook my head. "It's useless. Too bad we couldn't find him at the Phobos Bus Stop."

"What kind of Bus Stop?" Giles asked. "Where's that?"

"The Food Drop, I guess. Thaman said he heard Neils and Rod discussing the Phobos Bus Stop."

"Why did they call it that? I never heard of passengers getting picked up at the Food Drop. Maybe when Ginger moved to Phobos, but no one else."

"Is there another drop-off point that passengers might use?"

"I never heard of one," he said, then suddenly braked the rover. "Wait. Do you remember me telling you about shuttle sightings near the crater rim? Beth and I guessed what we saw meant there was another stop. Maybe that's the place Tham called the Bus Stop."

"You think someone built another stop without Milo or Luis knowing it?" I asked.

"Is that possible?" Giles asked.

I didn't know, but if Ray could speak to me from there, it couldn't be far away. "What can you tell me about the sightings that made you think there were two stops?"

"It was just the impression we had. The shuttle climbed south to north, flying over us at the food drop."

"And WayPoint is north of the equator. So, anything leaving the surface for Phobos should be heading south," I added.

He nodded. "If they are climbing back to Phobos, they should be moving south or following the equator to catch the moon, but not northward."

"Can this rover go off-trail?"

He shrugged. "I've only seen ruts, boulders, and lava tubes on the terrain of this crater. We can manage that. Should we notify Kaneko?"

"Solving this riddle is important, but there could be danger. What do you think?" I asked.

"So far today, I've been a race car driver and an ace detective. Why not add explorer to my skill list? I'm in. Let's go."

While Giles picked his way over the rocks, I spoke to Marvin. "Send a delayed message to Luis Kaneko, but only if you don't hear from Giles Cardiff or me in half an hour."

"What is your message?" Marvin droned.

"Tell him I ordered Giles Cardiff to drive me off-trail. But, I repeat, only if we don't message you in half an hour."

"Underst ... wait. Dr. Spring, are you undertaking a dangerous task? Could you be harmed?"

"Marvin, by my orders as an Administrative Official on WayPoint, override your caution and follow my directions."

"Oh yes, I detect a change of status memo. Congratulations, Secretary Spring."

"Thank you, Marvin."

"Complying," he droned. But an emotionless AI servant shouldn't sound unhappy about my orders.

Giles and I drove southward toward the curve, but then, while backtracking east, Ray appeared with me in our Blue Room. The expression on his invented silver face was relieved but upset. “Don’t put yourself in danger, Dr. Spring.”

“Aren’t you already in danger?” I asked.

“I am not as fragile as you. It is unlikely my captor can harm me.”

“Where are you?”

“I believe I’m underground. This place feels like Sanctuary Cave, but it’s elsewhere.”

“Can you detect other humans near you?” I asked.

“Only Neils Westergaard is near me now. But he is not adjacent, only reasonably close.”

“Can you direct me to you?” I asked.

“I can tell when you come closer or farther away.”

I turned to Giles, “Loop around this ridge to your right and toward the crater wall. Look for a cave entrance or anyplace that might be the Bus Stop.”

“This looks like the spot Beth and I found near where Hashimi died,” Giles said. “There. That looks like a cave,” he said, pointing toward a dark hole in the south wall. “Should I hide the rover?”

“If Neils is nearby, we don’t want to alert him, but we wouldn’t want to get far from the rover; we need it to survive.”

“Hide it as well as you can but as close to the entrance as possible,” I said. My Explorer Extraordinaire chose a spot hidden in a boulder group across the crater floor from the cave. We checked our power and oxygen levels and exited the rover.

Giles scanned the south crater wall. “This looks natural. There is nothing human-made here. Do you think this is a dead end?”

I waved him forward, but we entered with our lights on dim and the audio set to hear each other and surrounding sounds, should there be any.

Once inside the tunnel, we found signs of human workmanship. The main tunnel was over 30 meters long, but near the entry, an alcove to the right held a small, hatched enclosure where a feeble light escaped through a translucent shade. The airlock was decades older than anything in the WayPoint complex, and the light meant someone was inside. There was no sign of a vehicle; it had to be Neils. Who else could it be?

I signaled for Giles to keep silent as I visited the Blue Room to speak to Ray. "Are you alone? Is Neils with you?"

He was nearby, loud and clear. "My captor put me at some distance from him. I believe he means to hide me for a time."

"Are you still shielded?" I asked.

"Not fully," he replied.

I motioned for Giles to follow me down the tunnel. "Keep your lamp on dim," I said into the comm. "I'll leave mine off to make us less noticeable if Neils comes out of the safe room."

He nodded, and we followed the path to a new turn. Then Ray warned me that Neils was moving closer.

"Light out. Neils is moving our way," I commanded.

"How do you know that?" Giles asked, but he complied.

We huddled at the end of our alcove, listening as Neils approached. When he was a few meters beyond us, our dark hiding place caught a dim glow from the tunnel, and we heard a faint buzz. As the humming increased, my comm signal began to pop and crack. Some nearby humming electronic machine interfered with my comm system, not Ray's head-to-head.

I flattened against the cave wall and held a gloved hand before my face shield. Before Giles pressed against the wall, he bent low to pick up a heavy stone, the first weapon he could find.

I whispered to Marvin. "Relay our location to Luis Kaneko. We've found Neils Westergaard. He's south of the spot where Ross Hashimi's body was found."

"Complying."

It would take time for help to arrive, but if we did not escape, WayPoint would know where to look for us.

Then, there was a noise outside. But it wasn't the rumble of a lander's retro-jets or sand braking; it was more the sound of a rover rolling over the stony crater floor. It couldn't possibly be Luis so soon.

We dared not look with Neils in our path, but he heard it, too, and hurried toward the cave entrance, stuffing something into his vest pocket as he passed our alcove. Within minutes, he greeted a visitor, and they passed through the decontamination process and entered the safe rooms.

I motioned for Giles to follow me, and we felt our way toward the alcove Neils had visited. We found a small natural room to the left about twenty meters down the tunnel. The faintest setting on my helmet lamp was enough to find a gleaming white orb.

"You found me," Ray said.

"And I'm taking you home," I replied.

"Are you with Giles? The one who was bullied?" he asked. In our Blue Room, I nodded.

Giles held his rock at the ready while I picked up the melon-sized white cask that held Ray and hurried for the exit as silently as possible. We paused at the turn toward the safe room, now lit for company. When we heard faint conversation inside the room, we slipped outside the cave and hugged the crater wall, praying no one followed.

We held our breath when light brightened the cave's entrance, but when the footsteps went deeper into the passage, we had our chance.

"Go for the rover," I said. "I'll meet you behind the boulders."

He nodded, but when Giles was less than a dozen paces from the cave entry, I heard a disturbance inside. The two comrades had exited from the safe room, and their comms were still set to all nearby. The Martian air was thin, but I could hear them.

"It's gone," Neils said. "You tricked me. Who took my treasure?"

He must have meant Ray's cask. I slipped further along the cave wall, hoping for some shelf or outcropping to hide behind.

The partners heard Giles opening his rover door, and they shouted as they ran toward him.

"Run," I ordered through helmet comm, but Giles lobbed his boulder instead of hopping in and riding away. Unfortunately, his aim was as bad as mine. It flew over Neil's head and landed in the path of his visitor, who tripped and fell onto the crater floor.

Neils paid no attention to his fallen comrade and chased after

Giles, who set the rover in motion. Once he engaged the hover, dust swirled around the crater floor, blinding Neils and his companion.

"Go," I told Giles through the comms. "I have enough air, and they haven't found me yet. Go get help."

"I can't leave you," he replied.

"Go."

This time, he made a final sand-blasting spin around Neils and his visitor and headed toward the WayPoint road. Even men running on Mars couldn't catch his hover drive.

I was on my own and far from the safety of WayPoint facilities. I had air, and they hadn't spotted me, but where should I go? I set my comms for all nearby. Ray could speak to me, but I couldn't hide in his Blue Room. Hopefully, hearing what Neils and his friend planned would help me choose an escape route or a suitable hole to hide in.

Neils jerked his comrade off the ground, and they bickered as they returned to the tunnel.

"What now?" The visitor asked.

"We can't catch him with your ship," Neils spat. "All he carried was a rock. Maybe he hid what I found. Let me show you how this scanner works."

The delicate hum started again, and Ray spoke to me. "Don't let that thing get near you. It injured Collin and Tham."

"How?" I asked in our mental room.

The silver man shrugged. "Neils tested it near my cask. The closer he came, the louder the buzzing. It created such a disturbance that one of my controllers loosened. At first, he was thrilled, but as the sound grew louder, he moaned until he finally threw his machine to the side. It's dangerous for your kind. It would be best if you left," he said.

"I won't leave you with them."

"They probably can't hurt me," he said.

"*Probably* isn't good enough."

"They'll find me eventually. They can find me with the scanner,"

"Then I should go further away. I'll try for the boulders where

Giles hid the rover."

But after a few paces across the crater floor, the two thieves spotted me, and Neils gave chase.

"There it is. Stop that runner," Neils called.

I ran faster, but it wasn't enough. Neils Westergaard tackled my ankles, sending Ray's cask across the crater floor.

Neils retrieved Ray, and his partner pointed a weapon toward me. There were no predators on Mars; I had never seen humans fighting humans outside a gym. But I had seen this *gun*. It was a sandblaster used to free mineral specimens from layers of concreted regolith, and this one was built for high intensity.

"Looks like you lost, Dr. Spring," Neils said. "I've taken your prize."

I attempted to crawl up from the dust, but Westergaard's partner knocked me down with the butt of the weapon. So, I set my comm to all nearby and asked, "How did you vanish from WayPoint?"

"Oh, I don't owe you any answers, but I'm rather proud of that one. Mathis left a trove of tricks in his room, and I learned how they work. With AdMon, I found out when and where people were in the back tunnels, which helped locate this melon ball. Too bad you and Collin kept hiding it in different places."

I clenched my fists. "Did you kill Collin?"

"No, I can't take credit for that. I had a bigger prize in mind. My comrades and I sought power, and Mathis had power reserved for only the highest position on WayPoint. He could unlock any door."

"Yes, I heard Bernadette Duval say that once. That explains how you entered the memorial room and Collin's niche, but how did you vanish from WayPoint?"

Neils held up a wrist. "You can't find someone who isn't there. You'd be surprised how much I blend into a busy place like the transport bay when I dress and hurry like everyone else."

"But they looked for you. Your chip wouldn't be invisible."

"I had no chip when I robbed Collin's box, but I found a new identity with Ross Hashimi's chip."

"How could you have Ross' chip?" I asked.

"When Hashimi died, Mathis' duty was to extract and destroy his employee's chip, and the equipment was in his office. He failed to destroy Hashimi's, but I destroyed mine and taped Hashimi's around my wrist. Voila. Westergaard is gone, and Hashimi lives again."

"Wow, you got lucky being assigned to cover for our Prime Two," I said.

"Finding the car was a lucky break, but luck didn't play into the rest of it. It's all part of the plan."

"Whose plan?" I asked.

"You'd be surprised," he replied, a grin showing through his helmet. "And since you won't live to repeat it, perhaps I'll tell you, but you'll never get to tell Luis."

Westergaard bolted toward me, jerking me up with an arm around my neck. And he placed his lips near my helmet to whisper his secret. "Too bad no one else will ever know."

But then, lights from the east flooded the cave yard. *Giles! Why was Giles back?* He blasted the hover jets, giving me a fighting chance, but Neils held me tight while struggling in the swirling sands.

As the sands settled, Giles stopped the car and left the lights on as he climbed out.

The shorter thief, with the blaster in hand, ran toward Giles. But Giles quickly grabbed a good-sized rock, and his target fell to the ground this time.

"Take that, you bully," he shouted. "One down," he said, and he ran toward the thief, grabbed the weapon, and pointed it toward Neils.

"What are you playing at, Boy?" Neils said. "I know your training, and it's not with weaponry. Drop that sandblaster and be on your way."

"Not happening, you Bully," Giles replied.

Neils had me in one arm and Ray's cask in the other. Maybe I could grab Ray and run. Then we'd find out if Giles could use a blaster or, more likely, throw another rock.

Besides Vince's virtual boxing lessons, I was not trained in hand-to-hand combat, but I had seen a few movies. "*Horizontal force*," I reminded myself. Then I elbowed Neils in the stomach and kicked him hard where it counted. But sadly, none of the movies showed fights in Martian terrain suits, and my enemy was well-padded.

Neils fumbled Ray, and we both scrambled for the cask. But after Neils won the fight, he stood with his boot on my neck, holding Ray's cask close to his chest. But Giles still had the gun.

"Drop that blaster, boy, or we will see what my boot does to this gadfly's trachea."

Giles dropped the weapon, kicking it to his right, and Neils rolled me aside, pointing Giles toward me as he sidled toward the gun.

And when Giles was closer to me than the weapon, my captor picked up the gun in his right hand and shifted Ray to his left side, nodding for me to move.

After I crawled a few paces toward Giles, Neils added, "Keep away from me, or I'll see if I recall how to hit two with one blast."

Giles pulled me farther away from Neils but closer to his rock.

"Don't even think about it, lad. I'll take you out first and then take my time with that massive pain, Spring Graviston."

When I caught my breath, I whispered, "Why did you come back?"

"You told me to," Giles replied. "You were calling; I heard your voice. You asked me not to leave you with that bully."

"I must have been wishing for help very loudly," I replied.

"Shut up," Neils yelled.

We turned toward the enemy, wondering what he might do with us. We were hours from WayPoint. How long would it take Luis to find this place if Neils killed us?

"What will you do with them?" The shorter thief had recovered, and the voice was raspy and rough from swallowing sand, but it was female.

Neils didn't reply immediately, so his partner answered her own question.

"Leave them here," she said. "Someone will find them soon

enough, and they can use this camp to survive."

Neils turned to her. "They can't survive. They know too much."

Neils pointed the weapon again, and Giles stepped in front of me.

"Afraid of me now, wimp?" Neils asked.

"Not even if I die," Giles replied.

"Very well." Neils stared down the sights.

"Collin," I whispered, wondering if I'd see him again soon.

"Don't worry," Ray whispered back.

Then I heard a voice from Niels' wristband. It was faint and familiar, but I couldn't place it.

"Marvin," the voice shouted. "Scanner on. Maximum power."

The screech from Neils' pocket pierced my ears. Then his pocket scorched, smoked, and the artificial fabric melted into his skin. Neils' lips curled like leaves in a fire. He screamed in agony, dropping Ray's cask to the ground, and the shrill tones ceased.

When Neils lay still with the same scorching hole in his pocket that I had seen on Collin's uniform, I grabbed Ray, asking mentally, "Did you do that?"

The silver man shrugged. "I did not."

"What happened?" Giles asked. "Did you give Marvin an order to save you?"

"No," I replied. "That would have been against his protocol, anyway."

"Then what happened?"

"Marvin?" I was nearly afraid to ask for his help.

"At your service, Dr. Spring."

"Message Luis Kaneko to send his men to this location, please."

"They are en route, Dr. Spring."

"Marvin, what happened to Neils Westergaard?" I asked.

"He experienced extreme physical damage, I believe, Dr. Spring. Medics are on the way."

"But who sent the message to go full power?" I asked.

"What message do you mean, Dr. Spring?" Marvin replied.

Giles shook his head. "This is going to take a lot of explaining."

"I hope your rover cam recorded this."

"When the lights are on, so is the cam, Dr. Spring."

I nodded. Then I examined Ray's cask, and there wasn't a mark on it, but one blue curve was missing.

"Search his pockets, please, Giles."

"I found this," he said. "Isn't this part of the necklace you used to wear?"

"Yes, it is. Neils stole it from me."

Giles passed my blue charm back to me, and I fitted it into its spot on Ray's cask, where it flowed and hardened, becoming part of the cask again.

"Are we going to answer for this, Dr. Spring?" he asked.

"Giles, as long as you forget you ever saw this white melon, we won't have to explain a thing."

"What is that thing?"

"It was in Collin's memorial niche and should be returned."

He nodded.

Then we heard a rumbling not far away, and the vehicle I took to be a rover before became a shuttle lander gaining altitude as it headed north.

"Ginger got away," Giles said. "I'd know that voice anywhere. It was Ginger Welsh,"

"Kaneko will certainly be interested in hearing that," I said.

He nodded. "So will Beth."

41 Debriefing

Giles and I could have returned to WayPoint immediately, but Kaneko said we should wait for his men to escort us home. He also wanted to ask us about this unexpected bus stop in Echo Crater. So, Giles pulled the little rover close to the cave entrance, and we checked out the ration boxes in the safe room as we waited.

It was difficult to say how long the food had been there, but the use-by date was still ten Earth-years away. It probably wouldn't be delicious, but we could eat it. So, we picked out a few energy bars and some tea pouches to munch on.

"So that wasn't you calling me for help?" Giles asked.

"No. To tell the truth, I didn't think of it."

"Maybe you have ESP," he said.

"Maybe someone does," I replied.

"I saw you standing in front of me, but not in a terrain suit. You were in your normal clothes, looking small, afraid, and maybe bullied," he said. "But a different voice told me to save you. It sounded like Collin's voice, come to think of it."

In my head, Ray spoke to explain. "I couldn't let him go too far. I might not be able to reach him to return. I figured the word *bully* would persuade him."

Once Giles was comfortable in our crater camp, he had more

questions.

"Did you order Marvin to save us?" Giles asked.

"No. Did you?"

He shook his head, adding, "Somebody must have been watching over us."

Ray interrupted again. "That wasn't me," he said.

"Then who was it?"

Blue Room Ray shrugged. "I do not know."

When Giles finished chewing his chocolate bar, he said, "I didn't ask how you're managing without Collin. How are you doing?"

"Better," I replied. "It has been like living through a tornado, dodging one thing, righting another. At first, I was lost, broken, and foundering in grief, and I didn't know which world I was in. But my friends grabbed me by the fingers and toes and yanked me out of the abyss."

"Sounds gruesome," he said.

I sighed. "They tell me grief is the price of love. But, I wouldn't give up loving Collin, not even if I had known how his loss would grieve me."

"Maybe I'll love like that someday," he said. "Do you think Beth might ever love me that much?"

"You'll find out. And if it's real, it will make you stronger, no matter what."

"Are you over the pain yet?" he asked.

"No. It's a part of me now, but it changes. And in time, the pain doesn't make you cry as often as the love makes you smile."

"How does that work?"

"My friends helped. They stood me upright again, and there was work to do. The work distracted me, and after a while, I realized that the work gave me a goal. But I was only strong enough to meet my purpose because love had made me capable of it."

"Will you love again?" he asked.

"I don't know. I don't need to; Collin was enough love for forever. But if I do love again, it will be grand, and it will be because Collin made me fit for it. He's a part of me, too, and he overrides the pain."

"Hmph," Giles said.

While Giles picked out a cheese and sausage stick, I rummaged through boxes to find a container for Ray's cask. A yellow draw-string lantern cover fit perfectly.

"Is there anything else in there?" Giles asked as he started to rummage for himself. "Hey, look at this." He pulled out a small box the same size as two others I had seen. One was delivered to Rod Alexander, and the other Collin had used to wrap my blue charms. Mine was addressed to Garrison Mathis, but both had the familiar red, mint, and navy label used by Benjamin Hessling and Threshold Station.

"Don't lose that box," I said. "I bet an iridium signature will match one in Westergaard's vest pocket.

"Wow. Did we solve a murder?" Giles asked.

"I'm not sure we solved anything, but it is a piece of our puzzle. Keep it under wraps until we can show Luis Kaneko. The scanner we saw with Neils was probably a replacement we knew about. But if it was a replacement, where is the first one?"

"Destroyed?" Giles suggested.

"Maybe. We just saw one explode, but I doubt you can destroy iridium."

"What happened to Collin's hammer?" Giles asked.

"Hmm, if the cask was here, maybe the hammer is, too. Let's look around."

"It's not in the rover," he replied. "We checked that. But I wonder how Neils got Collin's things anyway. Wasn't Rod the thief?

I tossed my stale granola bar into the bin before replying. "I can only guess, but the easy answer is Rod passed it to him and dropped him off here. Can you think of any other way?"

"Nobody saw him in the Transport Dock," he replied, shrugging.

"But no one was looking for Neils then, and he showed us he had a false chip. If Rod got into the rover, maybe Neils did, too."

"That's a good theory, and I guess Kaneko will get the truth out of

Rod, and the mystery will be solved."

"Well, there is still one puzzle. If neither you nor I gave Marvin the order that stopped Neils, who did?" I asked.

"It must have been someone who knew that scanner could kill under certain circumstances," he replied. "Kaneko, maybe. He's been working on all the angles. Maybe he knew it."

"Yes, but he was too far away and didn't know where Neils was, much less that he had the scanner. How would he know to overload it, anyway?" I asked.

Giles shrugged, "Cobalt's investigators will work it out; they'll tell us sooner or later."

Giles had finished his cheese stick by then, so he went with me to examine the rest of the Bus Stop. There wasn't much to find. Besides the safe room and ancient transition closet, there were two or three small side caves, probably used for storage while workers decided where to build WayPoint Station. Nothing was left other than a few remnants of building supplies.

The room where Ray's cask had been was bare, besides a small table and a couple of stools. It was so dusty that we did no more than glance at it. But Giles saw a mound in a far corner, and when he brushed the dust aside, he uncovered Collin's hammer and passed it to me.

***

Eventually, Michelle, Luis, and Kaneko's men arrived. We showed them around the Bus Stop, and then Giles and I rested in the crawler. It had been a long day, but between the night's excitement and Giles' questions, sleep was impossible.

"That work you had to do, your purpose. Is it finished now?"

I shook my head, stuffing the hammer into the drawstring pouch at my feet. "No. There is still more to do."

"So, you're on Mars for a while longer?" he asked.

"Yes. I hear Lilith might leave us soon, though."

Giles grimaced. "Tham will hate that. He is his best when he's near her."

"Is he falling in love?" I asked.

"No, it's not that kind of friendship, but it's important to him. It wouldn't surprise me if he returned to Earth with her. She's as much his healer as his friend, and he still needs her."

The sun was rising when we reached WayPoint, but there was news there, too. Giles was right about Thaman and Lilith. She felt the same way as Giles had described. She wanted to shepherd him through his judgment issues, and the two agreed that time in the warm country air of France was just the place to do it.

"He says he'll be back," Fulbright told me. "And I think he will return."

***

The Kanekos caught me up on what they had learned from Bernadette's diary. It explained her adversarial relationship with her sister and told us something about who was behind the coup. Bernadette's orders came primarily from Garrison Mathis, but he answered to higher powers. The diary was scarce of names, but some of those pulling Garrison's strings were likely from Earth. Others might be hovering over WayPoint, and I had a feeling we'd hear more from them very soon.

We didn't have all the answers, and I had not completed my promise to Collin and Ray.

***

I was alone with Ray as I restored his cask to Collin's niche.

"What shall we do now, Spring?" he asked from his favorite blue chair. "Are we closer to finding my other half?"

"You tell me," I replied.

He opened a virtual bottle of my favorite Italian wine and poured a glass for me. "I believe we are very close," he said. "At least two enemies know what to look for now, and that's bound to lead to more clues."

"True," I replied. "If the seekers get closer to us, we must be closer to them.

"And to more danger," Ray said.

"You're right. The Seekers know what your cask looks like and where you used to hide. Hmm. Leaving you here might not be a good idea." I took the cask from Collin's niche and left only the little hammer. You'd better come home with me tonight."

"No matter where I hide, they can't reach our Blue Room. Finish your wine," he said. "The enemy has been here and in your house, too."

The first sip from my glass was as bright and refreshing as the glass he once poured for me on a Venetian gondola. I took a second sip before replying. "You're right. Luis will help us find a safe place tomorrow, but we'll be safe tonight."

"Why do you think so?" he asked.

I sipped as I considered the problem but sat straighter as a new threat dawned. "We chased Neils and Rod to get you back, but Neils met disaster, and Rod is in detention. We are safe from our known enemies, but there must be ones we don't know. Who and where are they?"

"So, our solution isn't clear yet," he said.

"No, but I'd say all clues point to Phobos.

"Are you sure? All?" he asked.

"Well. Mostly."

He raised his glass. "I've seen you and Collin toast your strawberry wine. I'd say our return here is worthy of a toast."

I wasn't sure our day had been successful, but we had survived it, so we tipped the glasses to celebrate. "What shall we toast to," I asked. "To Earth or Mars?"

"How about Collin and the great beyond?" he asked.

"To Collin and the great beyond," I repeated.

He nodded. "To Collin and to Spring beyond," he said.

It was probably due to my memories, but I imagined Collin's chuckle as we drained our virtual glasses.

What's Next for Spring?

Spring, stronger from her experiences with Collin, is ready for her next battle. She and Collin promised to help Ray find his complete form, and she thinks she'll find it on Phobos.

But will Ray keep his identity secret for much longer? Will he get the body he needs before all of Mars and most of Earth know what he is, where he is, and why he came to Mars?

There are new secrets to learn and powerful villains yet to meet as Spring discovers who is behind the plots on WayPoint. That's part of Spring's latest challenge. But to complete her destiny, she must know much more about Ray's plans and his distant world.

And her destiny may take her beyond Mars.

Watch for news about ***Spring Beyond***, Book 3 in the **Martian Spring Trilogy,** to be released later this year.

Get the latest at **Cooperspeak.com.**

I look forward to your comments and suggestions.
Email at **Cooperspeak@yahoo.com**, or drop in to **Cooperspeak.com**